For Mom and Dad

Thank you for always believing in me, even when I didn't believe in myself.

Today was going to be perfect. It was. Everyone got nervous on their wedding day. Maybe it was seeing my future in-laws spend more money on the reception than I had in my bank account, or hearing my mother chase the hair stylist down the hall to fix a loose strand my low bun. It could be that I spent so long planning this wedding, I couldn't enjoy it. I couldn't turn off the impulse to triple check every detail, when now I was supposed to focus on the biggest job of all — making today the best of my life. "It doesn't actually have to be your best day ever," my future mother-in-law, Melissa, told me at one of our wedding planning lunches. "You just have to make everyone think it is."

Melissa was a beautiful, blue-eyed socialite with perfect highlights and a magazine-worthy smile. To her, captivating a crowd was as simple as an offhanded comment over Cobb salads. I, on the other hand, could outthink Charlie Brown.

Over The Moon

Written by: Blake Richardson

Cover Artist: Sarah Luther

This is a work of fiction. All of the characters, organizations, and events portrayed in this novel are either products of the author's imagination or are used fictitiously.

ISBN 979-8-9922421-0-2 (paperback)
ISBN 979-8-9922421-1-9 (ebook)

www.blakerichardsonwrites.wordpress.com

For the past year, I spent every spare moment I had planning this wedding. Visiting venues, tasting cakes and catering menus, choosing a band, consulting with the florist, photographer, videographer, and pastor. At one point, I spoke to Melissa more frequently than my fiancé, and I lived with Matthew. It was a job on top of my job, a test of whether I could fit into the Tate family. So far, the Engagement Party, Bachelorette, Bridal Luncheon and Rehearsal Dinner all went off without a hitch. This was all that was left — the biggest event of all. I just had to be beautiful enough, charming enough, for Melissa Tate to feel proud as she paraded me beside her son in front of everyone she knew.

It was a lot of pressure. Of course I was nervous. Nothing worth reading into.

I kept my face still as I tried to control my breathing. I sat in a plush white bathrobe in a suite at The Mayflower Hotel while a makeup artist perfected my mask. She brushed blush over my cheeks as my bridal party waited nearby. Carter, my best friend from college, picked at a fruit platter on the mahogany coffee table in the middle of the room, while my mother and my sister, Gemma, bickered about her bridesmaid dress.

"I already talked to Alana about this," said Gemma, flicking her long, dark hair over her shoulder. "I don't like it, and she's making me wear it anyway. It doesn't mean I have to be happy about it."

"You don't need to have an attitude about it," my mom scolded, her blue eyes narrowing at her daughter. "Nobody will be looking at you anyway."

Gemma frowned at our mother's comment. "If nobody's looking at me, why can't I pick my own dress?"

"I don't care what you wear, Gemma," I said, careful to keep my face still so I wouldn't interrupt the makeup artist. Every piece of today was carefully partitioned down to the minute. A delay in the makeup would mean a delay in putting on the dress, in taking photos, in driving to the church, and who knows how the traffic would be. God forbid I show up late to my own wedding, with several hundred people waiting, most of them guests of Melissa's. "I *do* care what Melissa thinks. She picked that dress, so I need you to wear it. You can dress me up like

Little Bo Peep for your wedding, if it makes you feel better."

Gemma huffed a laugh and luckily let the issue die. There were more bridesmaids in here than I was comfortable with — an old co-worker, some college friends, Matthew's cousin. Melissa wanted a bridal party of exactly eight, more people than I was comfortable with hearing Gemma slander Melissa's dress (even if she was right). As Gemma scrolled through her phone, the bridesmaid small talk shifted to how perfectly the flowers matched Melissa's dresses, how excited they were to see me walk down the aisle in the exquisitely decorated church.

When my mother-in-law insisted on paying for the wedding, I was grateful, knowing my parents' budget couldn't accommodate the large guest list the Tate's intended to invite. I didn't consider that Melissa would take complete control. Everything became bigger than I wanted. The guest list ballooned, the floral bouquets swelled with blooms, the cake became the size of a toddler. Wedding planning overtook my life as we prepared for the large party and many side events that would accompany it, from the Engagement Party to the

Bridal Luncheon, Rehearsal Dinner, and next-day brunch. If I ever expressed concern about the cost, she'd brush it off by saying Mr. Tate *wanted* to pay for it. How could I tell her that made my stomach turn with guilt?

It was wrong of me to feel this way. I was lucky, really. Nobody's wedding was truly their own. I just wanted today to be worthy of the effort Melissa put into it. There were so many ways to let her down.

Deep breaths — why was it so hard to remember that? I thought of Matthew. I was doing this for Matthew. My fiancé with the golden hair and shy smile. We'd been dating two years, but it only took six months to realize I'd be happy sharing a life with him, anchored by his steady presence. He held car doors open, bought flowers for my birthday, and shyly shoved his hands in his pockets whenever he called me pretty. I moved into his two-bedroom apartment in Dupont Circle a few weeks before he proposed last Valentine's Day, and we built a peaceful life together. Complete with busy mornings sharing breakfast before work, evening drinks laughing with his colleagues, and quiet takeout dinners from the Thai place three blocks away. I was content to make this life my forever. Why wouldn't I be?

The door burst open, and music filled the room. I knew the song instantly, 'A Thousand Years,' by Christina Perri.

I looked toward the door to the suite, and there was Forrest, my maid of honor, swaying and waving her hands to the music with a portable speaker in one hand and something shiny in the other, our wedding videographer filming behind her. She turned sharply to Carter and Gemma mouthing, "SING," and the rest of the bridal party followed suit. Immediately, I was surrounded by my friends serenading me to the 'Twilight' theme song in bathrobes and slippers.

The makeup artist put down her brush. That's how I knew I was smiling.

Forrest turned off the speaker and placed it on the coffee table before turning back to me, flashing a wide smile framed by dimples. Even before putting on her dress, she was gorgeous. Her shimmery bronze eyeshadow accentuated her round, dark eyes and the warm tones in her brown skin, which reminded me of a sunset. She seemed to freeze as she took me in. My flawless makeup, my dark hair braided back into a low bun, not a wisp out of place, the satin bathrobe hugging my figure.

The joy in her eyes shifted to awe. Her mouth dropped open for a moment before she remembered that she was in the middle of leading a 'Twilight' chorus, and she grinned once again.

"I have your something blue," she announced, smirking conspiratorially as she presented the shiny object in her right hand.

I took the object in my French manicured fingertips. It was a hair comb, composed of intricately woven strands of rhinestone beads that looked like diamonds. There were two eye-shaped circles connected by swirling strands of rhinestone. Four tiny flowers with sapphire blue rhinestone petals poised delicately in the center of the clip. "Forrest, this is stunning. Thank you."

She pressed her lips together like she was biting back a laugh. "You haven't even seen the best part yet. Carter, would you do the honors?"

Carter's green eyes sparkled with mischief as he showed me his phone screen. There was a picture of the back of Bella's head from the wedding scene in

'Twilight: Breaking Dawn.' I squinted at it in confusion. Then I realized.

I was holding an exact replica of the hair clip Bella wore at her wedding.

I burst out laughing.

"It's a fitting gift because your wedding will replace Bella Swan's as the most iconic of our generation," Forrest explained. "Plus, if you ever have kids, it's a subtle naming challenge to do better than Renesmee."

Carter looked pained as he strained to keep a straight face. "We were thinking Cartorrest. But you can workshop it."

My laughter turned borderline hyperventilating when Forrest suggested the nickname 'Tory.' When I finally caught my breath, I told her, "It will also remind me of our 'Twilight' movie nights in DC." We were roommates for two years before she left the city to attend RISD, kickstarting her career as a professional artist.

"Well, that's an added bonus." Her eyes twinkled as she smiled.

I frowned, as a surge of anxiety washed over my stomach. I stared at the comb that I clutched with both hands. "Forrest, Melissa will never let me wear this." Every part of my outfit was cleared by my mother-in-law months ago, from the low braided bun that held my straight, dark hair to my simple but elegant wedding dress.

Forrest squeezed my shoulder reassuringly. "Actually, she already did," she said, her smile as soothing as the ocean. "I told her I wanted to surprise you with something blue, and she loved it. She told me the comb was 'gorgeous.' Obviously, she doesn't know its, um, unique history."

Gemma snorted.

"Everyone here is sworn to secrecy," Carter added, "including Kathy and Raveena." He gestured to my make-up artist and videographer.

"Yeah, Matthew's side of the family won't see this portion of the footage," Raveena said. "Don't worry."

I nodded as my shoulders sagged in relief. Matthew wouldn't care about something like a hair comb, probably wouldn't notice it, but he never did well with secrets. This one was safe with my loved ones. "Thanks, everyone," I said. I looked up at my best friend. "Thank you, Forrest."

"Of course." Her dark eyes shone as she smiled back, then stepped behind me to fasten the comb in my hair.

Melissa literally applauded when she saw me, a light golf clap, when she entered the back room where we waited for the ceremony to start.

I wore a long-sleeve, plain white mermaid dress that tastefully hugged my curves. I found it at a dress shop in New York City with Melissa. "Something timeless and elegant," she had said. "You'll look like Meghan Markle." Satin buttons lined the back, but otherwise, there was no fill. With a subtle spray tan, fresh manicure, and recently whitened teeth, I looked like I stepped out of a wedding magazine. It wasn't what I imagined my wedding dress would be, but it did the job. Most importantly, it earned applause from Melissa. I could see the twinkle of pleasure in her green eyes, the soft half-smile carving a faint wrinkle in her cheek. Like her son, my future mother-in-law wasn't one for grand emotional gestures. In Melissa's world, this was the equivalent of a sports fan ripping their shirt off and setting a couch on fire.

"Wonderful, Alana," she said, lifting her head appraisingly. "This is exactly what I envisioned."

She wore a midi-length, sleeveless gold dress that fit her slim figure perfectly, while her blonde shoulder-length hair was perfectly styled into place, falling around her shoulders in tasteful, swooping waves. She appeared even more glamourous than usual as she stood in the doorway with her arms crossed, quizzing me about details. Did I ask the wedding planner about the last-minute seating change at Table Eleven? Did I talk to Matthew's grandparents at the Rehearsal Dinner? Did the florist finish setting up the reception?

"We have everything handled, Mrs. Tate," Forrest said. "It's going to be a beautiful wedding."

Melissa turned to my maid of honor, and her eyes widened like she was noticing my bridal party for the first time. "Forrest Manning," she said, flashing a half-smile. "You look stunning."

I nodded in agreement as I faced my best friend. I almost forgot to breathe when I first saw Forrest in her bridesmaid dress. The dark blush pink dress brought out the candlelight tones in her brown skin, and the dress's thigh slit revealed a tasteful glimpse of her long, toned legs. Her hair was styled into passion twists that cascaded down her back, swinging slightly with each movement. Complete with the shy smile at Melissa's compliment and the kindness behind her piercing eyes, I was awestruck. I looked away.

"Thank you." She grinned at my future mother-in-law. Forrest was the only reason I survived a year of these Melissa interrogations. She always managed to diplomatically distract Melissa when her demands became too much. Without her, I would have floundered.

"Are you all ready for your walk down the aisle?" Melissa asked, turning to Carter and Gemma, who each carried a bouquet of pink hydrangeas that matched the dress and Carter's bowtie.

"I'll try not to trip," Carter teased, flashing a crooked smile.

"I should hope so." Melissa cocked an eyebrow at him as she crossed her arms, finding no humor in the joke. My friend shifted his feet uncomfortably, betraying the first nerves I'd seen from him all day.

"We're all ready," Forrest said, smiling. "The dresses you picked are beautiful."

Mercifully, Gemma disguised her snort as a cough.

"Thank you," said Melissa. She nodded at me. "Well, I suppose I will see all of you inside."

I smiled politely back. "See you inside."

When she left, Carter shuddered. "I was not nervous to walk until that. I swear, she looked at me like I was the Grim Reaper."

"Don't worry about her." I squeezed his shoulder. "We just need to get through the wedding ceremony, then we can relax at the reception."

Yes, I just put *get through* before *wedding*. But every bride must feel that way. Trying to breathe amid the tightening anxiety in my chest. Trying to pretend I wasn't on the cusp making the biggest commitment of my life. In planning my wedding, my excitement and dread were so intertwined, they practically rhymed.

After today, I'd be Alana Tate. Only Matthew's family was too different from mine for the name to truly fit. He grew up on vacations to his family's Cape Cod mansion, with a private school-to-

Ivy League education and a closet filled with Vineyard Vines. I grew up in a Raleigh suburb playing weekend soccer games, taking summer daytrips to the beach, and fighting with Gemma over whether to paint our room yellow or blue. What would happen when my life became his? I took a deep breath and tried to calm the shaking in my hands.

"Ally," Carter said suddenly, taking a step closer to me so he would whisper without the others hearing: "What's wrong?"

There was no hiding from Carter. That's why I loved him. I shrugged and squeezed his hand, suddenly overwhelmed by the urge to cry. "This is... a lot. You know."

I met his pale green eyes, which scanned mine in earnest. "I know." He spoke slowly then, weighing the gravity of his words. "Are you sure you want to—"

Just then, my dad appeared. When he saw the tears in my eyes. I saw panic arise in his. "I can come back?"

I shook my head as I blinked my tears away. My dad never did well with emotion. "I'm great," I said, forcing a smile. "Just excited for today."

He nodded, then asked Carter's opinion about the Carolina Panthers upcoming draft picks. My friend dutifully pretended he followed sports, a ruse he'd mastered since meeting my dad in college. He would Google the star player on any given team and tell my dad he needed more "support," to make the team "well-rounded." It was true of just about every pro team in North Carolina, so it worked like a charm.

The charade was oddly comforting, drowning my thoughts of wedding details with something I understood (Carter, not the sports.) Their whispers deflated the silence as waited together, until the footsteps died down and there was only violin music outside, indicating that it was time to start. One by one, my bridal party left the room, squeezing my hand, wishing me good luck, calling me beautiful. Forrest whispered, "See you on the other side," as she left, offering a hint of a smile before she disappeared.

It was just me and my dad, waiting for my wedding planner's signal. He awkwardly fidgeted with his bowtie as we stood together in silence. I took deep breaths as I closed my eyes, straining to calm my nerves.

Soon, I'd see Matthew, and everything would be okay, because my nerves had nothing to do with him. I loved Matthew. I really did. My anxiety stemmed from the anticipation of carrying out this ceremony according to plan, not from the fear of pledging my life to his. Anyone in my shoes would feel the same. It didn't mean anything.

It was fine. I was fine.

I took another deep breath.

2

We left our hiding spot and stepped into the lobby of the church, the guests silent as violins ushered the bridal party down the aisle. The wedding planner flashed a thumbs up as I approached the mahogany doors leading inside. I smiled faintly back, then turned toward the entrance. She whispered, "now," and I stepped through.

Everyone in the church rose to stare at me. My breath hitched at the sight of so many eyes at once. I fought the blush creeping up my neck and was grateful the bouquet hid my shaking hands. This was the moment I'd been preparing for, all this time, the reason I'd lost weight and lengthened my lashes and spent the whole day being styled to perfection. I calmed myself by counting my footsteps, to match the pace Melissa had tapped out once over coffee, knocking the knuckle that held her wedding ring against the wooden table. *One... and-two... One... and-two.* Not too fast, and not too slow. When I perfected the rhythm, about a quarter-way down the aisle, I let my eyes drift to my fiancé.

Matthew ran a hand through his short, blonde curls as his wide eyes ran over me. He looked like a deer in oncoming traffic, but he forced a smile, anyway. It reminded me of the first night we met, at his friend's house party in Arlington. I could feel him watching me from across the room half the night. When I finally stepped up to ask his name, he looked the same way. Dilated eyes, lightly parted lips, Adam's apple bobbing as he swallowed his beer nervously. He could be trite with his words, but his eyes never lied. He was so reassuringly easy to read.

I smiled for him. I wanted him to know I was entering our marriage grateful to be his bride. I wanted him to know I was enjoying *our* moment, and he had nothing to fear. Maybe I wanted myself to know that, too. I suppressed the nervous flutter in my chest. Matthew needed me to be a rock in this moment, and so did I.

As my dad and I reached the altar, I turned to Forrest to hand her my bouquet, and my mouth fell open at the sight of her. My best friend was crying. She didn't even bother to brush away the tears that streamed silently down her cheeks. When we locked eyes she smiled, but the tears continued to flow, even as she kept her face composed. They couldn't be joyful, not with that haunting sorrow in her eyes. Before I gave the bouquet, I grabbed her hand and squeezed. She squeezed back hard, like I was pulling her from the edge of something.

"Forrest," I said, studying the tears that shined on her lashes. "Are you—"

"I'm just happy for you," she whispered, dropping my hand to take the bouquet. She took a deep breath as she flashed a smile, and all traces of sadness were gone. Then she lifted her eyes to mine, her gaze piercing as she said: "I love you."

Of course. Of course she was happy for me. That was so Forrest. She cared for her friends so deeply the emotion oozed out of her. I must have imagined her sadness, a product of my own anxiety. I smiled back as I kissed her on the cheek. "I love you, too."

I returned to my father's side, who performed the final ritual of passing my hand to Matthew's, officially handing me over to my husband. When the deed was done, my father returned to his seat, and Matthew and I turned to face the altar. His hands gripped mine loosely.

They were sweaty.

Very. Sweaty.

He mumbled something about how I looked beautiful, and I whispered, "Thanks," suddenly shy. The effect of the crowd staring us down made Matthew feel almost like a stranger. I wondered what he made of it, to see our quiet life shrouded in glamor, subject to the scrutiny of all our family and friends.

The pastor said, "Please be seated," and the crowd obeyed. The Reverend Dominic Townes was tall with perfect posture, rosy cheeks, thinning gray hair, and ovular spectacles that rested halfway down his nose. He spoke like he was ready for retirement, with a soothing, steady voice that lent itself well to tuning out. Melissa was right in choosing him. It was the perfect semi-forgettable sermon on love — calm but uplifting — to warm the crowd up for the reception.

I sighed as I shifted my weight between my feet. I didn't know if it was his voice, my exhaustion, or the frozen perfection of the scene around me, but I felt like I could almost fall asleep. I hadn't relaxed like this in months. Everything really had come together exactly as Melissa and I planned. All the late nights over my computer and afternoons in tears, all the phone calls soothing disgruntled bridesmaids who disapproved of the seating chart, or the food, or their dresses — somehow, it worked out how I wanted. Maybe I could finally enjoy myself, after all.

"As long as you have love," the priest said, looking from me to Matthew fondly, "you can face whatever lies ahead."

I smiled as I felt my shoulders droop. Everything would be okay. It really would.

The thought had barely passed my mind when Townes said: "If anyone here objects to this union, speak now, or forever hold your peace."

That's when I heard it — rustling. Shuffling feet echoed down the aisle, and before I could pass it off as an ill-timed bathroom break, there were gasps. Then crinkling paper. Someone had prepared a speech. My eyes widened, as heat flushed my face. I didn't want to turn toward the commotion, didn't want to acknowledge the disaster, but what choice did I have? On a day that I curated down to the minute, I was suddenly, terrifyingly out of control.

I turned.

A pale, wiry woman stood in the aisle I had just crossed with her hands shaking, clutching a crumpled piece of notebook paper. She wore a blue cotton dress that was too casual for a wedding, with navy Converse covered in scuff marks; her long brown hair was tied in a messy bun as her bangs fell unkept around her face. She had large hazel eyes and an endearing button nose that gave her face a mouse-ish quality. I recognized her from Matthew's old Instagram photos, from before we were together. Jessica, his college girlfriend. They dated for three years but broke up at graduation because they didn't want to do long distance. He told me about the relationship, but shared almost nothing about her. I thought she was a distant ghost in his dating past. Only, if that were true, why was she here?

She tucked a loose strand of hair behind her ear as she lifted the paper and began to read. Her voice trembled as much as her hands.

"I never thought I would be the type to interrupt a wedding," she said. "But—" here, she met Matthew's eyes. "But I think you're making a mistake, Mattie."

"Mattie?" I mumbled. Then I realized she meant my fiancé. *A mistake.* That was me. My jaw dropped, and I turned to him reflexively — I immediately wished I hadn't.

Matthew stared at Jessica like she just melted winter with one breath, as a blush turned his whole face petal pink. He was completely frozen, as if he feared one movement would make her disappear. As if everything and everyone else in the room had simply ceased to exist, me included.

He never looked at me that way. Not once.

"Ever since I ran into you last week," she continued. *What?* "I haven't stopped thinking about you, or what you said to me. How being with me, you finally felt like you belonged somewhere. Because I feel the same way. Like," and here, she quickly brushed a single stray tear from her cheek, "I was existing in the world as half of myself, and then I saw you and woke up. Just like that. I thought I let go of my dreams because I grew up, but now I realize that's not true. Because I see you and my world feels just as wide as it was when we were 22. You bring something out of me, Mattie. You make me the best version of myself and—" Another dramatic pause to brush a tear away. "And I just think, how can you feel that way about a person and let them marry somebody else?"

Matthew dropped my hand to brush away a tear. It was the first time I ever saw him cry. I gasped at it, and he didn't even look at me.

"I don't know how you feel," (Fuck. There was *more?*) "Or if what I said will even change anything. I just knew I had to say something, or I'd always regret it, because... I love you. I never stopped loving you. I don't think I ever will stop loving you." Here, she looked to the aisles for the first time and blushed, like she had forgotten she was giving this speech in the middle of a wedding I spent a year planning, in front of every single family member, friend, and acquaintance I knew. "So, yeah. That's all I had to say..." her voice trailed off, and she turned to go. For a few painful moments, the church was dead silent, except for her shuffling converse on the marble floor.

Then: "Jess — wait!"

There was no goodbye, no apology, not even a passing glance. Matthew just took off. He sprinted down the aisle, his expression shifting from awe to determination. When he reached Jessica at the back door of the church, he wrapped his arms around her waist, forcefully pulling her into him. I didn't know he could be passionate like that. I always thought he was shy.

"I love you," he said, cradling her cheek in his hand. "I love you so fucking much."

He kissed her.

A chorus of gasps rippled through the pews; beside me Matthew's best man muttered "Holy shit." The pastor made the sign of the cross over his heart; Forrest dropped my bouquet, and it tumbled down the steps. Meanwhile, Matthew and Jessica kept kissing. They kissed with a hunger that made me long to turn away, but the circumstances made that impossible. I was frozen, mouth agape, eyes wide, hands flat at my side. There was nothing I could do but watch.

They were still kissing when Forrest grabbed my hand dragged me out a side door of the church. So I didn't see them leave with their fingers intertwined, with matching grins, free from the chaos they left me to clean up. I didn't see every eye in the church pivot at once from the back door to the

altar wondering what this meant for the abandoned
bride.

Like I could give them answers.

3

Forrest pulled me into a dark room down a back hallway of the church and immediately locked the door. When we were finally alone, I sunk to the floor, burying my face in my hands. There were so many ways I could have prevented this, so many questions I could have asked, so many subtle things I could have done to make Matthew love me enough to stay. Or at least respect me enough *not* to leave like this.

Was this wedding a joke to him this entire time? Was I?

There were hundreds of people still in the church, waiting for an explanation.

"I have to go back out there," I said, dropping my hands to boost myself back up. "I have to—"

"No," Forrest said firmly, gripping my shoulders to keep me grounded. Her eyes dug into mine, then softened. She dropped her hands to mine and brushed her thumbs over my palms, as she whispered: "You don't have to do anything."

That's when I lost it. My head collapsed into Forrest's shoulder as I began heaving sobs. It was like every nervous wave I stilled in my stomach, every steady breath I forced myself to take, broke free. It hit me all at once — the months I'd spent torturing myself over wedding planning were only wasted time; my loved ones would consider me pathetic at best and a failure at worst. How would I show my face anywhere again? Where would I even live? I couldn't go back to Matthew's apartment. I couldn't even breathe. I couldn't —

"Hey, hey" said Forrest, stroking my hair. "I know." She dropped one of my hands and ran her fingers down my back, undoing the satin buttons caging me inside my cursed dress, freeing my lungs. All I could see was eyes. Watching Matthew. Watching me. My life was in tatters. "I know." Forrest unfastened the last button, and my torso was free. She moved on to meticulously pluck away the bobby pins that kept my hair in place. When my hair was free, she ran her hands through my hair, massaging my scalp with her long fingers, letting my hair fall loose down my back. I did not realize how uncomfortable my head had been until this moment. I sighed as I leaned into her, resting my head on the divot above her collarbone.

We sat that way for a while, until my sobs quieted, and my tears crusted under my eyes.

"I can't believe he did this to me," I whispered, my voice cracking again. "I thought he was my friend."

That hurt the most. Not that Matthew was in love with another woman, but that after everything we'd been through, he didn't respect me enough to tell me, or to even glance my way before he ran into her arms. All the late nights we laughed together, all the quiet takeout dinners, the lazy mornings chatting in bed, were nothing. I gave everything to our relationship because I believed the roses, movie nights and gentle handholding meant something. I thought we were friends. Today Matthew proved me wrong without even speaking a word.

"I thought so, too," Forrest mumbled.

I lifted my head, so our eyes locked. "Really?"

Tears sprang to Forrest's eyes when I said that. "Alana, *of course*. He always seemed like a nice guy. This isn't your fault." She squeezed my hands as a tear ran down her cheek. "The only person responsible for what happened is Matthew. And that asshole ex-girlfriend, who could have given her speech to him in private, literally at any point before the wedding." There was fire in her dark eyes, piercing mine. "You didn't do *anything*. Some people are just really good at hiding who they are." She leaned forward and kissed my forehead gently. "He fooled me, too, Al."

I threw an arm around her neck, and squeezed her into a hug, as my tears started flowing again. It was so easy to blame myself. Only Forrest didn't. Forrest, who was there, and *saw* it, was holding me on the floor of some random room in the church, telling me it wasn't my fault. Soothing me like I mattered.

Maybe one day, I'd believe it, too.

"I don't know what to do," I told her, my voice breaking. "I don't even know where I'll live. I—"

"Alana." Forrest's voice was firm as she locked eyes with mine, gripping my hands in her own. "I don't know what comes next, but I promise you won't face it alone." Her thumb rubbed my shoulder in reassuring circles. "You'll always have a home with me. No matter what."

"Thank you," I whispered. And Forrest told me not to thank her, that it was nothing, which was the most *Forrest* response she could give. I almost smiled despite myself.

There were feet shuffling outside; right outside the door, muffled voices wondering aloud where I'd gone.

"Just so we're on the same page," Forrest whispered, barely moving her lips. "We're not leaving this room until they've given up looking for you."

"Oh, no way in hell."

She smiled. "Perfect."

As she moved to sit next to me, I finally looked past Forrest to see what room she'd dragged us into. When I did, I flinched back toward the door and gasped, clutching a hand to my chest.

"What?" Forrest asked, facing me with wide eyes.

"Ruth Bader-Ginsburg."

"What?"

I pointed, and when Forrest turned, her jaw dropped. She nearly fell into me as she muttered, "Holy shit."

There, right in front of us, was RBG.

And above us, below us, to our right and left, you name it. RBG was all over this room. Photographed portraits, artists' renderings, and prints with 'Notorious RBG' in a gold crown plastered the walls; to our left, a large mahogany bookshelf carried dozens of biographies alongside her own writing. Her face appeared on a wall clock, on throw pillows, on the t-shirt draped over the desk chair in front of us. Behind it, her life-size cardboard cutout seemed to survey the room like a queen in her kingdom.

"Dude," I said, removing my clenched fists from my chest. "where *are* we?"

Forrest pressed a hand to her forehead as she pursed her lips. "Al, did you almost marry into an RBG cult?"

I stood up, and the justice's eyes followed me like the Mona Lisa. I crossed my arms over my unbuttoned dress, for modesty. "I need to investigate." I felt the wall until I found a lamp and flicked it on. It was even worse in the light. Every photograph, every item of décor, professed ardent devotion to the Supreme Court justice. There were pens, postcards, enamel pins, stickers, socks, even a deck of playing cards. Every Ruth-Bader Ginsburg product in existence was somewhere in this room.

Forrest shook her head. "Where did they even *find* all this stuff?"

"I recognize this finger puppet from Politics and Prose," I said, recalling a display at the DC bookstore as I approached the desk. "I don't know about the rest." I stared at a terrifyingly accurate metal bust of her face on the desk and ran finger over the metal ridges of her hair.

When Forrest walked around the desk to stand beside me, a loud laugh burst from her lips. "Al," she said, suddenly wheezing. "Look."

She pointed at a framed photo on the desk and slid to the floor, clutching her stomach. My jaw fell open at the only picture in this room that did not feature Ruth Bader-Ginsburg. In a family vacation photo with little blonde grandkids, adult children, and grandparents, there was one face I knew. The grey-haired patriarch in a Hawaiian shirt at the center.

"No," I gasped, falling to the floor beside Forrest. "Not the priest!"

We both howled with laughter until our stomachs ached. I felt hysterical, swept away by the shock of today. My best friend was in tears beside me, clutching her stomach as her dress pooled on the floor beneath her. "I have," gasped Forrest, "so many follow-up questions."

Before I could reply, banging on the door interrupted us. My stomach sunk. Our laughter must have served as a siren call to everyone who was looking for me. Sure enough, the sliver of light under the door flickered with leg-sized shadows, as a flurry of voices began calling my name. The anxiety that almost subsided became marbles in my throat. Forrest pressed her lips into a flat line and stared at the door with dagger eyes. Was she... angry? But then she turned to me, and her scowl melted away.

"I don't care if we're here all night," Forrest said. "We're not opening that door."

I nodded, but I could barely hear my own thoughts Outside, their voices carried through the door with merciless clarity.

"Alana, open up, honey!"

"The poor thing, she must be humiliated."

"Do you want to cancel the wedding?" (Forrest laughed at that.)

"Leave her alone, Mom!"

"She can't run away from this."

"Why not? Matthew did. Remember?"

"Don't do anything rash, Alana."

"About my office... I can explain!"

"People are confused, honey. They need to know you're ok."

"Melissa's handling it. Alana doesn't need to go back out there."

"Not now, Gemma."

"Then when?"

"We can figure this out, Alana. He'll come back."

"I'm a feminist! Just know I'm a feminist!"

Forrest's phone buzzed, and she looked down at the screen. "It's Carter," she said, turning the phone toward me.

Get Alana out of here. I will handle this hot mess! Xo

Tears rushed down my cheeks as I read it, overcome with relief. There was no way I could manage a clean getaway on my own. How would I have survived this without my best friends? I stared at Forrest in wonder. "You brought your phone?"

"I'm the maid of honor, Al! I have to be ready for anything." I brushed the tears off my cheeks as Forrest squeezed my shoulder. "Let's get out of here."

Forrest got to work buttoning my dress, so I could escape properly clothed. There was only one way out: A window behind the pastor's desk that Forrest and I could just barely fit through. We leaned against the desk and stared at it together.

"Matthew left me at the altar, and *I'm* the one who has to escape through a window," I muttered.

"The patriarchy shows itself in surprising ways," Forrest said, shaking her head. "Hold on one second." She stepped past me to the cardboard cutout of RBG, and picked up the Supreme Court justice with one hand. She placed the cutout squarely in front of the door. "That'll slow them down."

I laughed as she joined me by the desk again. "Ready?"

We left my veil behind and carried our heels as we took turns wiggling through the window, to an empty alley behind the church. Forrest carried my train as we picked our way past a dead rat, a crumpled Doritos wrapper, and an oily puddle I could only hope was water. We escaped in the style of countless runaway brides before me — only there was no groom left for me to leave, nobody to disappoint but my parents. I pushed those thoughts away. For now, it was enough to be free.

Forrest left first so she could catch me once I got through the window, her dress more mobile than mine. "You know, in retrospect, a mermaid dress was probably the worst choice I could have made, for escaping purposes." Forrest was supporting my full upper body as I said this, my arms clutching her neck as I slowly shifted my feet from the windowsill to the ground.

"Melissa chose the perfect bridesmaid dresses for this, though," Forrest answered as my toes touched the ground. "This slit in the side? Perfect for running. I feel like I could wear this in an action movie. Though I *would* trade out the stilettos for sneakers."

"I'd trade the stilettos for a getaway car." I sighed, feeling tired and small. "I put everything into this wedding, only to end up between a dead rat and dumpster with no way out."

Forrest grinned, her eyes gleaming. "I have a solution for that."

She led us down the narrow alley around a corner to the left. The alley widened, and a candy red corvette appeared, a "Just Married" sign fastened to the back with cans tied to the bumper.

I stared at the car, then at my best friend, my face growing hot. "You did this?"

Forrest clicked the keys, unlocking the doors. "You mentioned that Matthew loves old cars. I thought it'd be a sweet gesture. The escape feature is a bonus." She winked at me as she opened the driver's door.

I clutched the hem of my dress and slide into the passenger seat. "You are my hero, Forrest. For real."

"Shut up, Al," Forrest said with a grin. "It'll go to my head."

I smiled softly as we drove away, cans clunking behind us.

4

Obviously, I never told Matthew that Forrest and I slept together when we were nineteen.

It just wasn't relevant. He tensed his shoulders uncomfortably if a man checked me out on a street corner, grew quiet if I called a celebrity attractive while watching TV. How would he react if he knew I lost my virginity to my maid of honor? I told him the first man I slept with, a college boyfriend who was addicted to Fortnite and described the Red Hot Chili Peppers as a band "you probably haven't heard of." But I didn't want him to see my best friend as a threat. How could I expect him to understand my relationship with Forrest? I wasn't entirely sure I understood it. Not when a nervous flutter still flared in my stomach whenever she called me pretty.

We were junior counselors together at a summer camp after our freshman year of college, back when I still believed that boys were who you married and girls where who secretly made you blush during math class.

I met Forrest as I hauled my trunk into the cabin with my mom, sweaty from the summer humidity.

I was immediately self-conscious when Forrest barged out of the cabin and almost hit my mom with the door.

Her midnight eyes flared in surprise when she saw us holding my large black trunk. Her mouth opened slightly as she flinched back. I took in everything. Her long fingers and chipped indigo nail polish, her white t-shirt with a line drawing of wildflowers on the front, the cerulean tips at the end of her long hair, which she wore in corn rows back then. She had a long face with a delicately curved nose and defined cheek bones. Her large, expressive eyes shined invitingly, but I shrunk back, instantly shy. It scared me how easy she was to love, even then.

"I'm so sorry," she blurted, holding the screen door open so we could carry the trunk through. "I almost took you out!"

"Don't worry," answered my mother, ever the hostess. "Thank you for getting the door."

"No problem." Forrest turned to me. "Are you the other counselor for this cabin?"

I flashed a polite smile. "Yeah."

She answered with a radiant grin, all dimples and straight, white teeth. "Nice! I'm in this cabin, too. I'm Forrest."

"Alana." I set the trunk down by our bunk beds, and my hands rested awkwardly at my side. Should I wave? Shake her hand? My cheeks warmed at the thought of touching her. "It's nice to meet you."

"You, too," she said, with that smile again, unleashing a rollercoaster in my chest. This must be how vampires felt in the sunshine, I realized. On the one hand, the sight of it, the feeling of warmth on my skin, was glorious. On the other, I was certainly, hopelessly, totally dead.

I avoided her as much as I could. Not that it was easy. Forrest's very demeanor was light. Within a week, she made inside jokes with every counselor and had a small trail of campers tailing her everywhere, asking questions, sharing stories, fighting over who could hold her hand, doing everything they could to earn a burst of her musical laughter. I was a Graphic Design major at UNC, she a business student at Howard. We were both from the South, Raleigh and Richmond, respectively, we both had one sister, though hers was older. I absorbed every detail about her greedily, even if I wasn't brave enough to ask the questions myself.

I was especially shy at nineteen. I had come to UNC after four years as the shining star of my high school. Captain of the soccer team, class president, straight-A student, well-liked because I was pretty and kind but not popular in the traditional sense. I graduated with few close friends and the vague sense that nobody really knew me. UNC was my fresh start, a chance to make friends that would keep in touch.

Naively, I joined a sorority. They kicked me out six months later. When freshman year ended, I found myself universally hated by about 100 people who I thought would be my sisters. At the same time, I was gifted with something I'd never had before — one true friend. Carter. I was shy around new faces, mistrusting of just about everyone else. But for the first time in my life I did not feel wholly alone.

All this to say it was very easy to convince myself that my past was the source of my shyness around Forrest — not her magnetic beauty. The more I avoided her, the easier it was to believe it.

Forrest taught arts and crafts, while I was a swimming instructor at the lake, so we only crossed paths in the cabin or at camp-wide activities. I was friendly, but whenever I found myself alone with her, I'd realize with a start that I had nothing to say and no idea where to put my hands.

I had no inclination that Forrest noticed, let alone cared, until she caught me in the cabin with a bat.

In the back of the junior counselor's cabin was a small bathroom stall that I used to change before lifeguarding. I had just pulled up my one piece when I heard a soft clicking noise coming from the cabin. I wondered if it was another counselor texting.

"Hello?" I called. The clicking stopped.

I took a deep breath, quickly finished pulling up my bathing suit, and stepped out of the bathroom. Nothing was amiss. There were the bunkbeds with pastel colored blankets, surrounded by wide screen windows, offering a glimpse of the lazy summer day. Nothing was amiss, but—

There. A black smudge no larger than my fist, with large cartoonish wings flying crookedly around the cabin. It appeared and disappeared behind bunk beds as it circled the space, blocking my path to the door. I had never seen a bat before, and was surprised it looked so, well, exactly how I thought a bat would look, its darkness out of place in broad daylight. Bats were supposed to be nocturnal, though. Could this one be rabid? I shuddered.

It was then that Forrest pushed open the cabin door, about to step inside with the animal when I found my voice again.

"Don't!" I shouted, and she froze with the door propped open as her eyes darted to mine, wide with fear as I stood frozen in the back of the cabin. "There's a bat!"

Then it circled toward the front of the cabin, seemingly unaware of both of us, and she saw it. Her round eyes swelled as wide as mine. "We need to get you out of here."

"Go get Lee Ann," the head counselor who'd hired us both a few months ago. "She can call Animal Control, and I'll wait here."

Forrest shook her head. "I'm not leaving you."

"I'll be fine. I don't want you to—"

Forrest crossed her arms as her face formed a pleading expression. "I know you don't like me, but just let me help you."

"What?" My stomach dropped, and my ears burned red with shame. "Why do you think I don't like you?"

"You're friendly to every counselor except me, and whenever we're alone in the cabin together, you find an excuse to go see Martha next door."

"I didn't—"

"It's fine, you don't have to like me, just — I think we should talk about this when you're not at risk of being bitten by a wild animal."

Oh, yeah. The bat. "Right."

Forrest shifted her gaze from me to the bat, to our bunk bed, beside the door. "Ok, I have an idea," she said.

Without warning, Forrest lunged toward our bunk and grabbed my lavender knit blanket off the bed. She draped it over her head like shawl, leaving one thin slit for her to see through. Then she hunched low to the ground sprinted to the back of the cabin where I stood. I barely had time to blink before she was beside me.

I stared at her eye through the blanket. "You—"

"Get under here," she hissed, and I did. "Hold on. Once it clears the aisle, we run." I clenched my fist around a fold in her t-shirt and waited, the silenced punctured by our panting.

"Now!" she cried, and we ran. Or, rather, we ran as best we could while hunched under a blanket. I could only see Forrest's back and our feet shuffling toward the cabin door. Our pace was probably just slightly faster than a walk, but our urgency made it feel like an Olympic race. Forrest's eyes on the door, our hearts pounding, seconds passing like years. The only thing on my mind was escaping — and not gripping Forrest's t-shirt too tight, because I didn't want to leave it wrinkled.

Finally we halted, as Forrest pushed open the door.

We burst through, panting as Forrest lifted the blanket off us and shoved the door shut. Murmuring, "Oh, thank God," and brushing our hands over our hair like the bat touched us. (It didn't.) Restoring a socially acceptable distance between each other. Looking at each other, blinking, still gasping. Then... a laugh. Loud, sudden, and uncontrollable. Because I was convinced I would die in the cabin until my bunkmate with the dimples and electric eyes saved me. We must have looked insane, but now we were here, together, and Forrest was laughing, too. I thought it was all worth it — the fear, the awkwardness — to laugh with her like this, just this once.

"Thank you for saving me," I said when my laughter calmed enough to breathe again.

Forrest widened her grin, still panting. "Do you like me now?" she teased.

"I never didn't." My blush returned. Why did I always sound so lame around her? "I mean, I always liked you." But did that sound too strong?

Forrest dropped her smile and cocked her head thoughtfully. "If you like me, then why won't you talk to me?" Her wide brown eyes were stained with hurt, her gaze so piercing I felt weak in the knees.

I took a deep breath and spoke carefully. "The truth is, I—" *can't form two sentences around you.* "I think you're really—" *beautiful.* "Cool." *Vexing.* "And I get nervous. Sometimes."

My face burned with a blush, as Forrest blinked, her lips parting slightly. "What?"

"I'm sorry for making you think I don't like you. Sometimes, it just takes me a little longer to warm up to people. I don't know. I'm working on it." I wasn't. It would be two more years before I started therapy. I just didn't know what else to say.

Forrest raised her eyebrows. "You get like that around people... when you think they're cool?"

"Yeah." I stared at her toes, freshly painted violet, then back at her eyes. "I know it's stupid."

"No, no. It's sweet. And not what I expected. At all." Forrest started fiddling with the silver ring on her middle finger, which I'd later learn was a nervous tick. She studied me with an odd, soft smile, almost shy. "If I can convince you that I'm actually a weirdo, can we be friends?"

I smiled in relief, and... something else. No one had ever asked to be my friend. "Deal."

"Cool." Forrest nodded her head in a gesture that was awkward but endearing. "I'll go tell Lee Ann to call animal control. You make sure none of the campers go in the cabin."

I agreed, and in a flash she was jogging to find the head counselor, leaving me alone in the afternoon sun.

We were inseparable for the rest of the summer. Laughing with campers in the mess hall, sharing a look whenever Lee Ann spoke cultishly about the camp at bonfires, always finding our way to the other's side when we hung out with the counselors after Light's Out. All my hesitation with her vanished. Never mind that when I dressed up for a dance with a neighboring boys' camp and Forrest said I looked gorgeous, my stomach went into freefall. Never mind that sometimes, when I stole a glance at her, I swore she was one of the most beautiful people I'd ever seen. Forrest drawing on the beach by my lifeguard chair, delicate fingers shading a portrait. Forrest surrounded by embers roasting s'mores, her enthralling eyes watching a marshmallow burn.

She had a boyfriend who wrote her letters once a week. I'd often find her lying on her stomach on the top bunk, writing back. The nervous flutters she sparked in me were achingly hopeless, to my relief. I never had to know what she'd think if she knew I wanted her, never had to wonder what it meant for my life that I desired a woman. In doing nothing, I was safe.

I basked in her friendship, instead. I loved the way she pressed her eyebrows together when she drew, loved the way she nodded earnestly when we stayed up late whispering in my bunk. She carried herself with a kind, carefree air that awed me as I learned what she'd been through. Her parents died in a car crash when she was sixteen. After, she and her sister, Monique, moved from New Orleans to Richmond to live with their aunt and uncle. She loved them, but the loss of her parents ached like a phantom limb.

She told me everything in the middle of the night when I woke up to use the bathroom and found her sobbing silently in her top bunk. They sung "Silver Spring" by Fleetwood Mac at a bonfire — which her mother used to play on the guitar back home. I walked her down to the dock by the lake, and we talked until the sun came up.

I had no understanding of the pain that comes with losing your parents, and no concept of the closeness that fueled Forrest's grief for her mom and dad. My mother loved me the way she loved outwardly beautiful things; most of our conversations centered around what I could do to be prettier, smarter, more perfect. My father was a workaholic who avoided anything involving emotion. At home, I lived with my guard up, always afraid of failing them. I couldn't fathom growing up close to your parents, only to have that love ripped away.

So I asked her. She told me her parents were basically Pam and Jim from 'The Office,' co-workers at a non-profit in New Orleans who became best friends, then realized they were soul mates. They raised Forrest and Monique in a house filled with warmth, laughter, and plenty of art. Their mother playing guitar before bed, their father making frames out of plywood to hang Forrest's drawings, Monique leading family dances in the kitchen, the smell of jasmine wafting in through the windows.

"My mom's flower garden surrounded the house. She grew jasmine, azaleas and clematis, but her hibiscus was her pride and joy. Nobody understood how she kept them alive every winter — it was her secret. Though she told me once that you just need to let the flowers die and come back, that plants grow on trust and love like kids do.

"I used to sit on the back porch after school when she gardened. She tried to teach me, but I was hopeless at it, so I just watched. We talked about everything, she called them our fireside chats. She always seemed to know the right thing to say, no matter what I was feeling. At sixteen, I felt like I could figure out any problem I put my mind to, because *she* could. Now, I just feel alone. I don't know anything anymore."

I watched her for awhile, sniffling under the starlight, the lake rippling beneath us. This was the Forrest she didn't let anyone see, wise and weary from the weight of the world. Now I understood that her warmth was laced with hurt, that she clung to outward joy because she intimately knew despair. That sometimes, when the world was ripped from under you, the beauty of silver moonlight dancing on a lake was the only thing keeping you from hurtling over the edge.

"I can't help you figure out any problems," I said, and her tears shined like stars in her eyes when she faced me. "I don't know anything, either." A soft laugh escaped through her melancholy. I scoot closer and placed my hand over hers. "But I can promise you'll never be alone."

I pierced her eyes with my gaze so she'd understand — as long as I knew her, I'd never leave her to suffer alone. I meant it like a wedding vow.

When tears welled in her eyes, I thought I said something wrong. But then she smiled as she wrapped me in an all-consuming hug. "Thanks, Al," she whispered.

By dawn, as we yawned together and trudged back to the cabin in the blue-gray light, it occurred to me that I loved her. Seeing tears fill those deep brown eyes ignited an uncontrollable urge to protect her. I'd cross a desert for her, I realized, anything to bring her peace. My heart seemed to burn when I looked at her, and it wasn't just her beauty. It was the layered, complex pieces of her soul that made her Forrest, as rare and precious as sapphires. My very being sang her name, and the song grew louder the deeper I knew her. I loved her.

But... platonically. I reminded myself as I held the cabin door open and watched her shuffle inside. I loved her platonically.

That summer, Forrest was the first and last person I spoke to each day, the one I whispered jokes with, whose company I sought at every camp event. When the end of summer came, my stomach twisted in knots at saying goodbye. We agreed to stay in touch, but it wouldn't be the same.

She'd go back to her boyfriend. I'd go home alone.

The camp closed the evening with a bonfire by the lake, with s'mores and music, sparks flying in the sunset. Forrest and I stood on opposite ends of a log with campers between us, and I pretended I wasn't transfixed watching her from the corner of my eye. Then we fire died, we slipped into our bunks, and that was that. Or so I thought.

I was in a light, dreamless sleep, when I felt a hand lightly squeeze my shoulder. "Hey," Forrest whispered. I opened my eyes and could barely make out her figure leaning over mine. She jutted her head to the cabin door. "Come on." Wordlessly, I slipped on my flip flops and followed.

Behind the cluster of cabins where we slept, there was a narrow wooden trail paved with pebbles that lead directly down a hill to the lake. When I came here with Forrest earlier in the summer, it was cloudy, and everything smelled like fresh rain. But tonight the sky was clear. Moonlight reflected off the lake, as constellations illuminated the indigo sky. We sat together on the dock over the water and watched it as crickets hummed loudly around us. Everything was still.

Forrest said, "I'm gonna miss this."

"I'm gonna miss you." My breath caught at the confession. Why did I say that?

But she said, "me, too," so maybe I wasn't an idiot.

The moonlight coated Forrest in lavender hues, as she stared across the lake. One of her feet dangled over the water, while the other perched on the edge of the dock, as she hugged a knee to her chest. I was about to turn back to the water when Forrest turned to me, locking eyes, and opened her mouth to speak. My breath hitched. She said: "You never told me why they kicked you out of your sorority."

I sighed. "Oh." I didn't expect to tell that story here, watching starlight dance on the water. "One night, Carter and I went out to a frat on Franklin Street with some of my sisters. Only, while we were there, someone spiked his drink."

"Oh, shit."

"Yeah. Luckily, I was with him the entire time, so nothing happened, but he got really fucked up. He still doesn't remember anything. I took him back to my room to take care of him. The next day, another sister saw him in the bathroom and ratted me out. No boys were allowed to stay overnight in the sorority house, and they were super intense about it. They fined me, but I couldn't pay, so they kicked me out. I never fit in with them, anyway, though. It worked out for the best."

I shrugged, indicating the story was finished. Forrest blinked again. "You took care of your friend, so they kicked you out?"

"Well, it was a lot more dramatic at the time. We had a chapter-wide meeting where they called me a slut and voted me out, 'Survivor' style." My eyes dropped to the dock's wood grain. "I slept on Carter's futon for the rest of the year."

Forrest wrinkled her nose. "In a boy's dorm?"

I shrugged. "Carter's neat, and it was only for two months."

Forrest nodded and faced the water, her legs dangling off the dock. Our knees were half an inch from touching. I stared at her back, still resting on my elbows, and felt my shoulders tense. I wondered what she thought of me. The sorority reject. Finally, she turned back. "It's just so you," she said.

I sat up to face her, so our eyes were level. I blushed at how close we were. "What do you mean?"

"You are so giving to other people, no matter the cost to yourself. I mean, you were going to let a bat *eat* you rather than have me be in danger for just a minute."

I shook my head as I smiled at her. "That bat was way too small to eat me."

Forrest elbowed me playfully. "Minor details. The point is, I'm grateful that we found each other. You're funny, and kind, and... so beautiful, Alana." I stopped breathing at this point. Her gaze drifted from my eyes to my lips as she whispered, "You make me feel so heard, like I could tell you anything and you'd still have my back. I hope you know I'd do the same. I feel the same way about you."

I stared at her, realizing I was close enough to feel her breath on my cheek, to see desire flare in her eyes, and I couldn't help myself. I kissed her. Her lips were even softer than I imagined, and as she opened her mouth slightly, I could taste her peppermint toothpaste and coconut lip balm. I pulled away.

Forrest blinked. Her eyes were wide with shock, her mouth open, as she stared at me. My jaw dropped alongside my stomach as I studied her. I read this wrong. I ruined everything. What was I thinking?

"I'm sorry," I said. "I don't know why I—"
Only Forrest kissed me back before I could say anything else. Stole the breath, fear, and doubt right from my mouth, and filled it with her.

Gently, she slipped her tongue behind my teeth, like she was savoring the taste of me, as I pulled her into me. She moaned softly, deepening the kiss, and I savored the low, rich sound of her pleasure. She thread her fingers through my hair, and wrapped my hand around her waist, pulling her into me. I'd heard that kisses could be lightning, but never believed it until that moment. Only it was more than sparks with Forrest. She was the freefall and the parachute, the hurricane and the hideout. I had never felt so out of control and so safe at once.

It never felt so easy to be brave.

I slipped my hand underneath her pajama shirt, and grazed her satin soft cleavage with my thumb, eliciting another delightful moan. Forrest pulled her lips away briefly as she swung her leg over mine, straddling me. "This is better," she whispered, as she kissed me again. She dragged a finger lazily across the hem of my boxer shorts, as her other hand slide under my shirt hem, her fingers dancing up my spine.

My body curled into her touch. Every stroke of her hand was a dare, begging me to take this further, to feel her in all the places that I'd dreamed about. I obliged, peeling my lips away from hers to draw a line of kisses down her neck. I brushed my thumb tenderly over her nipple, which hardened at my touch. She gasped, and I whispered into her collarbone, "I love that sound." I wanted to make her moan and gasp until she screamed, until my ears knew nothing but the sound of Forrest.

Her hand slipped past my boxers to graze the fabric of my underwear, and I gasped to feel her toying with me in my most sensitive place. She whispered back, "I love that sound." Her eyes locked into mine as her hand dropped further; she pushed my underwear aside and slipped her hand between my legs — right where I wanted her. I throbbed at the whisper of her touch.

She smiled as she traced my folds, on the cusp of entering me. I watched her with wide eyes and heavy breaths, reduced to molten by her touch. "I've never seen anyone look as beautiful as you do right now, Alana." She stared into my eyes for half a second, then pressed two fingers inside me.

As I moaned, she covered my mouth with hers, swallowing the sound with a kiss. She explored me like she wanted to sear the memory of her fingers in my skin. I was utterly at her mercy. Then she pulled her hand away, and I was about to protest when she ripped off her shirt, exposing her breasts to the night. Her shirt balled in her hands, and her skin glowed in the blue moonlight. I had never seen anyone so beautiful. She shook her t-shirt flat and resting it on the dock behind me. "Lay down," she ordered, and I dipped my head away from hers until it rested against her shirt. Instantly, her face was upon mine. "Thank you," she whispered, and I could feel her smile against my lips as her fingers entered me again.

The only thought I could form as she overtook my senses was *more*. More of her taste, her firm touch taking over my body. More of our tangled feet hanging off the dock. More of the exhilarating sense of finding the universe in her eyes. More.

She sped up her touch, flattening her fingers against the spot that I craved as I arched my back into her. I surrendered myself fully to Forrest, and cried her name into her lips as she led me to release. Her hand slowed to the pace of my breath, dragging out my pleasure, so by the time she finished I was limp in her arms, sweaty from the humidity and the rush of feeling her everywhere.

"My turn," I whispered, and I explored her body freely, the way I yearned to all summer. Kissing the groove in her collarbone, running my fingers over the soft skin of her upper thighs. I continued until her knees buckled beneath me, until I had to quiet her cries with a kiss. Fatigue finally coaxed us into a deep, dreamless sleep; I spent the best sleep of my life holding her.

All I wanted was peace. I would kill for a nap, but my phone wouldn't shut up — summoning me from task to task when all I wanted to do was curl up and watch "Letters To Juliet." The movie was playing in the background of our hotel room, so I could enjoy Italian landscapes even though my honeymoon was canceled. I could barely follow it with all the phone calls taking my attention, begging vendors for discounts and refunds wherever we could get them.

Carter and Forrest split a room at The Mayflower for the wedding, and that was where we set up camp with sweatpants and complimentary room service, a gift from The Mayflower's wedding team. We spoke with vendors and parried nosey phone calls from wedding guests who wanted to make sure I was okay. Allegedly. I sat on the hotel bed between Forrest and Carter, while Gemma sprawled in front of us closer to the TV — the only one actually watching the movie. Considering she fended off my mother long enough for Forrest and me to escape, she earned the break.

Thanks to Gemma, my parents were driving home tomorrow morning. My mom was still texting pleas for me to hear "Matthew's side," but at least I didn't have to deal with that in person.

This latest call was from Matthew's co-worker, a notorious office gossip, so I passed my phone to Carter — the only person currently unoccupied. "Hello? Who is this? Hi, Page... This is Carter, her bridesmaid... Alana is asleep right now, but I'll tell her you called... She's holding up, yeah... Yeah, definitely unexpected, not that it's any of your business... I'm sure you are... Ok, well, I'll tell her you called. Bye." He hung up and rolled his eyes as he returned the phone to me. "If this happened to one of my co-workers, there is no part of me that would think to *call* their fiancé."

"She's insanely nosey, and she never liked me. So I can't say I'm surprised." Matthew's consulting firm worked long hours and spent most of their free time together. The company was like a family, in the sense that everyone fought incessantly and gossiped even more. They would unpack my wedding with the fervor of a conspiracy theorist researching the moon landing. My disaster was their Super Bowl.

"The Sunday brunch caterers are giving us a full refund," Forrest announced triumphantly. "Sorry for interrupting."

"This chef is ridiculous," said Gemma. "I will never give a man the time of day who gets this excited about mushrooms, unless he's at a music festival. I don't understand how he pulled Amanda Seyfried."

"The biggest plot hole in any love triangle plot is how the woman put up with her shitty first boyfriend to begin with," said Carter.

I sighed at the TV. "Is that what happened to me?"

"No," Gemma said, not looking up from the TV. "I never saw Matthew jizz in his pants over a mushroom."

Forrest leaned across the bed to stroke my hair with her long fingers, gently detangling any loose knots. "Matthew seemed perfectly likeable," she said. "If any of us had pegged him for a sleaze, *we* would've stopped the wedding."

"Thanks," I said, leaning into the tug of her fingers. This was the kind of hellish day that seemed to last multiple lifetimes. The nervous bride-to-be from hours ago felt like a painfully naïve alter-ego. "Ugh, they've probably finished having reunion sex by now."

Carter smirked, turning away from the TV to lean back on his palms. "You mean *he* finished."

"Carter!" I turned back to him, my cheeks coloring. But I couldn't help but grin at the mischief in his eyes.

Carter held his hands up in mock surrender. "Alana, you yourself said that Matthew was terrible at sex."

"Wait, really?" Forrest's eyes widened. "You never mentioned that."

My blush deepened. "I never said *terrible*. Early on into dating, I said there was... room for improvement. And he did improve."

"Marginally," Carter added.

"Marginally."

"*Marginally?*" Forrest said.

I tried to shrug nonchalantly as I recalled Matthew's awkward handling of my body. There was something about the way he fondled my breasts like they were foreign objects, how his eyes carefully avoided me when he came, that was decidedly impersonal. Like I could be anyone, and he'd still enjoy it. "I figured he'd improve over time," I said sheepishly.

Carter squeezed my hand. "When you're ready, you'll get back out there and have such mind-blowing sex with so many people that you'll forget all about Matthew."

I pressed my fingers into the white duvet, pinching the fabric. Sex with someone else was impossible to imagine right now. Wanting someone who wasn't Matthew, trusting them enough to sleep with them, feeling desired after everything I'd been through — it was unthinkable. That the thought even entered my head made me ashamed. Maybe if I had been more loyal, we'd be twirling through our first dance right now, kissing as relatives surrounded us with sparklers. I bit my bottom lip as tears blurred my vision. "I don't know," I mumbled.

Forrest kept detangling my hair, as Carter rested a hand on my knee.

"Thank you guys for helping me get through all of this," I whispered with a shaking voice. "I have no idea what I'd do if I had to handle this alone."

"Come on, Al," Forrest murmured as she laced her fingers in mine and Carter pulled me into a hug. "You'd do the same for us."

I would, but I didn't feel deserving of their kindness right now. The more I sat with Matthew's betrayal, the more I wondered if I was in the wrong. The wedding overwhelmed me to the point of exhaustion — answering Melissa's texts, researching vendors, cooking dinner each night, keeping our apartment clean — I lost sight of Matthew. Perhaps my absence drove him away. Perhaps he could sense the panic that chilled my bones in the moments of quiet, that it was easier to lose myself in the wedding than dwell on the thought of forever with him.

"Al," Forrest said gently, pulling me out of my thoughts. "What is it?"

I swallowed a lump in my throat. "I was a bad partner to Matthew, I think. I think that's why he left. Maybe he could tell that I was..." my voice trailed off. I couldn't say it.

"Having doubts?" Carter finished for me, after a moment. "Were you having doubts, Alana?"

My vision blurred with tears as I buried my head in my hands. "Today has been so *hard*," I said, choking on sobs to get the words out. "But I think he was right to leave me."

Gemma muted the TV, and the room was silent except for my crying. I could Feel Forrest's fingers in my hair and Carter's arms around my shoulders. A hand (probably Gemma's) patted my head awkwardly. Then, a finger tilted my chin upward, and I opened my eyes to find Forrest, inches from my face. "Alana," she said, quiet but firm. "People have doubts before their weddings all the time. It's normal. It doesn't mean you *deserved* to be left at the altar."

Easy for her to say. I had a feeling most people with wedding jitters were not so easily reduced to a blushing schoolgirl by their maid of honor.

"No matter what you were thinking or feeling before the wedding, you deserve to be treated with respect," said Forrest. "There is nothing you could have done to deserve this."

I laughed lightly, searching her dark, earnest eyes. "Are you sure?"

Carter shook my shoulders in response. "Of course we're sure, dummy!"

"You need to sleep," said Forrest, backing away from me. "You'll feel better in the morning."

I shook my head. "But we still have more people to call," I protested, patting the duvet as I fumbled for my phone. "We might still be able to get a refund on the honeymoon."

"I'll call Melissa about the honeymoon," said Forrest, snatching my phone away from my reach. "You need to sleep. You're running yourself into the ground." She squeezed my hand reassuringly. "I know you were too wired earlier, but do you feel like you can sleep now?" She spoke softly, her wide, brown eyes absorbing every detail of my expression.

I broke our eye contact as I dropped my head to Carter's shoulder. "Yeah," I said, returning my gaze to Amanda Seyfried as she scanned her notes from the back of a car. "I can try."

I awoke to knocking on the hotel door. I jerked up from my spot in the middle of the bed, wedged between Forrest and Carter, disoriented in the gray morning light. Forrest blinked her eyes open lazily, staring up as me, but Carter remained passed out, his arm draped over me with his mouth wide open, tufts of dirty blonde hair shooting out in all directions. Gemma snored peacefully from a cot by the window. I gently lifted Carter's arm as I slipped out of bed tiptoed to the door.

It was the last person in the world I wanted to see.

"Hi, Melissa," I said. I wore Carter's oversized t-shirt and boxers, my hair frizzy from sleep and my face makeup-free, revealing eye bags and a few stress zits that sprouted along my jaw. Normally, I'd never let Melissa see me like this. The woman's dyed-blonde hair was perpetually, meticulously sprayed into place, with a thin figure, clear skin, and shoes that *always* matched her purse. She did not tolerate dishevelment. Even this morning, her tan crocodile skin loafers were the same material as her Chanel purse. Her white slacks had a perfectly straight crease ironed down the front, with a powder blue blouse and a gold chain belt. There was no trace of yesterday's chaos in her demeanor.

I crossed my arms to hide that I wasn't wearing a bra.

"Hello, Alana," she said softly, with a strained smile. There, I could see it now. The wrinkle between her eyebrows as she spoke, the extra layer of makeup under her eyes, obscuring any sign of fatigue. There was a softness in her voice I hadn't heard before — a blend of pity and understanding that disarmed me. I was expecting Melissa to blame me the way I blamed myself, but there was no anger in her voice. Sadness filled her eyes.

I frowned at her. "I'm sorry we wasted so much of your money," I said. "I had no idea this would happen."

Melissa waved my words away. "First of all, it's Matthew Sr.'s money. And second, of course you didn't. None of this is your fault."

I blinked. My mind ran through everything she'd said to me before yesterday. There were the snippy texts saying it was "fine," if I preferred lilies, but everyone knows all the best weddings have hydrangeas. The late-night phone call insisting I swap chicken for steak at dinner, since it was Matthew Sr.'s favorite. The panicked call after Matthew told her I was considering sewing my own dress. She would pay if I wore Vera Wang. And, of course, throughout the planning, and all the tearful hours venting to Forrest on the phone, the constant insistence that I needed to control every aspect of the day. *At a wedding, everyone looks to the bride. You will decide how they remember the day. Don't you want those memories to be good?*

The pressure threatened to swallow me whole. It felt like a miracle that I never buckled under it, but in her eyes, it felt like I could only ever meet expectations, moving heaven and earth to avoid seeing her lip twitched to the side in disapproval. Now, the look I feared most filled her face, but I could tell it wasn't directed at me.

She was disappointed in her son.

I took a deep breath, trying to hide my shock. "Um, thank you."

She nodded, then dropped her eyes to my toes, still a perfect pale pink from my pre-wedding pedicure. "I wanted to apologize."

"I — what?"

She cocked her head gently to the side. "I'm starting to realize that perhaps I was too hard on you over the wedding," she raised her light blue eyes back to mine, a whisper of tears filling them, "and not hard enough on my son."

I blinked again. I'd never seen Melissa cry, and even this looked flawless. Her clear blue eyes seemed larger as exactly one wrinkle formed between her eyebrows, and a single tear drew a straight line down her cheek. Normally my would-be mother-in-law's perfection spiked my anxiety, her very presence a reminder I'd never measure up. This time, it made me sad. What would it be like to never allow mess, even when bursting into tears? "Melissa, you didn't so anything" I said. "Please don't blame yourself. I don't blame you *at all*."

"I'm grateful to hear you say that," she choked. "But I think you're being too kind."

"Melissa?" Forrest suddenly appeared beside me, and her scent filled my nose, like the woods after a thunderstorm, clean and teeming with life. She wore an old Howard t-shirt and boxers, her hair wrapped in her lavender bonnet.

"Hi, dear," Melissa answered sheepishly.

"Oh, Melissa." Forrest stepped forward and wrapped my ex-mother-in-law in a tight hug. Melissa, who I'd only ever hugged once (before I knew better), melted into it. For once in her life, her shoulders dropped, and she allowed herself to be comforted. "It's been an overwhelming twenty-four hours, huh?" Forrest said.

She shook her head. "Not compared to what Alana's going through."

Forrest squeezed her shoulders gently. "She'll be ok, don't worry. I've got her."

She sniffled as she stepped back from Forrest's hug, nodding at my friend. "Thank you."

"Thank you for coming by to check on me," I said awkwardly, my hands still crossed over my boobs. "Did Forrest tell you I was here?"

Forrest nodded as she returned to my side. "I'm sorry to interrupt. I just heard your voice and wanted to say hi."

"I'm so glad to see you, Forrest," Melissa said, then turned to me. "I didn't just come to see if you were okay. I was hoping we could talk?"

"Um, yeah." I shifted my weight to the other foot. "Did you want to come in?"

And that's how I ended up squeezed between Melissa and Forrest at the edge of the hotel bed — Melissa careful not to touch me — as Carter snored loudly behind us. "Forrest told me you were trying to get a partial refund on the honeymoon," Melissa began.

"Yes," I said quickly. "I think we can still get a lot of that money back, at least as credit. Maybe you and Matthew Sr. could move the and go for your anniversary? I was going to call this morning and ask."

"But you haven't called yet?"

"No, I'm sorry. I actually just woke up. But I can do it right —"

"No!" Melissa clutched my arm. She looked down, embarrassed, and released her grip. "I mean, that's what I wanted to talk to you about. I want you to go."

In my surprise, I could do nothing but stare at her, her mouth pressed into a resolute line. "On the honeymoon?"

"Yes."

I blinked, feeling my body flush with surprise, overwhelmed by her generosity. "I can't do that. You and Mr. Tate paid for that trip for Matthew."

Melissa placed her hand over mine, her eyes filled with the kindness she normally strained to hide. "We paid for that trip for you, too, Alana. Matthew Sr. agrees with me. It's the least our family can do, after everything we put you through."

I took a deep, shaky breath. I'd been looking forward to the honeymoon more than the wedding. The two-week trip to the Amalfi Coast would be my first time in Italy, where my grandparents were from. Deciding on the itinerary was my mental vacation from wedding planning. When picking the flowers, the table seating, the cake overwhelmed me, I'd picture myself eating gelato as I wandered Positano, or sleeping by the beach, drunk on limoncello spritz. On the other hand, Matthew's investment in the honeymoon mirrored his wedding planning. Always *that sounds fine*, without much input. He wouldn't care if I went without him.

But sleeping in the honeymoon suite alone for a week? "I don't know," I said sadly. "I don't know that being by myself for two weeks would help."

"Well, why don't you bring Forrest?" Melissa asked

It was my best friend's turn to drop her jaw. "What?"

Melissa shrugged. "Why not? You have an extra ticket. As a teacher, aren't you off for the summer? It makes the most sense." She raised her thin eyebrows as her eyes darted between me and my best friend.

"I don't know." Forrest fiddled with the silver ring on her thumb, her go-to nervous tick. "I don't want to intrude on Alana's honeymoon."

"It's not my honeymoon anymore," I said quietly.

"Exactly," Melissa said. "Besides, you worked hard to help plan the wedding, too. You *both* deserve a break. Look," she shifted her piercing blue eyes from me, to Forrest, and back again. "I've always admired the friendship you two share. Nobody has my back like that." She took a shaky breath, and I could glimpse tears returning to her eyes. "Nothing would make me happier than doing this for both of you. Please."

Forrest turned to me. Her dark eyes held universes before she blinked them away, took a deep breath, and said, "If you want me there, I'll go with you." Her lips remained parted for a beat longer, like there was something else she wanted to say. But she closed her mouth and nodded once, ending her thoughts, as she turned back to Melissa.

I kept my eyes on her, struck by the way staring at Forrest felt like standing on the edge of a cliff. I turned to back to Melissa, suddenly shy. "Are you sure?" I asked quietly.

Melissa nodded. "I haven't been this sure in years."

I gently squeezed her arm. "Then I would love to," I said. "Thank you."

She waved my gratitude away casually, the lightness in her eyes returned for the first time since yesterday morning. As we exchanged cheerful chatter, things were easier between us, now that we could see the truth of our relationship. She and I were not united by Matthew, but by months of phone calls, texts and deliberations, crafting the perfect day. The wedding fell apart, but we still built something. I could see it her smile, polished but genuine. Matthew left me without blinking, but she felt the loss. What I had with Melissa was real.

As I laughed with his mother, Matthew was probably lying beside Jessica in our apartment, with Forrest's art on the walls and my toothbrush in the sink. He disappeared without an apology or even a text. Now, as Melissa checked her phone and said, "I should be going," I realized this was the only goodbye I'd get.

Melissa certainly didn't have it easy. Her husband was always working late or traveling, her relationship with her son polite but distant. Matthew resented her for her overinvolvement on his sports teams and homework assignments growing up. Her obsession with perfection vexed him; like most men, he took pride in not caring what people think. But Melissa cared so much, it isolated her. She didn't seem to let anyone close enough to see her flaws. I understood Matthew's frustration toward her, but I never understood the bitterness. Even when Melissa twisted my stomach in knots, I could empathize with her. Sometimes I thought she must be the loneliest person I knew.

"Thank you for everything," I told her as I walked her out. "Not just the honeymoon, but helping me with the wedding, and coming here to say goodbye." Tears blotted my eyes again. "It means a lot."

Melissa gently squeezed my arm — her version of lifting me in the air and leaving sloppy kisses on both cheeks. "Alana, you would have been a wonderful daughter-in-law."

I brushed my tears away. "Thank you."

After all this time of daily phone calls with Melissa, it never occurred to me she'd be out of my life so soon. The goodbye hardly felt adequate, a dry kiss on the cheek, her Chanel perfume filling my nose as she wished me a wonderful honeymoon. There was no invitation for coffee when I came back, no illusion of staying in touch. She muttered something about getting back to her family, doing damage control with the gossiping guests, and was gone. She left behind a quiet I hadn't known since Matthew proposed.

There was nothing to plan, no one to please, no way to fill the silence. I just stared at the cream-colored hotel door, wondering how I'd carry on with my life from here.

I didn't have time to wallow any longer — we had a plane to catch. Once Melissa left, Forrest and I scrambled to get ready for our red eye to Naples. Carter volunteered to grab my packed suitcase from Matthew's apartment, while Forrest and I took the metro to Target to buy her some extra underwear, t-shirts, and a bathing suit. She only packed for a long weekend when she traveled here from New Jersey, where she taught art at a prep school. We were lucky she happened to have her passport in her purse.

"I always like to be prepared to flee the country," she teased.

By the early afternoon, Forrest finished packing while Carter returned with my suitcase in a huff. Matthew and Jessica were not home when he went — probably avoiding a potential confrontation. He launched into a rant about his hopes that Matthew missed every train he took by seconds, that all his lunch breaks got interrupted by last-minute Zoom calls, and that his toothbrush fell in the toilet every day for the rest of his life. "You, Ally," he said, his gray-green eyes brightened by anger, "deserve so much better than that." He shooed Forrest and me toward the door. "Now go enjoy your honeymoon." We gave him quick hugs and raced to the nearest Silver Line stop to ride to Dulles Airport. After checking my bag and racing through security, we reached our flight just before the final boarding call.

I knew I was supposed to sleep on the plane. It was a redeye, and Forrest passed out almost immediately; her soft breaths created a slow, soothing rhythm beside me. Still, I was restless. In some way, rushing to the airport was a comfort; the stress took my mind off the swirling anxiety and grief that threatened to pull me under. Now that we were settled on the plane, I had nothing to do but ruminate.

Matthew and I were together just under two years and were roommates for one. I worked from home every day at his kitchen table, people watching passerby on tree-lined street below as sunlight streaked through the vast windows. I'd time my cooking so we could eat dinner just as he got home from work; he'd tell me about his latest office drama, and I'd thank the heavens that my web design job was fully remote. Nobody at my company cared for drama when we only interacted on Zoom. I spent weekends exploring the city with a group of Matthew's work friends and their girlfriends. They were nice enough, but I was always on guard, always aware that they were *his* friends. Only now did I realize it wasn't just that friend group — my entire life centered Matthew — his schedule, his home, his daily habits. Kicking me out of his life upended every piece of my routine. I'd only be allowed back home to collect my things.

Of course, there were things I'd change. I wished Matthew would help clean around the apartment. I wished our friends felt like mine. I wished it was easier to ignore the nagging feeling that something was missing, that this didn't quite fit. But I liked what we had. I liked our Sunday trips to the Dupont Farmer's Market, our weekday happy hours at a nearby wine bar, our date nights at a Georgetown brasserie. Nobody could find perfect happiness, but I found something good. Better than most.

That's why it hurt so much to be left behind. My life with Matthew wasn't my dream, but dreams were meant to be unattainable. I gave up on hoping for more when I almost lost Forrest at nineteen. Now a rational adult, I was fine accepting something less in love. Nothing made me feel more worthless than realizing even the life I settled for, even the dampened version of myself that I crammed into Matthew's world, was too ambitious. That perhaps, in dreaming smaller, I was still dreaming too big.

Tears warmed my eyes at the thought, and I closed them to keep from crying in the middle of our flight. Even then, sleep wouldn't come.

All thoughts of a dream life began and ended in the span of the night I spent with Forrest — and for good reason. I couldn't recover from shattering a dream like that twice.

Not saying I didn't love Matthew, but it took me a long time to drop my guard around him. He never saw my stuffed animal until we moved in together, and I never told him I had nightmares about the rats in DC, or that I once flashed my tits in New Orleans to get Mardis Gras beads. Forrest knew everything. I immediately felt safer with her than I had with anyone else in my life, excluding Carter. I didn't think one lifetime with her would be enough, let alone one summer.

Waking up beside her that morning felt like deliverance. I laid on the softened wood and listened to the birds as I processed the night that shattered everything I thought I knew about myself. But I didn't care about that yet. The whole world was murky, and the only thing that made sense was how Forrest's body seamlessly fit with mine, so I clung to that, to her. I decided nothing else mattered, as I cast aside questions of who I was and what my family would think. As I watched her soft breathing, I vowed to hold onto this. No matter what happened, I would never let her go.

Then Forrest opened her eyes.

"Oh, shit," she said, eyes widening at me as she sat up. "What time is it?"

"We have another hour before the other counselors wake up," I said, placing my hand on her thigh. "Don't worry."

She flinched at my touch, and I pulled my hand back nervously. Her eyes flit from my hand to my face. "We had sex," she said.

The words were so clinical, nothing like how I'd describe it. I winced at their blunt edge like she dealt a real blow. "Yeah."

"That was... that was a mistake." She crossed her arms as she watched me sit up, my movements more lethargic than hers. While love seemed to split my chest open, all l I could find in her eyes was fear.

"What do you mean?" Hearing her felt like the kind of nightmare state that leaves you running from an avalanche with cement limbs, too slow for escape. I was helpless.

"I have a boyfriend, and I cheated on him. Don't get me wrong, I..." Her eyes broke from mine as she stared down the dock. "I enjoyed last night. You were great, but that was wrong of me. Wyatt is a good guy; he doesn't deserve this. I just wasn't thinking."

"You weren't thinking?" She took me apart, word by word.

"I got lost in the moment, you know? I've never done that before, with a woman, I mean. I guess I just got carried away."

I pressed my palms against the wood grain, remembering. *I've never seen anyone look as beautiful as you do right now, Alana.* "I've never done that before, ever," I said quietly.

"Oh, Al." Forrest rubbed her arms as her tears welled. "Al, I'm so sorry."

As I lifted my gaze to her crumpled figure and studied the guilt in her eyes, it finally clicked. When my heart shivered at her touch, when her whispered praise made me feel holy, when I found the universe in her eyes as I came — that was just sex. Of course it was. I knew last night couldn't be real. There had to be a catch, and here it was: Forrest liked my touch but loved her boyfriend. What we did last night was just physical. To her, anyway. "I'm sorry," I said, clearing my throat. "I misread things. I shouldn't have kissed you."

"Don't apologize, Al. It's my fault. I kissed you back." The regret in her voice was unbearable. I shuddered as I crossed my arms.

"So, does this mean..." I dropped my eyes to the water, whose deep sea green rippled had shifted from soothing to haunting beneath Forrest's words. "Are we still friends?" The question stung, but I had to know.

"I—" she studied me with her wide, dark eyes, her expression unreadable. "I don't know. I don't know anything." Forrest buried her face in her hands, then stood up suddenly from the dock. "I need to talk to Wyatt."

I nodded and followed her back to the cabin. We waited in our bunks for another hour in silence until the camp bell woke the rest of the counselors up. I stared at wooden beams of her bunk, desperate for answers I didn't have the right to know. She never suggested last night meant anything. It wasn't her fault I assumed more, all because my knees turned to butter when she looked at me.

When the girls woke and we lead them through their last day of camp, Forrest avoided me like I did to her at the beginning of the summer. She didn't say goodbye, didn't tell me what her boyfriend said, didn't even send a text.

She changed everything about my life, and she was gone as quick as she appeared.

I'd take Matthew leaving every day of the week, compared to the emptiness that haunted me then.

We arrived in Naples, Italy in the morning European time, exhausted by my restless flight. An older man in a fitted black suit greeted us just outside security, with a white sign that said "Mr. & Mrs. Matthew Tate" in printed black letters. His nose flared in confusion when he saw me and Forrest approach.

"Hi," I said, forcing a smile he didn't return. "Alana Tate. Matthew got sick, so my maid of honor is here, instead." It was easier to lie than explain everything to a stranger, but my stomach turned when I claimed the name Tate. Connecting myself to Matthew made me queasy, knowing he'd have nothing to do with me.

The driver clicked his tongue and nodded. "Right this way," he said, scanning me from head to toe before turning on his heel and leading us to the car. I could tell he was judging me for leaving my sick husband behind, but I didn't care.

The drive from Naples to Sorrento was supposed to take under an hour, but it felt much longer with the driver guiding us noticeably slower than every other car on the road, muttering Italian curses under his breath as drivers sped around him, laying on their horns. Forrest white knuckled my hand the whole way.

Outside, the city passed us by. Blocks of colorful, run-down apartment buildings were rimmed by vegetation, Mount Vesuvius' looming silhouette, and the occasional glimpse of the sea. The summer heat cast the scene in a pale haze, and the landscape shifted from suburbs to greenery as we neared the Southern coast.

Matthew wanted us to spend the honeymoon at one of the large, luxe resorts that dotted the Amalfi Coast and Capri. The kind where the honeymoon suite took up an entire floor, and A-list celebrities hid behind cucumber masks at the spa. But when I found the small family-owned inn located on a cliff's edge over Positano, I begged him to reconsider. The small, two-story building with thin vines snaking between the windows and a lemon tree shading the back patio captured my heart immediately. I could imagine myself lounging by the pool with a limoncello spritz as I watched the sunset over the sea. The owner, Jia Valeri, was delightful over email, going on about how much she and her husband loved hosting newlyweds. Our room was at the end of the second-floor hallway, with a small private balcony overlooking Positano and the ocean. It would be perfect.

Of course, I thought the same thing about my wedding, about my life with Matthew when he got down on one knee, about Forrest, when I made those stupid, silent vows watching her sleep years ago. My mind always went back to that morning at times like this, as if my brain was compelled to keep my hopes in check.

We would meet Jia's husband, Maximo, in Sorrento. He insisted on starting our Amalfi Coast adventure by showing us the city, which housed some of the region's best restaurants, according to him.

If the food was half as good as the views, we were in for a treat. As the shrubbery surrounding us cleared, a sweeping view of Sorrento emerged on our right. Lush mountains surrounded the city's colorful buildings, which were poised atop dramatic, slate gray cliffs. Foamy, turquoise waves slapped the shore far below, completing the landscape whose beauty felt effortless, shrouded in a summer haze. Forrest and I leaned toward the window in unison, our jaws hanging open. Our driver locked eyes with me from the rearview mirror, and nodded expectantly at our awe.

"Welcome," he said, "to the gateway of the Amalfi Coast."

Soon, we found ourselves part of the landscape, as the car wound through the narrow streets, past white, pink, and yellow buildings, closer to the town center. We passed tourists with big hats and cameras, locals ducking around them, and the occasional worker pushing a cart of boxes into a shop. We reached a roundabout surrounding a grass plaza, rimmed by packed restaurants where diners cut into pizza on narrow café tables. Our driver pulled over behind another car. "I cannot go any further," he said, gesturing to the pedestrian-only road ahead. A wide cobblestone road unfolded ahead, filled with restaurants, gelaterias, and souvenir shops, a glimpse of the diagonal cut of a mountain appearing at the end of the street.

"No worries," I answered. "This is where we're meeting our guide, anyway."

"I think that might be him," said Forrest, pointing to a man a few cars
up. He wore loose white pants and a powder blue linen shirt as he pointed a film camera in the opposite direction of the pedestrian street, at a brick red-painted church steeple that towered over the plaza traffic. His wavy brown hair fell over his eyes as he jerked the camera abruptly to the right, toward the expansive outdoor seating area of a restaurant. He trained the lens on two diners who raised their eyebrows pointedly at each other, but the photographer either didn't notice, or didn't care. He continued adjusting the lens.

"Are you sure?" I asked Forrest, but when he snapped the photo turned around, looking for his next subject, there it was. He wore a cardboard sign with 'Alana Morris' written in messy script around his neck, tied by a piece of string. "Oh."

Recognition flared in his eyes as Forrest and I stepped out of the car, our driver
placing our luggage on the curb. Before we could say anything, he flashed a wide grin as he began to sing the chorus of "Ironic" by Alana Morrissette. He stretched his arms out as he belted, nearly hitting a

middle-aged blonde woman in the face, though he
didn't seem to notice. He didn't stop singing until he
completed the chorus and a small huddle of tourists
gathered, filming the scene on their phones.

Forrest shook her head and rewarded him
with a dimpled smile as she shook his hand. He had
wavy brown hair that fell loosely around his ears and
dark eyes and sparkled with laughter as he saw us.
His smile grew as Forrest complimented his singing
voice. "The shower is my own 'La Scala,'" he teased,
shifting his eyes between us. "Which one of you is
Alana?"

I raised my hand bashfully.

"You are even more beautiful than your
mother-in-law said on the phone," he
said in a warm, paternal tone. "Or your almost-
mother-in-law, I mean. She explained
everything. I'm Maximo Carozza. My wife Jia owns
the Valeri, so that makes me — as
you say in America — the trophy husband." He
smiled as he paused comedically, like it was a joke he
made many times before. "My family is so excited to
have you both. Honeymooners are our favorite
guests, especially the newly single ones." He winked,

and despite my embarrassment, I couldn't help but laugh. Then he turned to Forrest. "What is your name, signora?"

"Forrest," she answered. "Thank you for picking us up."

He waved off her gratitude as he took our luggage and began leading us down the wide pedestrian boulevard that seemed to be the city's main street. We passed restaurants, souvenir shops, bakeries, gelaterias, and the occasional English pub. As we walked, we were hit with bursts of smell, from parmesan, to vanilla, to the Amalfi Coast's famous lemons. Lemon-themed products seemed to spill out of the stores housing them on shelves and hanging stands, as passerby picked through postcards, candles, and fridge magnets. "I always enjoy an excuse to see Sorrento," Maximo continued. "I take great photos that I can sell as postcards. Besides, they have the best restaurants. Say, have you two had lunch?"

Azz! Taverna was the only restaurant with a line. A row of people waited across the street as diners twirled pasta on the narrow tables packed together on the cobblestone. A small black dog flit between the tables begging for food, a sign that said 'Do Not Feed Me,' taped to his harness. "The line moves quickly," said Maximo, "and it's worth the wait. Trust me."

He was right. Diners filed in and out of the tables quickly, and soon we were seated in the back left corner outside, right next to an older Italian man that prompted Maximo to do a double take. "Giuseppe?" he asked.

"Maximo!" The man turned. He was the owner of a Sorrento hotel that displayed Maximo's photography in the lobby — a close friend of the Valeri's, since they worked in the same business. He was short and bald with thick glasses and a kind smile as his gaze shifted from Maximo to Forrest and me.

"Who are these beautiful women with you?" he asked.

"Alana and Forrest," Maximo answered, gesturing at each of us as he said our names. "New guests."

"You're staying at the Valeri?" he asked, cocking an eyebrow.

We nodded.

"Lucky you." He cut into the steak he was eating as he spoke. "It is the most beautiful place in Amalfi, and Nonna's pasta is the best on the coast — almost as good as the gnocchi at my hotel."

"That is high praise from Giuseppe," said Maximo. "He always says no food in all of Amalfi can compare to his Gnocchi alla Sorrentina, and he is right." He smiled playfully as he raised his eyebrows at his friend. "Except for Nonna's."

"You married well," Giuseppe continued. "You have a beautiful woman, a mansion in Positano, and the best chef on the coast for a mother-in-law."

Maximo beamed, his cheeks flushing slightly. "My favorite part is the beautiful woman, but the pasta is nice too, yes." He turned to Forrest and me. "You will see tonight. Nonna cooks family dinner every Tuesday night for the guests. We eat together on the terrace to watch the sunset, drink wine, get to know each other better. It is heaven."

"It is." Giuseppe nodded firmly, his expression serious, as it should be when discussing pasta. "They had me for dinner one night. I still dream about Nonna's Tagliatelle a limone. If the Valeri had a restaurant, I'd eat there every week."

"And Nonna wouldn't sleep." Maximo leaned back in his chair, crossing his arms.

"A small sacrifice," Giuseppe teased. "Think of my appetite, here." He muttered something in Italian, and they both laughed.

We ordered the special — lasagna and a glass of house wine for seventeen euros — at Maximo's recommendation. Giuseppe left by the time the food arrived on simple ceramic plates before the server disappeared to attend to another table. The lasagna's well-baked layers of meat and cheese tasted cozy but felt light on my tongue, like eating a cloud. The dog perched at Forrest's feet, then, drawn by the smell of her lasagna. But when he realized she would only give him pets, not food, he trotted away to the next table, his tongue hanging out the side of his mouth. She flashed me a pouting look as he left, her bottom lip stuck out adorably.

While we ate, Maximo told us the story of the Hotel Valeri, founded by his wife's great-grandfather. Giovanni Valeri grew up in a small fishing village further down the

Amalfi Coast, where everyone survived on the sea. They were fishermen who raised fishermen; everyone started their day by piling into fishing boats and returned at sunset with buckets of shrimp, redfish, mollusks, and sardines. Everyone but Giovanni.

The poor boy could not swim. They had never seen anything like it — a boy who sunk like a rock the moment his feet left dry land. His parents tried everything. But after he almost drowned for a third time, when they threw him off the boat at the suggestion of the town doctor, they begrudgingly gave up. They still needed a son to carry the family name, and Giovanni was all they had.

"There are some things in life that simply cannot be done, no matter how hard you work," said Maximo. "For Giovanni, swimming was one of those things."

When he turned sixteen and his classmates left school for the Tyrrhenian, Giovanni went inland, picking up odd jobs to scrape the living he couldn't earn on the water. Eventually, he found steady work in a beautiful hillside mansion overlooking Positano, where an elderly millionaire lived an isolated retirement. He was a sad, scornful old man; most workers hired to help around the house did not last long. But Giovanni softened him with his quiet work ethic, bizarre backstory, and a God-given gift at chess.

The man was losing to his grandson badly, one summer afternoon. He stared at the chessboard with a scowl etched onto his face, hardly noticing Giovanni as the boy cleaned the pool on the patio nearby. But when he reached for the rook, he caught something out of the corner of his eye: Giovanni, shaking his head.

He beat his grandson that day. It was the only time Giovanni ever saw the man smile. "See, the only thing he hated more than losing was his own family," Maximo explained. He would scowl at his own brother one moment and summon Giovanni to the patio for a chess match the next. They played nearly every day. Only then did the old man's pinched expression resemble something nearly pleasant. Still, it was a shock to everyone when he died and left half his fortune to Giovanni, including the house. The boy was only nineteen.

"His parents thought he was a fool for spending his newfound wealth fixing up the old house," Maximo continued. "They wanted him to hire a swimming instructor." But Giovanni had a vision — to create a hotel that welcomed the world into Positano, the city that gave new life to a boy who couldn't swim. "The inn has been in our family ever since," said Maximo, "passed from one Valeri to the next, carrying on Giovanni's legacy."

By the time he finished, our plates were empty. Forrest and I were lethargic once again from the meal, jet lag, and summer heat. "It looks beautiful in the pictures," I said, thinking of the wide patio and pool I saw online, where Giovanni once played chess overlooking the sea.

Maximo's eyes sparkled at the praise. "It's even more beautiful in person," he said, leaning back in his chair as he crossed his arms expectantly. "Just wait."

7

A lazy summer haze engulfed the coast, blanketing the road, greenery, and ocean in a golden hue. Maximo drove us past vineyards and lemon farms, through thickets of shrubbery along steep cliffs as we approached Positano. When the view ahead was sky, lemon trees, and a large, Tuscan-style villa made from sandstone, I knew we arrived.

Chirping birds were the only sound that greeted us as we left the car. The hotel was delightfully peaceful; a pebble roundabout cut through a lush green lawn with magenta azaleas in full bloom, their petals unfurling delicately before the villa. Forrest and I approached the cliff's edge, to the left, where Positano awaited below. The Valeri's high perch offered a vast view of the city, with yellow, orange, and white square buildings stacked atop each other below, surrounded by mountains and water. They looked like tiny dollhouses, layered against the mountain. The Valeri was less than ten minutes away from the city by car, but up here, it felt like we were a world away from it all.

I sighed as I scanned the horizon, taking in the landscape I'd spent the past year dreaming of. I was really here. Not married, not with my fiancé, but here. Coming to Positano was the one thing in my life that had not been turned on its head; the city seemed to be above any my own personal chaos. It stood centuries before I got here and would remain for centuries more — unbothered and alluring.

This was supposed to make me feel comforted, being wrapped in a beauty that was bigger than myself. But I just felt hollow. I was too emotionally shattered to fully enjoy the scene, and its stunning beauty only emphasized the empty place in my chest where joy should have been. It made me angry, that a view like this could elicit sadness, all because of the person who was supposed to be here, who didn't even care.

"Hey," said Forrest, nudging me gently with her elbow. "How are you feeling?"

I shrugged. "A little dead inside, I guess."

"Good." I turned to her in surprise, and she smirked. "A little dead, I can work with. All dead, not so much."

I huffed a surprised laugh, and she swung her arm around me. The faint earthiness of her sweat filled my nose, mingling with her citrus-scented deodorant. I rested my head against her shoulder, melting into her steadying grasp.

"Come on, Al," she said. "The sooner we check in, the sooner we can take a nap."

I followed her away from the cliff, toward the hotel entrance. "That," I said, "is music to my ears."

There were only fifteen guest rooms in the Valeri. The hotel formed an 'L' shape around a sprawling terrace and pool in the back that practically hung over the mountain cliff. The long end housed most of the rooms, a large indoor dining room, and front desk, where the other end was for the Valeri family, the kitchen, and a couple of the smaller rooms. The lobby was narrow but tastefully decorated, with a high ceiling, a blue and white patterned rug, and wide glass doors that opened onto the terrace. A young woman with dark hair twisted back in a claw clip was tapping her pen against a notepad behind the front desk. She lifted her gaze when we walked in. "Where have you been, Maximo?" she asked with a sigh as he strode toward the desk carrying our bags. "You were supposed to come back with the honeymooners two hours ago. Jia had to clean the pool because you were gone."

"Well, I couldn't just bring them here, after their long flight, without stopping for lunch," Maximo answered. As her hazel eyes narrowed, he shrugged innocently. "We were in Sorrento! What was I supposed to do?" She muttered a curse in Italian, and Maximo turned back to us. "You will have to excuse Bianca. She just got home from the city and isn't used how we do things on the coast, the slower pace of life."

"Where do you live, normally?" Forrest asked as she leaned her elbows on the front desk.

"I go to university in Florence," she answered. Her expression was flat, but her hazel eyes brightened as she studied Forrest. She wore a pale pink button-down that looked freshly ironed, and carried herself with a stoic professionalism that was the exact opposite to Maximo's playful, laid-back demeanor. "I have one more year left of school." She turned to me, then. "Are you Alana?"

I nodded. "It's nice to meet you."

"I'm sorry about what happened." She said it plainly, without pity or remorse, as if being left at the altar was just another run-of-the-mill bout of misfortune. It was refreshing.

"Thank you."

"Well, you don't need a man to have a magical honeymoon in Positano, especially not when you're staying at the Valeri." She handed me a key ring with two keys. "This one is to the hotel, and this one is to your room. You're on the second floor, end of the hall, in the honeymoon suite. We don't have an elevator, so Maximo will carry your bags, since he's so well-rested from lunch." Maximo huffed a laugh at that, shaking his head.

"Thank you," Forrest and I said at once.

"And ladies?"

"Yes?"

"Please let us know if there is anything you need," Bianca said, shifting her pointed gaze from me, to Forrest, and back. "We want to make sure you enjoy your stay. Just call the front desk."

"Thanks, Bianca." I smiled softly as I took the keys from her outstretched hand. "I appreciate it."

She nodded, then turned her attention to a computer behind the desk as Maximo led us upstairs. Down a long hallway with white walls, the occasional watercolor painting of the ocean, and a lightly scratched hardwood floor, we walked until we reached the simple wooden door at the end — the honeymoon suite. Maximo gestured toward the door with one hand, as if he were presenting a prized gem, and I turned the key to enter.

My mouth fell open when I stepped inside. It was even more beautiful than the pictures. A beige and burnt orange knit rug rested on the wooden floors, and the boho-style bed had a cream-colored duvet and sheer canopy. On the other side of the room, an azure couch awaited underneath a large photograph of Positano at sunset, taken by Maximo. Each crisp line of the city buildings and mountains glowed contrasted with the sky's gentle ombré. The bathroom door was to the left, adjacent to the bed, while the couch on the right was nestled between two tall windows. The back wall was covered with large windows framed with linen clementine curtains. On the far left, a glass door opened onto a large patio that wrapped behind the couch, offering a breathtaking view of the ocean. Baby pink rose petals blanketed the duvet, and an ice bucket of champagne awaited at the foot of the bed. Every detail of the room radiated cheerful comfort.

"Oh, wow," Forrest whispered. She had migrated under the photograph to study it, and now turned her attention to the view, with Positano bustling under our feet, as the soothing ocean stretched beyond.

Maximo beamed as he watched us take it in. "It was Jia," he said proudly. "All Jia. This room is her baby. Now that our son is grown, I mean."

"It's beautiful." Forrest ran a hand gently across one curtain, her deep brown eyes trained on the view outside.

Maximo accepted the praise with a shy smile, uncharacteristically bashful when he spoke of Jia, like a schoolboy with a crush. He mumbled something about going to check on his wife, and quickly slipped away, leaving us. When he closed the door Forrest collapsed onto the couch, sticking her feet straight out ahead as she kicked off her sneakers. She sighed loudly, rubbing her forehead with her fingertips.

I sat on the foot of the bed as my shoulders sagged. Waking up at The Mayflower felt like ages ago; the wedding, another lifetime.

"I'm exhausted," said Forrest, closing her eyes. "Maximo is nice, but like, he *talks.*"

"I know." I leaned back on my elbows. "A couple of hours in, and we already know all the tea on the hotels in Positano and Sorrento, *plus* the entire Valeri family tree."

Forrest laughed, flashing her dimples as she tilted her head to the ceiling. As she brushed a hand over her face, the sound shifted to a groan. "You can shower first," she said, turning to me.

I studied her round, dark eyes; the depth of them stunned me sometimes. She had the kind of gaze I could easily fall into, if I wasn't careful. "Are you sure? I'm fine to wait."

Forrest smiled weakly, a dimple denting her cheek. "Please, Al. I want to nap first, anyway."

It was the *please* for me. I could never say no to Forrest. By the time I returned from the bathroom, my hair wet and my skin soft from steam, she was fast asleep on top of the duvet, rose petals crinkling under her chest. One soft cheek was pressed into a pillow, while the other shifted slightly with each breath. Her long fingers curled open in front of her, like she was waiting to for me to hold her hand.

Not that I did. It was just an observation.

I turned my back to her when I lay down on the other side of the bed.

After camp, Forrest and I did not talk the entire fall semester. I flipped through her Facebook albums of nights out with her college friends and felt helplessly alone in my heartbreak. Most of my nights out ended with me alone in bed, mascara smudged under my eyes, drunkenly scrolling through Forrest's social media as I pored over each smile, the depth in her eyes, searching for signs that she missed me. I knew she was indifferent to me, but I couldn't believe it. Until I got her text over winter break. She missed me. She and her sister were spending Christmas in

Richmond with their aunt and uncle, and she wanted to drive down to see me. To apologize.

We met at a coffee shop in downtown Durham, where Forrest was staying the night with a family friend. It was a spacious establishment, with a sleek, cold interior that matched my nerves as I stepped inside and instantly came face to face with Forrest.

She looked the same, long hair and stunning eyes and a face that was living sunlight. Of course she came early. She wore an emerald green turtleneck sweater, mom jeans, and doc Martens, both hands shoved into the pockets of her unzipped coat. It took my last shreds of dignity to keep from ogling at this winter version Forrest, whose brilliant smile was subdued today. She offered a nervous, close-lipped smile when she caught my eyes — almost as if she were shocked I came to see her. As if I could ever say no to Forrest.

She gave me a quick hug, then we ordered hot chocolates and lapsed into awkward silence.

She asked about my semester, my parents, and Carter, but I kept my answers vague. My guard was up, of course. It seemed unfathomable that she'd be genuinely interested in me, after the fear in her eyes the last time I saw her.

She dropped her gaze to the small black table between us, then my face, then back to the table again.

"Alana, I'm really sorry for what happened this summer." Forrest met my eyes with an intense stare, as if she were determined to hold my gaze. "And I am sorry for telling you I regretted it, because I don't. I was surprised and confused, that's all. I never felt anything like that before, and I thought I betrayed my boyfriend by—" she blushed as she lowered her eyes; she seemed to force herself to meet mine again. "Not just by sleeping with you, but by *enjoying* it so much. I panicked. It was unfair to you. I know I hurt you, and I hate myself for it." Forrest lowered her gaze to her hands, wrapped around her mug. "It was wrong. I'm not asking you to forgive me; I know I don't deserve it. I just wanted you to know that I'm sorry."

For the past five months, this was everything I wanted to hear — well, almost everything. Sure, my desire for her was one-sided, but at least she was sorry. At least she didn't blame me anymore. For months, I'd lie awake trying to dream up some scenario where I could have been right about her, where she really did care about me; each time, I had nothing. Only she did care. Just not in the way I wanted.

Now I had to choose — to let her go, or to make this care, this friendship, be enough.

I never had a choice when it came to Forrest.

"I understand," I said finally. "I was scared, too."

Forrest shook her head. "You were scared, but you weren't an asshole."

"I also don't have a boyfriend."

She laughed, but it felt forced. "Yeah, that did complicate things. But we worked it out." She studied me shyly. "I mean, we broke up. It wasn't meant to be."

"Oh." I tried to calm the faint, stupid hope that flared in my chest. "I'm glad everything worked out."

Forrest met my gaze with an expression that was anything but peaceful. "Well, I wouldn't say that."

My heart thundered at her words. "What do you mean?"

"I mean, you're one of my best friends." She began fidgeting with her rings. "I acted recklessly, and I hurt you. There's not a lot of people that I feel comfortable opening up to, the way I did with you. Our friendship means a lot to me, and I almost lost you." She shook her head softly, eyes trained on her rings. "Nothing is worth risking that."

She raised her gaze to meet mine. "Of course, if you never want to see me again, I understand. I deserve it. But if you do want to be my friend, I promise I won't hurt you like this again." Her eyes flicked back and forth, searching mine earnestly. "Would you ever consider letting me prove it to you? One more chance is all I need — I promise."

I studied her clasped, fidgeting hands, her earnest eyes, her slightly parted lips. It wasn't much of a question. "Of course, Forrest," I said breathlessly. I could live with being her friend, but I couldn't live without her. I knew it even then. "Considering you saved my life, I think I can forgive you."

She looked giddy when she grinned back, squeezing my hand. "You won't regret this, I promise," she said with fire in her eyes.

I already knew that, so I smiled back.

Forrest kept her word, approaching our friendship with an almost religious observance. I thought it would take time to lower my guard with her, but trusting Forrest again felt like fitting back into an old, favorite pair of jeans. Every time I doubted her, she proved me wrong with a thoughtful text, a shared belly laugh, or the tenderness in her eyes when she looked at me. I fell far more in love with her soul than with the way our bodies fit together — a memory that faded but was never truly gone. Not that it mattered. I no longer allowed myself to entertain the thought of something more. I cherished our friendship too much. I cast my feelings out of sight, out of mind.

That was the furthest thing from my mind right now, of course. I was stewing about how Matthew left — not about how I ended up in a honeymoon suite with my first love. Lying in bed with Forrest snoring peacefully beside me, I could hardly sleep. It had been this way since the wedding. I managed to drift off for a moment, but every time I woke up, I'd remember. Matthew dropping my hand, kissing Jessica in the aisle. Forrest dropping the bouquet, dragging me away from the scene.

I rolled over restlessly, but now I was eye to eye with her. She hadn't moved since she collapsed into bed earlier. The soft curve of her lips moved slightly with each breath; her long hair spread out behind her like she was floating in water. Her long eyelashes resembled the delicate brush strokes of a Renaissance painting, casting shadows above her cheeks. I wished that I could paint like she did, only to capture her like this. Of course, now I was watching her sleep, and that wouldn't do, for obvious reasons.

I sighed as I rolled over again.

8

We didn't leave the suite for the rest of the day. Bianca brought us Prosciutto sandwiches, and we ate dinner as we watched the sunset from the upstairs balcony, staring at the view of Positano below. We sat together in comfortable silence — Forrest knew I didn't have the energy for talking — as the sky faded from blue, to golden, orange, pink, and cobalt, and night emerged.

My sleep was dreamless and sporadic, interrupted by a useless stream of replayed memories as I wondered whether my relationship with Matthew was a lie. The house party where we met, when we talked about our favorite TV shows over beer cans on the back porch. Our dinner date at L'Ardente, when he asked me to be his girlfriend over a flaming tiramisu. The Trader Joe's flower bouquet he bought me after work, our first week living together. It was a lily bouquet, framed by smaller flowers in shades of magenta and lavender. He said the colors reminded him of me.

All those shared memories, and he didn't respect me enough to say goodbye. He called off our wedding at the most humiliating moment possible; he didn't even look at me before sprinting into Jessica's arms.

How was I supposed to reconcile that with the man I thought I knew?

Like I said, I couldn't sleep. But maybe it was just the jet lag.

The pool was a long, turquoise rectangle with a narrow line of orange cushioned lounge chairs behind the shallow end, separating the shorter 'L' of the mansion from the water. Forrest and I took the two chairs closest to the cliff and the stunning views below, shaded by a blue and white striped umbrella. I was too tired to venture into town on our first day here, but Forrest convinced me to join her at the pool, to at least leave the suite.

She read a historical romance by Carli St. Helen while I lay on the lounge chair as my eyes fluttered closed. The sun soft-baked my skin while the June breeze lulled me to a slumber that eluded me the night before. Positano stretched peacefully ahead in a pale blue haze, utterly infinite. Even when

I closed my eyes, I could feel this place slow my breaths, easing my anxiety.

It felt like I was melting into the day, lulled by chirping birds and the faint sound of crashing waves far below.

I could have been dozing for two hours or twenty minutes. Everything seemed to fall away in the summer sun, including time itself. I stretched my hands above my head as I woke, and turned toward Forrest. She was holding the book slightly closer to her face, to hide the text from any passerby, her fingers spread over the cover. Her legs were crossed, her lips parted, and her pupils dilated as they flitted across the page. I smirked. I knew what that look meant. It was adorable.

"It's the honeymooners!" Maximo called, and Forrest startled so sharply, she nearly fell out of her chair.

"Hey, Maximo," I said, waving at him while Forrest shoved the book under her towel.

He ran a hand through his dark brown curls. "Would you girls like a drink as you enjoy the pool? As the Valeri's resident bartender, I make a fantastic limoncello spritz."

The one thing that would make this day better. "I'd love one." I turned to Forrest. "But is it too early?"

Now it was Forrest's turn to smirk at me. "We're on vacation. Plus it's 3:00."

"Really?" I checked my phone. Sure enough, above the flood of new texts from loved ones expressing condolences, there it was. 3:06. "I slept longer than I thought."

"I'm glad," said Forrest, eyeing me so tenderly, it was an effort not to blush.

"That's the whole point of the honeymoon," Maximo said with a grin. "After our wedding, Jia and I didn't leave bed for four days. I mean, we weren't only sleeping, of course..." his eyes seemed to glaze over at the memory before he snapped his attention back to us. "Don't tell Jia I told you that."

"Don't tell Jia what?" the Valeri's owner appeared beside her husband smiling at us as she placed two limoncello spritz's on the small wooden table between us. "These are for you two, on us."

"Thank you," we said together, and Forrest added: "You didn't have to do that."

"It's the least we can do, after what you've been through." Jia shook her head.

"If my son left a girl at the altar, I'd string him up by his feet," said Maximo.

"The next time you complain about Gio being single, I'll remind you of that," Jia teased, as she tucked a strand of her shoulder-length wavy hair behind her ear. "Our boy has integrity."

Maximo's eyes twinkled with mischief as he grinned at his wife. "That is true. But I only nag him because you'd be such a wonderful grandmother."

I could have sworn Jia fought off a blush as she waved him away. Then she clasped her hands together as she turned back to us. "So, are you joining us for dinner tonight?"

At our confused expressions, Maximo said: "It's Tuesday. Nonna cooks dinner for all the guests Tuesday nights. Trust me, you don't want to miss it."

I forced a polite smile as I nodded. "I'll think about it, I'm sure it's delicious. I just don't know if I will have the energy. I've been so tired since the wedding."

"Sure." Jia nodded. "You can just call the front desk and let Bianca know."

Forrest watched me silently, with an odd look I couldn't quite place. I returned a small smile before changing the subject. "Your hotel is even more beautiful that I imagined."

Maximo turned to face the Positano view before us as he ran a hand through his dark hair. "I have lived on the Amalfi Coast since I was nineteen, and it still feels as if I am seeing it for the first time."

"You don't get used to it?" Forrest asked.

"No," he answered. "I don't think you can ever get used to beauty like this." He smiled at me, eyes twinkling. "Imagine how sad life would be if you could."

Maximo and Jia left to attend to hotel business. I closed my eyes, and Forrest returned to her novel. The quiet shifted from peaceful to restless. I felt tormented by my past and future at once, haunted by hurt and unknowns. One minute, Positano's beauty was a welcome distraction, the next it seemed to heighten my loneliness. I felt disconnected from the city and afraid to be a part of it. Maybe I shouldn't have come at all.

I stood from the chair and jumped in the pool.

The cool water quieted my thoughts as I sank below the surface. I wondered what Matthew was doing right now. It was hard to imagine. The life we built together already seemed like a distant memory, something that was never even mine.

I moved into his apartment six months after we started dating, because it was the logical next step. My lease was up, and Matthew insisted. When he proposed at a Georgetown brasserie on Valentine's Day, it was the same. I was silent at first, overwhelmed by the massive diamond and the weight of what it symbolized, as Matthew studied me with eager, expectant eyes. He rose from his knee to the restaurant chair and gently explained all the economic benefits of marriage. "We're as good as married already," he said softly. "We live together, and we love each other. This would just make it official." I couldn't see a reason to turn him down.

A lot of our relationship was like that, now that I thought about it.

But it was easy to lose myself in the splendor of it. I started dating Matthew shortly after Forrest left the city to get her MFA at RISD, and I was melancholy without my best friend. I missed the contently sleepy look on her face when she'd take that first sip of Earl Grey tea in the morning, the coconut scent of her favorite body lotion, the way she'd call "Night, Al!" across the apartment before retreating to bed. I mourned my once-sacred place among her routine that had always been temporary. I knew we would have stopped being roommates eventually. I knew I wanted more than she could ever give. With Matthew, it was nice to feel like an object of adoration, for once — even if I sometimes felt like an object too much. Like the entire relationship was something that happened to me, outside my control.

Maybe Matthew wasn't the perfect guy, but he was good. At least, I thought so, before our wedding made him a stranger to me.

I swam to the far edge of the pool, closest to the cliff, and stared out at the sea. The vast landscape daunted me, taunting me with beauty I felt too fragile to explore. My exhaustion suddenly overwhelmed me. I turned back, swimming toward Forrest.

I rose from the pool, water forming a puddle at my feet. I left a trail of dark footprints on the terrace leading to my lounge chair. As I dried off, Forrest shut her book and lifted her head, giving me the same odd look from earlier.

"I'm tired," I said, wrapping myself in a towel. "I'm going to go back to the room and take a nap."

"Why don't you lie down here?" Forrest tilted her head.

I shrugged. "I want to lie in bed, and I need a shower."

She frowned but offered a tight nod. "Sure, whatever you need." I left her for the quiet, sorrowful safety of the room. After a hot shower, I curled up under the covers thinking I could spend the whole trip like this, as I drifted off to sleep.

I pretended I was still dreaming when the suite door clicked closed. Forrest must have come back from the pool to freshen up for dinner. The day was almost over, then, putting more distance between me and my most humiliating moment. I wanted to fast-forward time, only to put it behind me. Somehow, doing nothing made today feel longer.

I felt the mattress sink beside me as Forrest sat on the bed. I turned toward her, opening my eyes.

She placed a hand on the covers over my thigh. "You're going to mess up your jet lag if you sleep too much."

I frowned. "I know. I just don't have the energy."

"Alana, I've never seen you this tired before."

"I've never been left at the altar before."

"Fair." She rubbed the duvet where my thigh was. "But you've been hurt before, and staying in bed has never made you feel better."

I smiled dryly. "Maybe it's because I haven't stayed in bed long enough."

Forrest chuckled as she shook her head. "Al, I'm being serious. I've been giving you space today because I know you need to process what happened. But I think that was a mistake." She frowned at me, but her words were gentle. "You're not processing, you're stewing."

I struggled to blink back tears. Forrest could always see to the heart of my feelings, bravado be damned. "What am I supposed to do?"

Forrest brushed a loose strand of hair off my forehead, and my breath caught in my throat. I was engaged two days ago, and now I fended off a blush because Forrest touched my face. No wonder Matthew left. "Let yourself live, Alana." Forrest squeezed my knee. "You've been dying to go to Italy since we were kids. If you don't enjoy it, you'll always regret it. I know that's easier said than done, but moping in here isn't going to help you heal. I don't even think you're moping." She looked at me with hurt in her eyes, as if I personally offended her. "I think you're beating yourself up."

I looked away from her eyes that seemed to see everything. Of course I blamed myself. If I had been more loyal, more perceptive, harder to leave... "It's hard not to."

"I know it is. But that's my best friend you're ragging on, and I won't allow it." Forrest smiled at me. "Come to dinner with me, with the Valeri's. We'll have a nice, relaxing meal downstairs, enjoy the sunset, maybe watch a movie. Then, tomorrow, let's see Positano."

I smiled faintly back at her.

Forrest brought her hand to my shoulder as her dark eyes searched mine. "Come on, Alana. Talk to me."

I lifted my eyes back to her, let her see the lingering tears in them as I struggled to hold myself together. "I can't help but think that I did this to myself by ignoring the signs that he was doubting the wedding, and by doubting it myself. I walked myself into a trainwreck, all because I was so focused on planning the perfect wedding, I blinded myself to everything else. I was practically begging for disaster."

Forrest shook her head as she rubbed my shoulder reassuringly. "Of course you were worried about the wedding being perfect, Al," she said. "That's what happens when you work hard on something — you want it to go well. You're not a bad person for caring. Besides, I remember you being more concerned about doing right by Melissa than anything else." I smiled softly, because she was right. Most of my worry was for Melissa's sake. Forrest leaned closer, captivating me with her intense stare when she asked: "Do you think every person who gets cold feet on their wedding day deserves to be left at the altar?"

I crossed my arms as I leaned away from her. "Of course not!"

Forrest crossed her arms back. "So, why do you think that about yourself, Al? Why are you holding yourself to a standard you would never expect of anyone else?"

I said nothing, because of course, she was right. "That's what I thought," she said. "Let's go to dinner. I know you must be hungry." She leaned toward me again, her eyes piercing mine. I tried not to think about how close we were. "You deserve to have fun, Alana. Please."

The moment she asked, it was decided. I could never turn her down. "Deal."

She beamed at me like I hung the moon with that word. "Perfect. Let's get dressed."

9

Nonna's Tuesday night dinners were one of the main reasons visitors stayed at the Valeri. You had to be a guest to eat here, and everything was served out of family-sized bowls passed up and down a long wooden table on the terrace, half the length of the pool. The menu changed every week, depending on Nonna's mood and the ingredients she procured from local farmers and fishermen, and the recipes spanned generations. Forrest and I sat together facing the pool, so we could watch the sunset over the city and ocean. I surveyed the pool that ended at the cliff's edge directly, the glowing buildings of Positano, lit up against the fading light, the green mountains, and ocean beyond. It was breathtaking.

To our right were a few empty seats that one woman told us were reserved for the Valeri family — Maximo, Jia, Bianca, and Nonna herself. To the left, seats filled up quickly with other guests. Forrest wore a long olive-green tank dress that was on sale at Target, while I wore a white spaghetti strap sundress that fell halfway down my calves, covered in printed blue flowers.

An older couple made their way toward the empty seats across from us when the man stopped dead in his tracks. His blue eyes were wide with terror as his jaw hung open, hands hanging limply at his sides, his face so pale it was almost gray. He wore the same Hawaiian shirt from the family photo that he kept on his desk, right beside a hauntingly accurate bust of Ruth Bader-Ginsberg.

It was Reverend Townes. From my wedding.

"Lord have mercy," he whispered, as Forrest and I blinked at him, our jaws falling open.

"What's the matter dear?" his wife asked behind him. She wore a simple pink sundress, her graying blonde hair tied into a low ponytail.

"It—ah—it just occurred to me," the reverend sputtered, "that we can't see the sunset from these seats."

"Don't worry, love. There will be a sunset every night we're here."

"But not *this* sunset. Maybe if we go down to the end of the table—"

"But those seats are already taken. See, there's a family taking the seats on that end. I bet those two empty chairs are for the dad and the little girl."

"But—"

"Dominic. We're not separating their family. These seats are fine." At last, he nodded, cheeks flushed cherry red as he and his wife sat in front of us. Mrs. Townes smiled warmly at Forrest and me as she introduced herself as Peggy. The reverend became suddenly transfixed by the empty plate in front of him. Just then, Jia appeared from the doorway in a simple blue cotton dress, her sparkling blue eyes framed by mascara. She held a platter of Caprese, while Maximo appeared with a basket of focaccia. They set the food down on opposite ends of the table, and we began serving ourselves. I reached into the breadbasket and sighed. The focaccia was warm and light, with rosemary and flaky salt baked into the crust. I felt a hand on my shoulder, then.

"You made it," Jia said, smiling warmly at me. "We're so happy you could join us for dinner.

"Thank you, Jia." I smiled up at her. "We couldn't miss it."

"You are kind to say that. These dinners mean a lot to Nonna." Her gaze shifted from me to Forrest. "It's a hotel tradition."

"I can see why," Forrest added. "It's a great way to get everyone together."

Her smile dipped, slightly, when she turned back to me. "I know the circumstances of your trip are a bit..." she glanced around the table to make sure the other guests weren't listening, "complicated. But we are so happy to have you both here. We like to make our guests feel like this is their home, too. We'd love to help you with anything you need. Just say the word."

"Thank you," I answered, touched by her kindness. "I will." For once, there was no shame in my voice as I said it.

"Good." She smiled, squeezed my shoulder, and gradually drifted to another guest before settling down next to Forrest to fill her own plate with the starters. As she did, Peggy turned her attention back to us, as she reached into the breadbasket for a second piece of focaccia.

"So, where are you girls from?" she asked.

"DC," I answered, smiling back at her. After the initial shock of seeing Reverend Townes, I was feeling at ease again. It was clear he was infinitely more mortified by this run-in than I was.

"No kidding!" She beamed as she patted her husband's chest, who still refused to lift his gaze from his plate. "So are we!"

"What a small world," Forrest answered, grinning back at her. She squeezed my knee, and I stifled a flutter in my stomach.

"It really is." Peggy nodded firmly, eyes boring into Forrest's. "Dominic is a reverend at an Episcopal church back in DC. He meets all kinds of people through Sunday services, baptisms, weddings. We run into people Dominic knows all the time. It makes DC feel like a small town sometimes. I bet you and I would know someone in common if we tried to connect the dots. I won't press, though." She lifted her hands in surrender. "Dominic had a stressful bout at work recently, and he wanted to get a break from all of that. Enjoy some rare anonymity."

"What happened?" I asked innocently.

He crossed his arms and glared — actually glared — at me.

"Oh, you know how it is for pastors," she answered with a wave of her hand. "Nothing about their life can be private. You are essentially a public figure in your community. For me, I can take the occasional Sunday off, and I have friends who don't go to our church, but Dominic is so immersed in everything. He just needed a break." She patted his knee affectionately.

"This is definitely the perfect place for a break," Forrest answered, gazing out at the city. "I can't believe people actually live here."

"It is unbelievable, isn't it?" Peggy shook her head.

"You never get used to it," Jia said grinning, as she brought out dinner — tagliatelle with shrimp in a lemon sauce — with Nonna behind her. the woman was a little more than half the height of Jia, with her hair tied back in a white cloth as she wore a faded blue-gray dress with flour dusting her thighs. She nodded at Forrest and me.

"That looks heavenly," Peggy muttered as guests began passing around the pasta bowls. She turned her focus back to Forrest and me. "So, what brings you two to Positano? I heard you're staying in the honeymoon suite. Is that right?"

I tensed at the question, until Forrest squeezed my knee again, under the table. It was comforting to sit beside someone who seemed to understand my every thought. Maybe that was why I felt brave enough to be honest, at last, because she was right. I needed to spend this vacation out of hiding. "Yeah," I said, "This was supposed to be my honeymoon." I straightened in my chair, and Forrest kept her hand on my knee. "My fiancé left me at the altar on Saturday, during the wedding." The table quieted down as I spoke, and soon my words were the only sound beside clinking plates. "It was awful, as you'd imagine. I'm still processing it. But the trip was already paid for, and my fian — I mean, my *ex*-fiancé's mother insisted I go. Forrest was my maid of honor." I looked at my friend, whose brown eyes shined with pride as I spoke. I kept watching her, lest I lose the courage to speak. "I guess I'm here to figure out how I can put my life back together, after something like that."

Peggy burst out laughing.

Jia dropped her fork, and Bianca watched Peggy with a horrified expression that mirrored the everyone else at the table. Reverend Townes' whole head was crimson. But Peggy only laughed harder, until tears were streaming down her cheeks, until she sank so low in her chair we could only make out the top half of her head as she doubled over, clutching her stomach.

"You," she wheezed, "That was you!" She howled as her head dipped over the table. "I can't believe it!"

"Ok, love, that's enough," said Dominic, his tone tense. His face was so flushed he almost looked purple, but his words only made Peggy laugh harder.

Forrest cleared her throat, her hand still on my knee, her face pinched in a taut frown. "We didn't want to say anything, because we didn't want to make their vacation awkward, but Reverend Townes officiated the wedding." She gestured toward the pastor with her free hand. "I think Peggy just realized that."

Peggy got control of herself long enough to choke out, "I'm sorry!" before she glanced at her mortified husband and started laughing again.

Bianca muttered a curse under her breath, while Nonna signed the cross with her hands. Jia's face went ghastly pale, but Maximo clapped his hands together and smiled. "It's Italy," he said cheerfully, "nothing goes according to plan, but we make the best with what we've got." He studied the guests' bewildered expressions with an easy grin. I wondered if he was touching his wife's knee, the way Forrest was touching mine. "Who wants dessert?"

After we polished off another glass of wine and Nonna's homemade cheesecake, and after we reassured Jia that she had nothing to apologize for — that we found the whole thing a bit funny, too — Forrest and I retreated to our room. A few guests smiled politely, but most kept their distance, understandably. We were steps away from the honeymoon suite, and its promised privacy, when Peggy called behind us, "Girls! Wait!"

Forrest stifled a groan before she turned around and forced a smile.

"I'm so sorry about dinner," she panted when she caught up. Her face was flushed, and a few strands of hair had come loose from her ponytail. "I don't know what came over me."

"It's ok," I said, overcome by my impulse to reassure her. "It's totally understandable. I was shocked when I saw him, too."

"It is a weird coincidence, isn't it?" She shifted her weight from one foot to the other, and crossed her arms as she looked at us with a suddenly determined expression. "It was very kind of you," she said breezily, "not to mention Ruth Bader-Ginsberg at dinner."

I blinked at her, unsure how to respond, until Forrest said, "Of course. We didn't want to make him feel embarrassed. We want to fly under the radar here, too."

Peggy sighed. "I'm so relieved to hear that. You see, nobody in the congregation knew about his, um, interest in the justice until your wedding. It's caused quite a stir for him back home. People want to know why their pastor owns more items with RBG's face on it than Jesus — no false idols, and all that. There's this junior pastor who's vying for his position, and he's started going through Dominic's old sermons to find all the times he quoted RBG. As you can imagine, it's a lot." She shook her head. "He just cares about women's rights. It's what I love about him. But the church is having a hard time accepting him now that they know this side of him. It's all been very stressful on Dominic."

"Of course it is," said Forrest. "The church was his community, and now that they know who he really is, they won't accept him. It's not right."

I nodded solemnly. "It's the opposite of what you'd expect from a religion that claims to be based on love."

Peggy's eyes widened at our words. "Exactly! It's so refreshing to talk to someone who gets it. I mean, the way the church is acting came as such a shock, but none of my friends seem to really understand." She smiled warmly at the two of us. "You two girls are wonderful. Dominic and I would love to buy you dinner one of these nights that we're here. There are a ton of incredible restaurants along the Amalfi Coast. It's the least we can do."

Forrest raised her eyebrows, and I offered a noncommittal response about how we'd have to check our schedule. "I'm sorry the wedding caused all of those issues for him," I said.

"Oh, don't apologize." Peggy waved away my concern. "It's not your fault. If you girls hadn't seen his office, someone else would have, eventually. If anything, it's my fault for telling him to keep his RBG stuff at work. We have one painted portrait of her in the living room, but I thought anything more would be tacky."

Forrest smiled back at her. "I mean, having seen his office, I think you made the right call."

All three of us laughed at that, and Peggy apologized one more time before she left to find Dominic. When we were safely behind the closed door of our suite, Forrest buried her head in her hands and fell face-first on the bed.

"Alana," she groaned. "I'm so sorry."

I tilted my head as I sat beside her. "What do you mean?"

She rolled over to face me, her face full of guilt. "I gave you this whole pep talk about putting yourself out there and enjoying the trip, pushed you to go to dinner. Then, your first moment in public since the wedding was Peggy laughing in your face about it."

"You helped me face my fear of public humiliation." I cracked a smile. "It was good exposure therapy."

Forrest frowned back, her arms wrapped around a pillow.

"Oh, you really feel bad about this."

Her eyes widened as she studied me sadly. "I do."

"Forrest." I squeezed her hand. "It's not your fault. That was bad luck, and it *was* kind of funny." I sighed. "Also, you were right. I was beating myself up in the room, and I needed to get out. I'm not going to let my guilt keep us from enjoying this honeymoon, and I won't let Peggy Townes get in the way, either."

Forrest smiled at me. "You're amazing, Al."

"I mean, I'm no Ruth Bader-Ginsburg..."

We dissolved into a fit of giggles, tangled limbs folding into each other on the bed. "Al," she wheezed, her brown eyes flickering like candles. "What sad, strange world have we found ourselves in?"

Laughing in bed with my beautiful best friend, a two-week vacation stretching promisingly ahead, I realized I would treasure this trip. Even if the scars of the wedding never healed, I would always have this time with Forrest, eyes dancing at our own private joke. I smiled back at her. "Fuck if I know."

10

Triangles of yellow sunlight streaked across the rumpled covers in the honeymoon suite. Forrest and I got up early to force ourselves out of our jetlag and to make the most of our day in Positano. We got dressed and tucked sunscreen into a purse with a phone charger, lip balm, and some euros in cash. Luckily, we didn't see any other guests on the way out.

I arranged a Vespa rental for the duration of the trip, and thanks to Bianca, our ride awaited us outside the hotel. The mint green motorbike was parked near the azalea bushes, on the edge of the cobblestone roundabout that made up the mansion's entrance. I drove. I grew up driving ATVs with my dad in North Carolina, and a Vespa wasn't so different. Forrest wrapped her arms around my waist and clung to me the whole way. The ride to the city was short, down a narrow, winding road lined with lemon trees with a stunning view of the ocean. Within ten minutes we were sitting at a Positano sidewalk café, sipping cappuccinos as we watched tourists wander past us down the street. The morning breeze cooled us as we sat, stalling the heat from singeing the city this afternoon.

The tension that had overtaken my senses for the past six months melted away. I thought I'd forgotten how to relax, but I found myself rapt by the city's calming spell. That was Positano. It seemed the entire landscape was designed to transport visitors to a permanent state of peace — removed from the rest of the world. Maybe coming on this honeymoon wasn't a mistake, after all.

The city had the same effect on Forrest. She leaned back in her chair and sipped espresso from a shiny white mug with her eyes half-closed, squinting at the colorful buildings and mountains behind them, the morning light turning golden on her brown skin. She wore a sundress I made her in college as a welcome home present when she studied abroad in Barcelona — a mid-length tank dress whose colorful patchwork mimicked the stained-glass windows at La Sagrada Familia. She wore it every chance she got. Now, she met my gaze with a warm expression that reminded me of melted butter. Her dark eyes glowed in sunset tones as she studied my face with impossible tenderness, a ghost of a smile curving her lips. It was both unsettling and reassuring — how well she could see to the heart of me, and how gentle she was when she did. I wanted to freeze the image in my mind.

"What is it?" Forrest asked, her brow wrinkling in concern.

I smiled back, breaking the trance. "I'm excited for today."

She rewarded me with a radiant grin, her dimples flashing. "Me, too."

We explored Positano into the afternoon, aimlessly circling the alleyways and storefronts. We dodged the summer heat that sweltered by the hour by ducking into the different stores lining the shaded streets. There were bakeries that smelled like custard, shops selling colorful dresses and bathing suits, lemon scented candles, soap, oils, and ornaments, shelves filled with postcards of the Amalfi Coast. There seemed to be an art gallery on almost every block, boasting modern pieces, ceramics, and seaside landscapes by Italian artists. We wandered through each one, admiring the intricacies of the art, balking at the prices, and moving on.

The only thing more breathtaking than the art was Forrest's awestruck face as she beheld it. Each time we encountered a new gallery, Forrest would freeze, eyes searching the window before shooting me a shy, questioning glance that I'd answer by leading her inside. Up close with the art, her lips would part slightly as she shifted from piece to piece, contemplating each composition, bringing a hand to her chin, then to her elbows, then back at her sides. Her eyes seemed to glow as she studied them, timidly tucking a twist behind her ear, as if the art were looking back. My favorite part was when she was nearly finished examining the piece. She'd step back and smile softly, like the art just told her a joke, then move on to the next one.

Whenever Forrest turned to comment on the work, on the colors or composition, she whispered as if we were in a church. I followed her lead, regarding the art with reverence, even if I didn't understand it the way she did. Of course, I admired the colorful Italian ceramics and intricate landscapes, but the best part, to me, was how they made art out of

Forrest. The real beauty was not the work itself, but the quiet awe it inspired in her.

We were looking for a place to stop for lunch when something different caught Forrest's eye. "Al!" she cried, pointing at a storefront beside us. "We have to go in!"

It was a fabric shop, with rolls of bright patterned cloth hanging from the window invitingly. There was one covered in bright red hexagons, another pale blue with lemons, and white lace fit for a wedding veil. The hexagons would make a stunning pair of pants; a patchwork with the lemons could spruce up an otherwise boring pair of jeans, or maybe accent a blouse; and the lace... Who was I kidding? "I don't know, Forrest," I said. "Maybe another time."

"We'll just pop in!" She smiled again, but it felt forced. "You've put up with me wandering art galleries at a sloth's pace. We have to check out at least *one* store for your passion."

"Watching you wander art galleries at a sloth's pace *is* one of my passions," I teased.

"And watching *you* ogle over fabrics while you plan out clothing designs is one of mine." She grabbed my hand and tried to gently pull me toward the store. My feet remained planted, but my cheeks flushed as I dropped my eyes to the ground. Forrest stopped tugging.

"Why not?" Her dark brown eyes looked even rounder as she stared at my planted feet in confusion.

"I'm too tired for sewing," I said quickly, so the words ran together. "We don't have any materials for that at the hotel, and I don't think the fabric will fit in our suitcase, anyway."

Forrest's expression shifted from confusion to understanding as she dropped my hand in resignation. But somehow, her acquiescing just made me sad. "Okay," she said slowly. "I guess we can always come back."

"Of course," I lied, grateful to leave the store behind us.

We stopped for lunch in a small restaurant down one of the side streets, where outdoor seating spilled into the alleyway and waiters served limoncello spritz with the afternoon sun directly overhead. I ordered gnocchi alla Sorrentina, while Forrest opted for tagliatelle in truffle sauce. We ate in silence at first, enjoying the effortless perfection of our meal, before Forrest finally asked, "Why didn't you want to go in the fabric store, really?"

I nudged the gnocchi with my fork. "Why do you think—"

"Room in your suitcase never stopped you before." Forrest shook her head. "Remember our trip to New Orleans, in college? You found a roll of fabric you liked for cheap and carried it with you the whole night out, to every bar on Bourbon Street. And you've never been too tired for sewing. I used to watch you finish a long workday designing websites just to plop in front of your sewing machine." She leaned forward in her seat, her piercing stare softened by concern. "Tell me what's going on, please. I'm worried."

I nodded as I took a bite of my meal, stalling for time as I shrugged lightly, trying to appear nonchalant. "It's been a little while since I last sewed," I said. "I'm rusty."

She nodded gently, aware of my hesitation as she leaned back and twirled her tagliatelle, mimicking my casual air. "How long?"

That was the worst part. I couldn't remember. My sewing gradually became more sporadic when Matthew and I got serious. Somehow, seeing my hobby through his eyes dampened my passion for it. There was the awkward head tilt when I first told him about my clothing designs. There were the loud sighs when I left his bed early on weekends to go thrifting for fabric, questions about why I didn't want to sleep in. And of course, there was the happy hour he told his co-workers, "Alana *loves* clothes." Nothing wrong with that but the way he said it, like an inside joke I couldn't grasp. All of it was vague enough that I never confronted him.

It got worse when we moved in together. He hated the noise of the sewing machine and the tiny scraps of fabric and thread that covered the kitchen table while I worked, even though I cleaned up afterward. I switched to knitting and crochet to lessen the mess, as my machine gathered dust in the closet. I used to sell my clothing designs on Etsy for an income that rivaled my full-time salary, but by the time we got engaged that business dried up. Knitting, too, dwindled a meager hobby to distract me between work and wedding prep.

I never questioned it, never resented him, because I thought it was my choice. It was easier to tell myself my dreams changed.

"A while," I told Forrest.

She pressed her mouth into a flat line, then dropped her eyes to her food. We ate in silence. I thought perhaps this conversation could be behind us. Then, she said softly: "Is that why you didn't make your wedding dress?"

I dared to meet her gaze, and cracked at the tenderness that awaited there. Her expression was frozen, but her eyes were on fire, swimming with anger and a softness that melted by embarrassment. I could wrap myself in that gaze and sleep for days. She blinked and took a slow, steady breath. "Even before you met Matthew," she said, "I wondered what your wedding would be like. Not that I buy into the patriarchal bullshit about how a woman's life peaks on her wedding day, or whatever. I just always wondered what you'd do with your dress. Even the jean shorts you're wearing right now are unlike any pair I've seen before. So for your wedding? I knew that dress would be the most beautiful piece of clothing I've ever seen in my life."

As she met my gaze, her eyes darkened with hurt, as if I betrayed her, personally. "I was really sad when you invited me to go dress shopping with you and Melissa, when I realized I wouldn't get to see that dress. The one you chose looked nothing like what I imagined. It was so... minimal. Don't get me wrong, you looked stunning. You're always beautiful. But the dress wasn't *you*. I hated that I'd never know what you would have done if you had true creative freedom over your wedding." She squeezed my hand under the table as tears clouded both our eyes. "I'm sorry for making you cry."

I shook my head. I barely noticed the tears that now coated my cheeks. "No, no, you're right," I said. I had wondered, too, how I'd design a wedding dress, before I agreed to marry Matthew and that dream became impossible. It was easy to give that up when I thought no one else would care. Clothing was superficial, anyway, and it felt disloyal to complain about my fiancé. But Matthew was gone, and this was Forrest. It was safe, I realized, to tell her the truth.

"One of the most romantic parts of a wedding is your fiancé's face when they see you walk down the aisle," I shrugged, as I hung my head in shame. "I didn't think I could make a dress that would give him that face. Not to mention I was way too busy planning the wedding to design something like that."

Forrest smiled softly, sadly, but said nothing.

"I told myself it was about starting our life together on the right note, by honoring what he and his family would want," I continued, staring at my bare ring finger, "but... I don't know. Now it feels like I took what's supposed to be one of the most important days of my life and lived it in a way that was wholly counter to who I am. I can't tell if Matthew didn't realize what I gave up, or if he didn't care."

The quiet rage behind Forrest's eyes stunned me, when I was brave enough to meet her gaze. But the softness in her expression returned when she squeezed my hand.

"I really hope," she said, "that one day, I'll see *your* wedding dress."

"You will," I vowed. "Even if I have to marry myself."

We bought two gelato cones at a seaside café to eat by the water — strawberry for Forrest and pistachio for me. We stood among the tourists on Positano's promenade, as swimmers floated in the waves before us. Golden hour was just starting, and flecks of light danced along the sea, disco ball style.

The gelato stuck to my tongue like taffy, its creaminess punctuated by the subtle spice of pistachio. The crowds around us moved at the pace of the lazy waves that lapped the shore. The buildings tinted yellow from sunlight grew more golden with each breath. Forrest and I watched in comfortable silence, until something caught her eye in the distance.

"Look over there," said Forrest, squinting toward the other end of the promenade.

"What?"

She pointed, and I saw the woman, standing in front of an easel, further down the sidewalk. She had long, curly brown hair that was lost to the wind behind her as she puzzled over her art, pulling her brush across the canvas in long, wavy strokes that had to be the ocean. There was no hesitation in her movements, as if painting were as simple as signing her name.

I turned back to Forrest the same time her eyes jerked to me. "Can we?" she asked.

We walked toward her together until we reached the canvas. It was a minimalist, abstract take of Positano. The brilliant colors and hurried outlines of the ocean, sun, mountains, and boat-shaped triangles only alluded to reality. Still, she captured the essence perfectly. The sunset hues took my breath away, as enchanting as the real ocean. Forrest was enthralled, her gelato melting down her hand forgotten as her wide eyes studied the woman's brush strokes.

"Um," I said shyly, and the woman turned. "*Tu arte... Bella.*"

I couldn't muster the adequate words in English, let alone Italian. Still, the woman beamed at me. "Thank you," she said. Her glittering eyes mirrored the water, while her accent made the words sound like music. "This is my favorite place in the world to paint."

"I can see why," said Forrest. "You capture it perfectly." The woman introduced herself as Stella, as she and Forrest launched into a conversation about how she captured a landscape that was shifting before her eyes.

"I'm capturing the experience of watching the sunset, start to finish. I will paint the sun at different heights and add more pink as the sky changes. When I'm done, there will be colors from every hour on here."

"It looks incredible," I murmured, and she laughed as she mixed a sherbet orange and began blending it into the sky.

"That's brilliant," said Forrest. "Instead of painting one moment, you're painting time itself."

"Exactly," she said. "I don't like painting frozen moments because that's not how we experience life. Everything has context, history, even a sunset. Every moment of the sun falling is as beautiful as the last, and I like to put them all in my paintings. There is nothing in the world like an Amalfi sunset. I like to think I am capturing them for others to enjoy — or just for myself to remember them on the next rainy day."

"Is that why you paint them?"

"That, and this is my home." She shrugged. "I was born here, and while I've lived in other places, there is only one Positano. Nothing makes me happier than painting my home."

She asked Forrest about her art, and my friend showed Stella some iPhone photos of her work. Forrest specializes in portraits in abstract colors that capture the emotion behind each scene. Her sister in blue and orange with her eyes closed in the sun. Her uncle in fuchsia and lavender, flashing a smile over his shoulder. A close-up of my hands in indigo, fiddling with my engagement ring. Her portraits depicted a person's essence, and underlying truth of a scene. It stunned me, sometimes — how much she could see.

My favorite is a self-portrait she created just before graduating from RISD. Forrest was an explosion of teal and cerulean in the center of a lavender background, her head tilted back and hands in her hair as if she were rinsing shampoo. Her dimples carved valleys in her cheeks as smile lines bloomed from the corners of her eyes. The painting perfectly captured Forrest's euphoria at finally becoming an artist, her hope and liberation evident in each stroke. She called it *Rebirth.*

Forrest had been a free-spirited, creative child who filled her family home with drawings; her aunt and uncle were more pragmatic. After her parents died, she threw herself into school and landed a lucrative job as an analyst at a hotel conglomerate in Washington, DC.

Forrest hated that job. She hated her long workdays in a cubicle, the plain blazers and work shoes that cut up her ankles. She hated that she barely had time eat lunch. Any time I spent sewing she passed in front of a sketch book or easel, creating some new art piece for our apartment. Then the pandemic hit, and she was laid off. All she had left was the emptiness that job carved out of her life, from straying so far from her passion. There was no hiding from her inner 12-year-old who loved to draw, who didn't care about anything else.

"What am I even doing with my life?" she cried as we lay in my bed together. Tears ran down her cheeks as she squeezed my stuffed animal to her chest.

"We're twenty-four," I said gently. "You don't need to know the answer to that."

For the next few months, she lived off severance and painted. She seemed to spend every spare moment she had creating art, paint smears covering her arms and clothing. I had never seen her so joyful. When she told me she was leaving DC for art school, I understood. Even as I cried myself to sleep that night.

It wasn't the worst thing, really, to no longer live with her. After two years as her roommate, I started to catch myself slipping. I'd notice how delicately her fork balanced between her long fingers during dinner, or how deep her dimples bloomed when she laughed, and I'd be suddenly overwhelmed with longing to kiss her. Just once. The thought alone of her lips on mine, of our bodies pressed together, was enough to leave me blushing, even as I lay alone in bed. I shook the thought away, of course. I always did. But that didn't stop my gut from sinking when she started dating her then-girlfriend, knowing she'd never see me that way. That didn't stop the hope from fluttering in my chest when they broke up, only to learn she was leaving. I couldn't bear the thought of losing her, but my feelings threatened to topple me.

When she went to RISD, I missed her desperately, but part of me was relieved, too. I doubted our friendship would survive if she stayed. Being close to her was becoming unbearable. I feared I'd one day snap, confess my feelings, and ruin everything. It was safer to say goodbye.

It was safer to back away as Stella proclaimed her awe at Forrest's self-portrait, safer to pretend my old desire didn't flare at the flush in Forrest's cheeks as Stella praised her talent. Forrest exchanged a glance with me, her eyes sparkling, and I brushed the thought away. I needed her now more than ever. I couldn't afford to lose myself in the past.

11

I knew my problem was the second I woke up the next day, to chirping birds, golden sunlight, and the honeymoon suite's sweeping view. Exhaustion. I was jet-lagged and completely drained from months of wedding planning, and by yesterday evening my delirium put me in a tailspin over feelings long forgotten. Now, I could see clearly again, as Forrest lay beside me. One hand was tucked under her pillow, while the other reached toward me, her legs hidden by the white duvet. Watching her sleep, it was easier to stifle my dread. She was beautiful, but she was my best friend. Being with her was enough.

What a relief.

I flipped a curtain of messy hair out of my face as I slipped out of bed, eager to see the morning balcony view. As the door slipped open, I heard Forrest stir behind me. "How'd you sleep?" she asked, her voice raspy from sleep. My stomach fluttered at the sound.

"Good." I turned around to smile at her, leaning against the doorframe. "I'm starting to feel like a person again."

"Me, too." Forrest sat up and stretched her arms. "I know this is your honeymoon, but I really needed a vacation."

"I know." My wedding, her teaching job, and her upcoming exhibition kept Forrest busy the past few months. "How is the art coming?"

"It's getting there." She shrugged. "There are a couple old paintings I'm bringing to showcase. I'm just struggling with getting inspired to make new ones, probably because I've been so busy. I think the trip will help, so I can come back with fresh eyes."

I nodded. "Can I see photos?"

"Not yet." Forrest smiled wearily. "It's still a work in progress, but maybe later."

Odd. She normally showed me everything, no matter what state it was in. "Sure."

As we got dressed, I caught myself up on the text messages I missed since arriving in Italy. I cringed as I scrolled through them — friends, co-workers and acquaintances offering their condolences on what they witnessed (or heard about) at the wedding. I'd answer those later, once I could clear my head. Only three required a response now:

Mom: I really think you and Matthew should talk when you get back. Maybe he will look past this. You could have at least invited him to Italy…

Gemma: Idk what unhinged shit Mom is texting you… just know I'm handling it.

Carter: I am rescuing your sewing machine (and other items) from Shithead's today. Will keep you posted on this hostage crisis. You better drink an aperol spritz in my honor! Love you, babe. Xx

I told Mom "Ok," thanked Gemma, and sent Carter some photos from yesterday's outing to accompany my gratitude. I would have continued replying, making my way through the condolence notes, if I didn't find Forrest standing in the bathroom door, eyeing me suspiciously. "You better not be comforting random acquaintances right now about how well you're doing," she said. The sight of her in a high-waisted blue bikini was enough to make me lock my phone and flipped it face down on the bedside table. "Not texting anyone but Carter for the rest of the day," I announced. "Let's go to the beach."

Jia was waiting for us at the front desk when we came out. When she saw us, she rose from her seat and rounded the mahogany desk, wringing her hands as she approached. "Girls, I'm so sorry for what happened the other night," she said, shaking her head. "I don't know what Peggy Townes was thinking."

"Don't feel bad about that," I said, shaking my head back. I think Peggy was just surprised, and y'all had no way of knowing any of that would happen. We're both having an amazing time here. Your family has been wonderful to us. I'm so grateful."

Jia nodded, but she looked unconvinced. "Do you two have dinner plans?" When we shook our heads, she continued. "We're having family dinner tonight, just the four of us. We would love to have you join if you're free."

"Oh, we can't do that," I said instinctively. "It's your family night. We wouldn't want to intrude."

"Our family is always together," Maximo answered as he passed through the lobby, carrying a full laundry basket. "Please, intrude!"

"We wouldn't invite you if we didn't want you there," Jia said gently, offering a soft smile.

"In that case, we'd love to," answered Forrest, flashing her dimples at Jia. I added a shy "thank you," and Jia asked our day Positano. We told her how the city enchanted us, wandering the art galleries and shops, indulging in a decadent lunch, meeting a local artist, and ogling over our Vespa ride up the coast as we made our way back to the Valeri. She listened with the pride of a local in love with her home, her expression softening as a smile spread across her narrow face.

"This place is incredible," she said. "I love watching guests fall in love with it."

"We are definitely in love," I answered, thinking of Forrest's hands on my waist as we rode the Vespa home yesterday, an endless sunset blanketing the cliffs ahead. "I can't imagine living here."

Jia smiled knowingly, eyes shifting from me to Forrest. "I can't imagine living anywhere else."

We beat the crowds to find two lounge chairs on the Positano beach, where we decided to spend the day relaxing with novels in hand and pastries from a bakery we passed on the way. While we sat, I told Forrest about the texts from back home, the way Gemma was handling my mother's chaos without complaint.

"It's a little... surprising?" I said. Normally, Gemma left me to fend for myself against our mother. I grew up chasing straight A's, exceling at sports and student leadership, all at my mother's urging — even though I yearned to spend my weekends in, sewing in peace. Meanwhile, Gemma scraped by with B's and snuck out to parties, untouched by my mother's judging eye. We didn't have a lot in common. I was intimidated by how easily she moved through the world, while she grew impatient with my compulsion to please.

Forrest nodded slowly as she ate a croissant, turning over the words in her mind. "I think you learn a lot about your family when shit hits the fan," she said. "I didn't connect with my aunt and uncle super well growing up. I'm a free spirit, and they're like, the polar opposite." She shrugged. "But when we lost Mom and Dad, they showed up. They didn't have or want kids, but they became parents to me and Monique. They never made us feel unwelcome, even though we turned their lives upside down. We were family. That's all that mattered."

Together Forrest and her family endured over a decade of grieving. I did what I could to support her, but Monique, Aunt Pat and Uncle Artie were the only ones who truly understood her loss. Their relationships reflected that. They loved each other with everything they had, because they were all they had. "I love your aunt and uncle," I said, and Forrest smiled in agreement. "I didn't realize my family could be like that, too."

"Maybe she just needed to see that you were human." Forrest shrugged as she tapped her fingers on her lounge chair.

"What do you mean?"

Forrest stared into my eyes for a moment, weighing whether to tell me something, then shrugged again as she answered me. "The morning after the Bachelorette, I woke up early to watch the sunrise on the balcony. Your uncle's beach house had the best view. Gemma was there, too, watching the waves crash, and criticizing one of the surfers on his form." Forrest chuckled. "I can't remember what we were talking about, but there was a lull in the conversation, and then she said, out of the blue, 'What do you think of all this?' I told her I was happy for you, that Matthew seemed nice, and you seemed content. I asked her, and she said Matthew was the type of guy she thought you'd end up with."

I cocked my head to the side. "What's that supposed to mean?"

"Perfect," Forrest answered. "She said, 'I guess it makes sense; he's perfect just like her.'"

I shook my head. Our entire relationship, I strained to fit the role of a perfect girlfriend, to convince Matthew and myself that I deserved him. It came naturally. I lived my life straining to appear put together, to meet my mom's expectations. I never thought my own sister would buy the act. "What did you say to her?"

"I told her you're not perfect. You think Shrek 1 is better than Shrek 2."

I laughed in equal parts surprise and relief, knowing my best friend understood. "It *is*."

Forrest shook her head. "I'm sorry, but the one Shrek movie that does not have Puss in Boots *cannot* be the superior Shrek. That's science." She waved her hand dismissively, pushing the thought away. "The point is, I think she misjudged you. I hope things can be better between you two, now."

"Me, too." Our mom pit us against each other, growing up. I was the 'good girl' my mother always wanted. Gemma was thinner, which Mom liked to point out when dropping hints about my diet, but unlike me, Gemma never bought into my mother's snide comments. She refused to reshape her personality to please. As kids, it felt like we spoke two different languages. "I always wanted to be close to her. But when I tried, she'd roll her eyes and go to her room. I thought I embarrassed her."

Forrest watched me silently, her eyes going soft as she tilted her head and smiled, dimples flashing. "For the record," she said, "You're the shit, Al. I doubt Gemma ever found you embarrassing." The gentleness in her voice made me blush, but she just shrugged as her eyes drifted to the sea. We watched two kids bob in the waves, laughing when the sea lifted them off the ground. Finally, Forrest said: "The circumstances are obviously terrible, but I hope all this can bring some healing."

"I hope so, too." I leaned back against my lounge chair and closed my eyes. "Then, at least some good could come of it."

We spent the whole day at the beach. Sleeping on the lounge chairs, reading our novels, floating in the waves. Forrest ordered lunch from a café and picked up prosciutto sandwiches wrapped in wax paper to eat by the beach, while I fetched us two gelato cones in the late afternoon.

It was a relief to be unproductive. I couldn't remember the last time I lazed the day away, and there was no better place to do it than Positano. The city's historic buildings stacked on the hill behind us — the church's green and yellow-tile dome an intricate contrast with the simple buildings surrounding it, all in white and warm colors. The mountains cocooned the city like a protective mother, while the ocean stretched endlessly ahead. It felt like we were wholly removed from the rest of the world, tucked away in the landscape.

Tourists wandered the scenery mesmerized, while kids laughed in the waves and other sunbathers napped beside us. Everyone was on vacation, and their tranquility was contagious. As I dozed in the sun and floated in the sea, I felt lighter than I had months. By the time we returned to the Valeri, my body was completely drained of tension. I met the Valeri family with wet hair, a baggy sundress, and no makeup, at peace. Judging by her soft voice and gentle smile, Forrest felt the same.

Each member of the family greeted us with a wide smile and a kiss on the cheek as we met them. A pan of lasagna awaited us on the table alongside caprese salad. Nonna's own nonna taught her the recipe, deliciously thin layers of pasta, ricotta, and Bolognese baked until the top turned golden. The fluffy layers were cozy and timeless, like being carried to bed by your mother after falling asleep in the car. They paired the meal with a deliciously light pinot noir from a vineyard nearby, owned by Jia's childhood best friend.

Unlike last night's meal, this one was indoors, on a scratched wooden table in the mansion's large kitchen, where the family enjoyed some privacy from the guests. There was a large stove and oven in the back and a wide wooden counter in the middle of the room that ran parallel to our dinner table at the front. The ceiling light glowed in candlelight hues against the cream-colored walls. The room spacious and homey, especially when filled with the smell of lasagna and the Valeri family's laughter.

Talk of the inn was forbidden at dinner, a family rule instituted by Jia's father decades ago. Instead, they spoke of Bianca's friends at university and Maximo's photography, of which neighbors were pondering retirement and whose kids might move back to the coast. They spoke of their son, Giovanni and his work at a museum in Rome, as they teased Nonna about her own youthful days in the capital. When they slipped into Italian, Maximo or

Bianca would quietly translate for Forrest and me, since Nonna did not speak much English.

When Nonna's gaze landed on me, I pointed to my plate. "*Molto bene*," I said shyly, ducking my head as I nodded to her.

"*Grazie*," she answered, her hazel eyes twinkling.

"It really is," affirmed Forrest. "Better than any restaurant." When Bianca raised her eyebrow at her aunt and uncle, my best friend asked: "What?"

Bianca shook her head, smiling apologetically at Forrest. "It's nothing. That's just what I've been telling them for the past two years. We'd do so well if we opened a restaurant."

"Bianca." Maximo shook his head. "Not at family dinner."

"Weekly dinner with the guests is our hotel tradition," Jia said, tucking a shoulder-length curl behind her ear. "My father liked it that way, because then we can get to know everyone staying at the hotel. Besides, I don't want to give my mother more work."

"We could hire cooks to run the restaurant," Bianca said as she ate. "Nonna could teach them her recipes, then she wouldn't have to cook the weekly guest dinners. We can afford the help, especially with the profits we'd bring from a restaurant. I've been looking at the numbers, and—"

"We don't want to talk about numbers now." Jia waved Bianca's comment away. "That would have to be a much longer conversation with Nonna."

"I'd be curious to see if Giovanni will make any changes like that when he takes over the Valeri," Maximo said, leaning back in his chair with his hands behind his head. "I often wonder if he will lead with his city education or his romantic heart. Maybe a little of both."

"*Zio*, you already know this," Bianca sighed as she put down her fork. "Giovanni doesn't want to run the Valeri."

"Why do you think that? Who said that?"

"*He* did."

The two began arguing in Italian, waving hands and forks in the air with their words. From the head of the table, Nonna shook her head and chuckled. Then, she winked at me, her eyes full of mischief. It was so surprising, I laughed too, then covered my mouth so the others wouldn't see. That only made Nonna laugh harder. Somehow, no one else at the table seemed to notice.

"This," Jia sighed, "is why we don't talk business at dinner."

"I'm so sorry," Forrest said. "I shouldn't have said anything."

"Oh, it wasn't you." Jia waved Forrest off with a loose hand. "Why do you think we have the rule? Every week, we somehow end up talking business, and every week, the only way to get them to stop arguing is by reminding them that we don't talk business at dinner." She paused to shout at them in Italian, which promptly ended the argument. "See?"

"Forrest and Alana," Maximo said, forcing a smile back to his face. "How long are you two staying with us, again?"

"We leave next Sunday," I answered.

"Oh, wonderful! You will meet Giovanni. He comes home for a few days. You know, he loves art history. I bet you two will have plenty to talk about." Maximo gestured at Forrest. "He always gets so excited when he meets an artist."

Forrest blushed as Jia started telling us about the art museum where Giovanni worked. His schedule was more relaxed in the summer months, so he could visit the coast more often. They were hosting a slew of neighbors Thursday night for a welcome dinner. It was always a celebration when Giovanni came to town.

Between bites of dessert, a soft lemon cake with soothing citrus taste, Jia told us stories of Giovanni and Bianca as children, treating the Valeri as their personal playground. Giovanni jumping out the second-floor window because watching Glinda in 'The Wizard of Oz' convinced him he could fly. Bianca dressing up as a ghost to prank a guest into thinking the hotel was haunted. The stories were so outlandish, especially in contrast to Bianca's present day temperament, that soon the whole table was in tears.

After showering Nonna with a flurry of *Grazie's*, Forrest and I retreated to bed, mumbling to each other tiredly about how thoroughly we were enjoying this. The beautiful coastline, the food, the warm, hilarious family we were staying with. "And we only just got here," I murmured.

"It makes me so happy to see you like this," Forrest said as we lay in the dark together. "It's been too long."

I furrowed my eyebrows. "Since what?"

"Since you were happy." I couldn't see her, but I could hear the warmth in her voice. Her tenderness was strong enough to make me tipsy, drunk on the feeling of her breath on my face as we whispered.

She squeezed my hand under the covers and said: "I hope they let Bianca run the Valeri, when the time comes."

I squeezed her hand back, to return the affection, and to anchor myself. "Me, too."

12

The invitation came with a knock on our door the next morning. Bianca, in her standard button-down and khaki shorts, told us she would be helping Nonna make tortellini tonight, and we were welcome to join. "Unless you have plans?" she asked uncertainly.

"No plan of ours could beat helping you and Nonna make tortellini," I answered as I tied my hair back into a high ponytail. Forrest was in the bathroom, brushing her teeth. I thought back to the laughter in Nonna's eyes last night, during Bianca and Maximo's bickering. "We'd love to."

We took the Vespa to Fornillo Beach, the quieter sister to Positano's main beach. We curved along the winding roads of the Amalfi coast, the mountains to our left and the ocean to our right. Forrest sat behind me, clutching my waist. I relished the press of her fingers above my hip, her breath tickling the back of my ear when she whispered a joke or asked how close we were. This vacation had to be the best decision I ever made.

We reached a beach surrounded by cliffs and lush greenery, where bright turquoise waves and white foam lapped at the rocky shore. We passed the morning on a pair of lounge chairs under a bright blue umbrella, reading, napping, and periodically cooling off in the water. Forrest sketched a mother holding hands with her toddler as they walked into the ocean and gifted the drawing to the family when she finished — prompting an older French couple to ask for a portrait of their grandson in exchange for a swig of limoncello. They came from Toulouse for vacation; we traded stories about our trip so far and mulled over ideas for where to hang Forrest's portrait when they got back home. They carefully slipped the completed art into their tote bag between two beach reads, and added us both on Facebook to stay in touch. The grandson said goodbye with the shy, jerky motion of a toddler still learning to wave, his blue eyes wide with curiosity.

"This is why I love drawing," Forrest told me, eyes drifting shut as we returned to our lounge chairs. "I've been so busy, I think I forgot."

"Why you love it?" I asked.

She shook her head. "Why it matters."

We shared a pizza from a shop in downtown Fornillo, a light lunch to satiate our hunger without ruining our appetite for the afternoon. A certain lightness settled into my bones, the vacation healing my tired soul piece by piece. We returned to the Valeri soothed and sun-kissed, ready to cook and, more importantly, eat.

Of course, I didn't expect making pasta to be quite this difficult.

Bianca explained the process to us as Nonna mixed and kneaded the dough. It was the kind of recipe that was impossible to replicate, the ratio of flour to eggs determined by the temperature outside and a gut instinct Nonna developed over decades. It was a wonder to watch her work, utterly relaxed as the mixture became dough beneath her fingers. She winked at us as she used a pasta machine roll the dough flat, teasing Bianca in Italian.

"It took me months to convince Nonna to get a pasta machine," said Bianca. She was uncharacteristically casual here, in a t-shirt and loose cotton shorts with her hair tin a messy bun.

There was laughter in her eyes that she normally kept hidden at the front desk. "But now she loves it."

Nonna lifted her eyes from the dough. "I like, how you say, *tradizione*." She looked admiringly at her granddaughter. "Bianca is a smart girl."

Bianca rolled her eyes, but squeezed Nonna's arm affectionately as she replied in Italian. "She works so hard," she said. "And there are so many ways to make her life easier. The weekly dinners are hard work. I like to give her a break where I can." She smiled coyly at us. "That's why we're here."

We were making tortellini to freeze for next week's dinner, folding each pasta by hand. Bianca cut squares for us to fold into tortellini with a spinach and ricotta mixture Nonna prepared earlier. Then, she walked us through the steps. How much ricotta to place on the dough, where to brush egg wash and pinch the corners to securely seal the mixture, how to fold it into that familiar, round tortellini shape. Bianca made tortellini the same way she seemed to do everything, diligent and efficient. Her pasta was impeccable; any miniscule variations only showed they were handmade, making them more beautiful.

I, on the other hand, could not fold tortellini to save my life. I'd over-flour the dough, so it wouldn't stick together, or under-flour so it stuck to the table. I struggled to keep the ricotta from spilling out the edges, and pinching it into a neat circle seemed impossible. My lumpy, uneven ovals took far longer to shape than they should have.

Nonna shook her head and chuckled when she saw my work. "You're really Italian?" she asked

"She's half Italian," Forrest answered. "She got her tortellini skills from the Southern half."

Bianca burst out laughing as she translated, and Nonna soon joined her. I scoffed in mock offense and flicked a dusting of flour at Forrest. "Rude," I said.

"You're just jealous because I'm a natural," Forrest teased, and it was true. She'd already folded twice as much tortellini as I did, in neat, artistic circles that rivaled Bianca's.

"You have an unfair advantage!" I said. "You literally make art for a living."

"So do you, Coco Chanel." Forrest flicked flour back at me, and I scoffed again.

"Double rude!"

Nonna laughed to herself as she chopped basil for the tomato sauce, shaking her head. Bianca smiled too, as she placed another perfect tortellini on the tray. "Why'd you call her Chanel?"

"I make my own clothes," I answered as I scooped some ricotta for another tortellini. "It's a hobby."

"*Not* a hobby," Forrest said firmly, placing a tortellini beside Bianca's. "She made the dress I wore yesterday. She has her own Etsy shop and everything."

I shook my head. "The Etsy shop isn't active right now."

"So? That doesn't change anything." She nudged me with an elbow. "She took a break to plan her wedding, but she's incredible."

"Wow," said Bianca, eyes widening.

"Right?"

Bianca tilted her head as she faced me. "How long have you been making clothes?"

I fought the blush spreading across my cheeks. "Since I was fifteen." It started as tailoring. I'd take a too-big pair of jeans from Goodwill and make them hug my curves, or relax the waistline of a corduroy skirt to fit the soft folds of my stomach. A few stiches here and there, and nobody would know I couldn't afford Abercrombie jeans. Only, what if I made the pants into a skirt? Or added a patch of patterned fabric above the knee? Over time my designs became too intricate to be mistaken for department store ware. People would gawk, "you *made* this?" then ask if I could do it for them. In school, I worked tirelessly toward overachieving, but clothing was my outlet. Sewing a precise line of stitches was the most satisfying form of perfection. Unlike in life, there was no deadline on getting a pattern right, no one else who would notice, or care, but me. There was no pressure, only the soothing hum of the sewing machine as I ran the neat cuts of fabric between my fingers. There was only the joy of making something new.

Over time, I learned to respond to praise with a business card. I took commissions and partitioned my time on a color-coded calendar to juggle school and designing. After graduating, I started selling my clothes on Etsy and at local markets in DC; the sales supplemented my entry level salary and fulfilled me in a way work never did. Forrest joined me at every market, bringing a tote bag of snacks and two oat milk lattés from the closest local coffeeshop.

"I loved that dress you made her," Bianca said. Then, she turned toward the corner of the room. My eyes followed her to a small wooden table under the window that I hadn't noticed before, where a clunky sewing machine sat beside a basket of different colored threads. "You know, you can use the family sewing machine," she said. "It's a little old, but it runs well. Sometimes, Jia patches up holes in our clothes or in the bedsheets, but it's mostly unused."

Nestled in this cozy kitchen, buoyed by the homey scent of dinner and unquestioning confidence from the women beside me, the thought wasn't as scary. Maybe I'd been too hasty outside the fabric shop. It was instinct to balk at the risk of embarrassing myself. I spent my entire relationship with Matthew chasing comfort and logic and called that adulthood. Only I couldn't remember why I was so desperate to grow up. Not with a standing invitation to try my passion again. "Thank you," I said. "Maybe I will. I'll let you know."

Forrest beamed at my answer, and that decided it. At some point, while I was here, I would try sewing again, if only to make her smile like that. My cheeks heated at the pillow-soft tenderness in her eyes. I hurriedly dropped my gaze to the tortellini, folding and re-folding until I got it right.

"*Bellisima*," said Nonna, as she inspected Forrest's neat rows of tortellini. She turned to mine and smiled wryly as she said, "These will do, too." She squeezed my bicep, then Forrest's, leaving light flour handprints behind. We packaged most of the pasta into a container and placed it in the freezer. The rest Nonna boiled and mixed with tomato sauce — our dinner, with leftovers for Jia and Maximo to eat later.

The four of us sat together at the kitchen table as we ate. The light ricotta filling seemed to dissolve on my tongue, contrasting deliciously while the sharp tomato sauce. As we ate, I asked Bianca about her experience at Valeri, if she grew up in the hotel like Giovanni did.

Bianca shook her head as she took a bite of pasta. "I grew up in Naples," she said. "That's where my parents live. We'd come here for the summer, and I spent the whole time following Giovanni around. I'm sure I was annoying. He's nine years older and would meet his teenage friends at the beach with his little cousin in tow. But he always seemed happy to have me there. When we got older and he moved to Rome, I started helping with the hotel. At thirteen, I thought answering the phone for the Valeri was the coolest thing in the world.

"I used to beg my parents to move here, but they didn't want to. It was too expensive, too isolated from the city. My father grew up here and hated it. He associated the hotel with busy summers and weekend chores. But I always knew I wanted to join the family business one day. That's why I'm studying hotel management at university, and why I spent so much time learning English."

"Your family is lucky that this is your dream," said Forrest, smiling softly at our friend. "You're a natural at it."

Bianca shrugged away the compliment. "This place is my family's history, and it's paradise. I want to make it even better. There's so much we could do to modernize, expand — that's how we'll stay successful in the future. I just want to help. It's all I ever wanted."

She spoke quickly with a firm voice, almost as if she were preparing for an argument. I reached out to where she sat next to me and squeezed her arm reassuringly. "You don't need to defend your dream to us," I said. "We think your ideas are amazing."

Bianca shook her head. "Sorry, it's a habit. All I've ever dreamed of, since I was a kid, is one day running this place. But I've never been able to convince my aunt and uncle that I can do it."

She sighed and leaned back from the table as she crossed her arms in resignation. "Jia wants to see Giovanni take over because he grew up here, and he's her son. I also think she does not like my ideas. She's more like Nonna; she likes tradition. Maximo is more open. He always asks me, 'Why can't you run it together?' Only I know how that would look. We would share the work, but Gio would be the face. I don't want that.

"I also think they want Gio to do it because he's so good with people, like Maximo. I'm not. Interacting with the guests doesn't come naturally to me. I get it, I need to work on that. But so much more goes into running a hotel."

"I think you're being too hard on yourself," said Forrest, shaking her head. "I mean, we're guests, and look at how great you've been to us. Doing the job differently than Gio or Maximo would doesn't mean you're doing it wrong. There's lots of ways to connect with people."

Bianca offered a half-hearted smile. "Thanks."

"Besides," she said, taking another bite of tortellini, "didn't you say Giovanni doesn't want to do it?"

Bianca sighed. "That's what he told me, but he hasn't told his parents. I keep asking him to talk to them, and he keeps putting it off. I don't know what to think anymore." She drummed her fingertips on the kitchen table. "I am graduating university next year. I just want to know the truth by then. If Giovanni is going to run the Valeri, I will take a job at another hotel. I don't want to spend my career in his shadow when I've been working my whole life for this."

I nodded. "Do you have a job in mind?"

"I've been interviewing with this five-star hotel in Milan. They're a chain with locations all over the world. The program is a sort of apprenticeship." Bianca shrugged. "If I get it, I could be managing my own hotel in five years, but probably not in Italy."

"Milan," said Nonna, shaking her head as she muttered a curse in Italian.

Bianca laughed and reached across the table to squeeze her grandmother's hand. "Nonna doesn't want me to go."

"What do you want?" I asked.

"This," she said, her eyes growing sad. "I want this to be my life, all year round. It's why I went into the hotel business in the first place. But even if I could get a job at another hotel in the area, I don't want to work for a competitor. I want to work with my family, but if I can't have that..." she shrugged. "The apprenticeship is an incredible opportunity; I'd be a fool to turn it down."

I cracked a dry, half-smile. "I thought I'd be a fool to turn down Matthew's marriage proposal, and look how that went." I shrugged. "Sometimes it's better to follow your heart."

I turned back to Forrest and paled at the look on my best friend's face. Wide eyes, slightly parted lips, flushed cheeks, like she could see right through what I said about Matthew. Like she knew my first thought was *what about Forrest?* when Matthew presented the ring. I fought a blush. I said too much. "B-but I know sometimes you have to make the best of the choices you have," I added, hoping Forrest couldn't read the meaning in that, too.

After we washed the dishes, and our conversation became interrupted by intermittent yawning, Forrest announced that we should probably all go to bed. We hugged each other tightly, like old friends, and kissed both cheeks, the Italian way. "Alana and Forrest," Nonna said affectionately, eyes shifting between us. "Thank you." Then she said something to Bianca in Italian.

"Nonna said she loved seeing the three of us together, in the kitchen," Bianca translated, tucking some loose hair behind her ear. "It reminded her of when she used to make pasta with her two best friends, before she married my grandfather."

I looked from Bianca to Nonna, flushing at the older woman's smiling face and damp eyelashes. Something about them felt like family, the way women in a bar's bathroom instinctively feel like friends. "Oh, Nonna," I said, stretching my arms toward the other two women. "Can we?"

Bianca smiled as she pulled us into a group hug. "Tell her she's going to get sick of us," said Forrest, "because we will definitely be bothering her in the kitchen again." Nonna chuckled at Bianca's translation. We promised to come back soon, and often.

As Forrest and I took turns in the bathroom and slipped into bed, we didn't talk much. I was relieved she didn't ask me about Matthew, that I didn't have to lie to her about my doubts before the wedding. I needed to be more careful. The honeymoon was dredging up old feelings I thought I'd mostly resolved. I needed to be more careful about keeping myself in check. I needed to remember what was real — and what wasn't.

"This cannot be real," said Forrest, shaking her head. "I mean, look at this place." The bread crust-colored dirt trail wound through the grassy hillside, hugging the cliff's edge. We left the Valeri at sunrise to the hike the Path of the Gods, the region's most famous trail, before the heat set in. Forrest and I maintained a steady pace, a soft breeze cooling us as we hiked the terrain. Before the wedding I was painfully connected to the world, fielding texts from vendors, guests, and Melissa. It was a relief to have my phone on 'Do Not Disturb' in my fanny pack, surrounded by nature with nobody but Forrest nearby. Now, the Valeri was just a dot on the horizon behind us as we hiked through the mountainside. The late morning sun was starting to scorch, but with these views, we didn't care.

The trail led us over cliffs and mountains, through the remote coast beyond Positano. I could see why it was called the Path of the Gods. The human world felt blissfully irrelevant, alone with the countryside and vast views of the sea.

I stopped beside her and stared out at the green hills and gray cliffs, framed by the baby blue sky and cerulean sea. "Maybe we can stop here for a bit and enjoy it."

Forrest nodded. "I definitely need a water break" She squeezed my shoulder affectionately. "I'm not sporty enough to easily keep up with you, but I'm still loving this. It's so beautiful."

"I wouldn't exactly call myself *sporty*." I shook my head as I sat on a large rock, shaded by a short, evergreen tree, and opened my water bottle.

"Because you're humble." She beamed at me with butter-soft eyes that used to make my stomach flip with false hope. (*Used to.* Who was I kidding?) "I still remember the first time I saw you play soccer at camp. You made it look like dancing." She plopped on the rock beside me, breaking eye contact to face the sea.

"You remember that?" It was a good thing my face was already flushed from heat. I barely remembered that game. I barely remembered anything about camp beyond the time spent with her. Not that I'd tell Forrest that. Instead, when she nodded, I muttered "thanks," and we stared at the view in silence.

Even in this heat, Forrest was gorgeous. Her hair was tied back into a low ponytail, and the late morning light emphasized the warm tones in her skin. Her brow was barely damp, and the musky scent of her sweat mingled with her coconut-scented lotion. She wore nothing but spandex and a sports bra, revealing the cleavage she normally kept hidden under t-shirts and halter tops.

Which was when I realized I was checking out her boobs.

I shifted my gaze back to the ocean. I always did this with her. It was even worse when we lived together. We'd be whispering in a coffee shop, watching Netflix in our apartment, or reading books together in silence at Malcom X Park, and suddenly I'd remember the time I kissed her. I'd imagine what she'd taste like now, how soft her lips would feel, the electricity that would ignite my body as her fingers trailed down my back. Like now, nothing about this hike was romantic, but her sweat and sighing set butterflies loose inside me. My mind teased me with the thought of our hands touching, of—

So long. It had been so long since I thought this way around her. When she moved out of DC, my hope left with her. Later, my loyalty to Matthew kept my feelings safely buried. I knew they'd never go away — I'd never known adult life without wanting Forrest — but they were as dormant as they'd ever be. Not even a week after the breakup, and here I was, fantasizing again, even when I knew it was hopeless. She already made it clear we were just friends, and even if she hadn't, I couldn't imagine her wanting me now. My life was a disaster. I wiped sweat from my forehead with the back of my hand and sighed.

"Ugh, I sweat so much," I said, shaking my head. "Matthew used to think it was so gross."

"Seriously?" She furrowed her eyebrows as she turned to face me. She watched me appraisingly, eyeing my red face, tank top, and ponytail. Then she turned away, rolling her eyes. "That is so dramatic of him. Everybody sweats."

I shrugged and sipped my water, marveling at how easily she reassured me. With Matthew I was always looking over my shoulder, trying to correct some flaw. "There's a lot I'm starting to second guess."

"Like what?"

I shrugged again. "Like why did my entire life revolve around him, when he was always too busy to pick me up from the airport?" I thought of all the happy hours and networking dinners I attended with his co-workers, the Saturdays spent at brunch with Melissa in Georgetown when she came to visit and Matthew was too busy to see her. When my own parents drove up from North Carolina, Matthew tolerated one dinner before saying *I think we've had enough family time for the weekend.* "He made me feel like his life was more important than mine, and I believed him."

"I felt that way with Melanie." Forrest's last ex dumped her a month after she lost her job, when Forrest decided to leave the corporate world to be an artist. Melanie said they were on different paths, and she needed someone with "real ambition." What she meant was that she was a Hill staffer, and Forrest's unproven art career was not prestigious enough for a girl with political goals. Still, it took me weeks to convince Forrest that she was not unmotivated, that becoming an artist was bad ass — no matter what some Congresswoman wannabe had to say.

"She never realized how lucky she was," I said, "to be with you. That's why I didn't like her."

"Oh, really?" Forrest smirked. "It had nothing to do with 'Twilight?'"

Really, it had something to do with the way my heart died a little every time I caught them stealing a kiss in the living room. It had something to do with the way Melanie treated Forrest like an accessory to her life, instead of a whole person. In Melanie's eyes, everything about my best friend mattered only in terms of how attractive it made her to Melanie. Her grief made her interesting, her lucrative job impressive; her kindness was a bit boring, her art frivolous. Melanie treated Forrest's personality like a pro-con list to be sorted as she saw fit. It tormented me that Forrest couldn't see she deserved better.

Obviously, I didn't say that. How could I tell Forrest that dating her would be like dating the sun? How could I platonically say that I would be wholly devoted to her, if given the chance, and she shouldn't accept anything less from anyone else? Something like that would cross a line. Instead, I bought her a jumbo-size bag of peanut butter M&Ms and said: "You deserve better than someone who hates 'Twilight.'"

I repeated that opinion now, which got us laughing about the time we thought it was a good idea to include Melanie in a 'Twilight' marathon. We didn't make it past the first movie. She complained the whole time, dumbfounded that we could love something so objectively terrible. "It's iconic *because* it's also terrible," I said. "What about that is so hard to understand?"

Forrest shook her head somberly as she screwed the cap back on her water. "What was I thinking, dating her?"

"I can answer that," I said, and Forrest froze, her round brown eyes watching mine cautiously. We were sitting so close, our knees touched when I turned to face her. "You're kind, loyal, and you see the best in everyone. You can't help it if someone takes advantage of that."

Forrest smiled at me, her eyes going soft again. Then, she blinked quickly, as if snapping herself out of it, and looked back at the sea. "Well, whoever takes advantage of it next will not work in Congress, that's for sure."

I nodded at the word *whoever*, which implied, decidedly, *not me*. A reminder. "Good."

We stood from the rock and took a couple final photos of the view before continuing the hike. I zipped my phone into my fanny pack, and when I looked up, Forrest was watching me with sad eyes. She said: "If I had any sense, I would have dumped her that night, with an audience of you and Edward Cullen."

"Maybe." I nudged her playfully, desperate to bring her smile back. "But what would love even be if you had sense the whole time?"

"Healthy."

I laughed as I started walking down the trail. "The correct answer is *boring*."

A few months into living together in DC, Forrest and I were watching *Pride and Prejudice* when she let out a bored sigh. "Why don't we do stuff like that anymore?" she asked, biting into a pizza slice.

I raised my eyebrows at her remark. "Get drunk while wearing corsets that could crack a rib?" I teased.

"Ha, ha." She knocked her shoulder into mine playfully, as she took another contemplative bite of our takeout dinner. "Go out in style. Be classy. Do a hand flex after helping our crush into a carriage."

I smiled softly as I pictured it. Inviting Forrest to dance, squeezing her hand as I guided her onto the floor, feeling the rest of the crowd vanish as we lock eyes. Only it wouldn't be like that. We were friends. Still, I shrugged. "Who says we can't?"

We called those nights a turnabout the room, named for the scene when Caroline Bingley invites Elizabeth to join her walking circles around Mr. Darcy. As Darcy stated, the whole point of taking a turnabout the room was to share in each other's confidence and show off our figures. In today's terms, that meant drinking wine and looking hot.

We would treat ourselves to a fancy night out in the city — dinner at an upscale restaurant, nosebleed seats at a play, Prosecco on our apartment's rooftop, something that felt impossibly bourgeoisie without breaking the bank. We'd don our best dresses, get drunk on wine, and spend half the night doing period romance impressions. Before she moved, I surprised her with tickets to *Hadestown*. Just as the lights dimmed, she whispered, "Oh, my dearest Alana, how I delight in the theater!" I laughed so hard I earned glares from several rows of theatergoers.

We were lying by the beach that afternoon, using the ocean to cool off from our hike, when Forrest said, "You know, Alana, it's a real travesty.

We've been in Positano for four days now, and we still haven't taken a turn about the room."

I turned to my friend. She was watching the waves crash through her sunglasses, a soft smile playing on her lips as we lay on beach towels together. We were at Maori, one of the only sand beaches on the coast. The long, white beach was surrounded by peach-colored cliffs and green hills; square white houses dotted the greenery beyond. Forrest's smile was even more breathtaking than the view behind her. Beads of ocean water dotted her skin as she lifted her head toward me, propped on her elbows. Her dimples were cavernous against her rounded cheeks, and she tilted her head to the right as she awaited my reply. She looked utterly, beautifully content. My lips parted at the sight.

The tradition was dated, now. We hadn't taken a turn about the room since *Hadestown*, a couple months before I started dating Matthew. "You remember."

She waved away the question. "Of course I do. I never forget matters of such consequence."

I grinned, leaning into the bit. "Well, you must be a truly accomplished woman, to boast such an impressive memory."

She threw her head back as she rewarded me with her laughter. Soothing and musical, the sound reminded me of honey. All the thoughts in my head scattered, replaced by awe at her magnetic confidence, her long mermaid hair and fiery eyes. "I draw, I read, I *remember*. Dare I say, I'd even meet Mr. Darcy's standards of accomplishment."

The soft smile that lifted my lips shifted from playful to awestruck, as I watched her. "I *know* you would, Miss Manning," I murmured.

Her eyes widened at my expression; her smile stilled. Something passed between our shared, quiet look — or maybe I imagined it. Because after a moment Forrest shook her head and was grinning again. "As would you," she said. "A truly accomplished woman only surrounds herself with the most suitable of companions, and you are that. Smart, talented, beautiful. You're everything, Miss Morris."

I forced my smile to return, trying not to read between her words. "I'm grateful to be considered so… distinguished, in your eyes."

"Of course you are." Forrest shrugged, standing from her towel to return to the sea. I caught a glimpse of her rib tattoo, hibiscus and two hummingbirds, meant to symbolize her parents. She turned back, and her tone returned to this century. "Maybe we can ask Bianca for a dinner recommendation."

I nodded, and she smiled as she strode into the waves.

14

Forrest wore an outfit I made her a few years ago — the same one she wore to the rehearsal dinner. Before I dated Matthew, before my creativity floundered, my favorite thing in the world was creating clothes for Forrest. I loved to see her figure fill out my designs, loved how her lips parted when she beheld a new creation. But my favorite part was filling up her closet. I loved that my work lived in her wardrobe, that a piece of myself could be part of her everyday routine.

This one was a sleeveless rose-colored jumpsuit with a deep 'V' neck and intricate hibiscus flowers embroidered into the bodice. I made the outfit in honor of her mother's garden, where they used to have fireside chats. It was always one of my favorite pieces I'd made her — and not just because she cried when I gave it to her. In that jumpsuit, she wore her mother's love like a badge of honor. It was beautiful to see. Unlike the rehearsal dinner, she dressed it down with a pair of brown leather sandals.

She added a few gold bangles to her wrists and for her ears, large, gold hoops, decorated with a small pink bead at the bottom.

She was always stunning, but tonight, she was radiant. As she stepped into the jumpsuit and touched up her makeup, it was an effort to look away so I could get ready myself. My outfit was... different. I brought the short, red spaghetti strap dress because I wanted something sexy for my honeymoon. It was a bit more skin than I'd normally show on a turnabout the room. Nothing about it mimicked period wear, Still, it was the best I could do.

I slipped into the dress as Forrest finished applying her mascara. When she turned around, her jaw dropped. I crossed my arms bashfully. "It's the fanciest dress I packed," I mumbled. She stood and slowly walked toward me, still holding her mascara brush as her eyes raked over me, as if lost in a trance. I frowned. "I was trying to go for the hot newlywed vibe when I packed, but I don't know. I think you're right. It might be too much."

She blinked sharply, as if my words snapped whatever daze she'd fallen into. Then, she grabbed my wrists, gentle but firm, and raised her gaze from my chest to my eyes. "Stop it, Alana," she said breathlessly, her brown eyes glowing like gemstones. "You look hot."

My lips pared as I studied her, deeply aware of where her thumbs pressed my wrists, how we stood close enough that I could smell the coconut lotion on her skin. I froze as I lost myself in her, desperate to bask in her proximity.

But then she dropped my wrists and turned away, sitting down to finish her mascara. "Want to leave in five?" she asked.

"Yeah," I said after a breath, my voice less composed than I'd like. "That sounds perfect."

We made our way to Chez Black on the Positano waterfront, per Bianca's recommendation. The upscale restaurant served seafood and pasta by the beach; it was the perfect place to people watch as the last day trippers boarded the ferry. We sat in cushioned teal chairs under an awning, sandwiched between other diners with an unobstructed view of the sea. A waiter brought us water, bread with olive oil and balsamic, and two limoncello spritzes as we watched the sunset unfurl over the waves.

The rich olive oil and sharp balsamic paired deliciously with the bread. In Italy, even the simplest cuisine could deliver euphoria; every ingredient tasted homemade. I closed my eyes involuntarily as I ate. "Wow," I told Forrest. "Whenever I eat with you, we always end up at the best restaurants."

She smiled coyly. "It is my superpower."

"It really is." I shook my head at the trove of memories that flooded me. "I still dream about that sushi place you found in NoMa, for that one turnabout the room. I wanted to go back with Matthew, but he doesn't like sushi."

"That is how we should have known he was a knave." Forrest lifted her head haughtily. "A true gentleman is capable of appreciating fine cuisine, like sushi."

I laughed at her shift to Regency English. "It's true. You can hardly call yourself a proper member of high society if you lack the refined palette needed to enjoy such delicacies." As Forrest laughed, I tilted my head to the side. "Do you really think he was a knave?"

Forrest dropped the joking tone and watched me tenderly, as if she could tell I was only half-joking. "No," she said finally. "I don't think he's a knave. I just think he didn't deserve you."

"Didn't deserve me?" She was the only one who felt that way. After all the comments from my mother about how lucky I was to find a nice, wealthy man, after all the lectures from Melissa about what it meant to marry into *this family*, after all the acquaintances who ogled over imposing diamond on my left hand, the thought was laughable. I might have had issues with our relationship, but I always knew Matthew was the ideal man. It was easy to overlook his inadequacies when I believed I couldn't do better.

"Yes, Alana." Forrest's eyes looked even darker as they studied mine, her jaw tense. "Because he didn't. If I'm being honest... I felt that way early on. But you seemed happy, and he was a nice person. I thought maybe I was wrong and just j—" she stopped herself from finishing that thought as she reached for her spritz. After taking a slow sip, and placing her glass on the table, she met my gaze again. "You pushed me away when you were with him, Al."

Her brown eyes softened with hurt. "By the time I realized I should say something, I didn't feel like it was my place."

"What?" A lump formed in my throat at the realization that Forrest, of all people, felt that way. But she was right. I *had* pushed her away. Put off phone calls, delayed visits, kept pieces of my relationship to myself because I feared she wouldn't like Matthew if she knew everything. Maybe, too, some part of me thought it'd be a betrayal to keep her close, when I my feelings for her were so strong they sometimes threatened to topple me. "Oh gosh, you're right." I shook my head. "You're right, and I had no idea. I'm so sorry, Forrest."

Forrest raised her eyebrows back. "Alana, are you kidding me? *I'm* sorry. I might not have known everything, but I could see what he was doing, how he made you feel. I wanted to be wrong, so I told myself I was. But I should have said something."

I shook my head as I fidgeted with a corner of the tablecloth. "No, you made the right choice," I said. "He wasn't so bad, and you only had a hunch that I could have been happier without him. I needed to see that for myself."

Forrest smiled sadly, and we sat in silence. It was only after my glass was mostly melted ice that I spoke. "As embarrassing as my wedding was, I don't regret what happened." I shrugged. "I'm already happier here with you than I would have been if this really was my honeymoon. I think about the life I would have had with him, and... I feel grateful that I lost it, somehow. Does that make any sense?"

Forrest's eyes snapped to mine with a focus that startled me, as her breathing seemed to halt. Her eyes widened, glowing amber in the sunset, as she tilted her head to the side. She looked... hopeful, maybe? Only, that didn't make sense. "It does." She blinked, opening her mouth to say something else, when two steaming plates clattered onto the table between us. Forrest nearly jumped out of her seat.

"*Grazie*," I said, and our waiter smiled as he offered us a topping of parmesan. (Who could say no to that?) By the time he left, Forrest was composed again, whatever she was going to say long forgotten. Forrest twirled her shrimp scampi noodles, while I dug into the seafood risotto. Both carried a cozy citrus scent, with ample garlic, shrimp, scallops and clams. I groaned when I took a bite of my meal. "Holy shit. This is delicious."

Forrest released an answering sigh as she tried her pasta. "Holy shit is right."

We ate in silence for a moment. When I began to accumulate a small pile of shrimp tails and empty clam shells on my plate, I asked Forrest: "Has it been stressful for you? Leaving home for two weeks without notice?"

She wouldn't tell me if it had been, so I watched her eyes for the truth. There was the relaxed droop in her shoulders, her warm eyes, and an answering smile that left a single dimple on her left cheek. "Not as bad as you would think." Forrest shrugged, and I was at ease. "School's already out, and I was taking the summer off to focus on getting ready for my exhibition in the fall, at the gallery. I would have spent the time puttering around my house and trying to scrounge up inspiration." She frowned down at her pasta at the mention of the gallery. "This is much better than that. I think it helps to take my mind off of it, and come back with fresh eyes."

My gaze softened at her words. "You'll get your inspiration back. This year was insane for you, and it's basically impossible to be creative without rest. You just need to take some time to yourself." I smiled as I sipped my second spritz of the night. "I've been obsessed with your drawings ever since you showed me your sketchbook at nineteen. You might be in a creative rut, but you're sensational, Forrest. Talent like that doesn't just go away."

As I spoke, her eyes dropped to her lap. I could tell she was fidgeting with her rings the way she always did when she was nervous. But now she met my eyes. "You really believe in me?"

"Devoutly." I beamed at her. "Like Reverend Townes and RBG, minus the memorabilia."

Forrest rewarded me with her honey laughter, echoing across the boardwalk. "I don't know if I should be flattered, or if I should sign up for the Witness Protection Program."

"Definitely both." I propped my chin on my palm and leaned forward, tilting my head as I flashed a horror movie smile. Forrest giggled again.

"Such devotion is quite remarkable." She picked up her spritz glass and stuck out a prominent pinkie, in keeping with the theme of the night. "And what do you plan to do with this passion?"

I smirked back at her. "Perhaps I shall write you a sonnet, or compose a ballad on the pianoforte."

"How romantic." Then, Forrest blinked and shook her head, as if correcting herself. "You are quite the accomplished companion, Miss Morris."

I puffed my chest out haughtily, ignoring the flutter her words stirred in me. "Why even take a turn about the room, if not to bask in one's accomplishments?"

"To bask in yours." Forrest smiled dreamily. "I find I quite enjoy it."

I laughed and changed the topic with some comment about my imminent food coma. Really, I couldn't bear her compliments. I couldn't bear how close we danced toward something more than friends. To Forrest, our night together at nineteen was a sexual awakening and nothing more, but in moments like this the past felt as simple to touch as folding paper in two, bringing opposite corners together. It was necessary, but agonizing, to snap myself out of it. My face would never inspire the quiet reverence I still felt when I beheld hers; I accepted that a long time ago. That should have been the last thing on my mind now. I needed her friendship like I needed air. I couldn't risk anything that would push her away.

These daydreams were dangerous. They made me feel like I could burst.

"Is it possible to explode from being full?" asked Forrest as she leaned back in her chair and sighed.

For dessert, we split a slice of Tiramisu and exchanged contented hums with each bite of the light mascarpone, layered with lady fingers and espresso. I was tipsy from the limoncello spritzes and lulled into tranquility by my full stomach and the gentle rhythm of the waves. It had been months since I experienced any sense of peace, but on this trip, that was the dominant feeling, confusion surrounding Forrest aside. The sun fully set now, and across the ocean, the glowing moonlight painted a path across the water, like I would walk into the night sky if I wanted. Something about that pathway to the moon, surrounded by rippling waves and stars, soothed me more than anything else.

I was about to reply to my friend when the performers began to play.

Three musicians had set up on the boardwalk with a guitar, a keyboard, and a saxophone. As they played soothing jazz music, the guitarist sang in Italian, his rich voice carrying over the boardwalk. Their melodies perfectly complimented the evening, filling the beach with the quiet joy that could only be found in a place like Positano, where just about everyone was on vacation.

Unsurprisingly, my gaze drifted from the music to Forrest, who closed her eyes as she listened, her shoulders swaying almost imperceptibly to the beat. I thought — not for the first time — that there was nothing more beautiful in the world than an awestruck Forrest. Her whole being seemed perfectly soothed by her delight at the performance, the sea breeze, and the night sky overhead. It seemed like the entire city breathed a collective sigh in the darkness, and Forrest relished all of it. I couldn't help but feel elated, seeing her so relaxed. Then her eyes snapped open, immediately locking with mine, and I realized I'd been caught staring. My best friend just smiled.

"Alana?" she said, and my lips parted involuntarily. My heart always stuttered a bit, to hear her say my name.

"Yes?"

She beamed at me, flashing both dimples, and reached out her hand. "May I have this dance?"

"Oh." We never danced when we took a turn about the room, because it was never a date. There was always an unspoken strain between us to keep it an activity between friends. Only tonight she said I looked hot, that she wanted to bask in me, and now she asked me to dance. The daydreams were dangerous, but I couldn't help myself. "I'd love to."

I stood up and took her hand.

Forrest led me from our table to the center of the boardwalk, dropping a couple euros in an upside-down hat by the musicians as she did. She kept our hands clasped as she wrapped her other arm around my lower back, pulling me close. I could smell the limoncello on her breath, and the hint of sweat underneath the lingering scent of her lotion. I drew in a sharp breath and looked out at the ocean while we swayed; the sight of her up close was too much when I could feel her against me like this. Only she took that as an invitation to press her cheek against mine, drawing closer. We never danced like this before, like a couple. It was more intimate than we'd been since... but I couldn't think about that now. At least she couldn't see my blush.

The sky jut downwards and filled my vision as Forrest abruptly dipped my head back. As I rose again, she broke away and twirled me so suddenly I nearly tripped over my feet. But she caught me. Her arm returned to my waist, at once gentle and protective. She swayed into me laughing, and I could hardly see anything past her smile. "You look graceful even when you're falling," she teased. I laughed, too; her joy was infectious.

I realized with a start how close we were, again. Only this time, I couldn't look away. I was wholly lost in her; in her wide, dark eyes that held galaxies, in her flushed cheeks and parted lips, in her fingers pressed firmly into my back. The music stopped, and I kept standing there, awestruck, unable to break whatever this dance had ignited between us. She was motionless, too, until a flurry of applause burst around us. Apparently, a few pedestrians had gathered to watch.

Immediately, Forrest broke into her winning smile and offered a shy wave to the onlookers, and a "*Grazie*" to the band. She stepped back from me, then wrapped her arm around my shoulder in a sideways, platonic hug. That's what finally broke me from my trance. I squeezed her back and smiled, reminding myself it was only a dance. As the band began a new song, several couples joined. Forrest and I continued, but without the fervor from before. I was careful to keep space between us, dampened by the gnawing knowledge that whatever her touch sparked in me was a one-sided feeling, unnoticed by her.

That night, when we returned to our suite tipsy and giggling as we wiped off our makeup and exchanged dresses for pajamas, I was taunted by the memory of her fingers on my back, the way her gaze seemed to swallow me whole as we danced. As we lay in bed, the gentle hum of her breath, her arms flung carelessly over the sheets, were irresistibly close but painfully out of reach, all at once.

It took a while before I could surrender myself to dreams. When I did, her smile found its way into everyone.

15

We left the Valeri early in the morning, bound for Furore at Bianca's recommendation. Yesterday we asked her what she'd recommend seeing of the coast beyond Positano. "As much as I love this city, it can get a bit touristy," she said. "There is so much more to the Amalfi Coast. You'll love Furore."

The town was known for its narrow, picturesque beach, sandwiched between two mountains underneath an arching medieval bridge that connected two cliffs. We came early to beat the crowd to the water, taking photos of each other in the turquoise waves before floating on our backs in the water, feeling ourselves drift with the current. I sent a selfie to Carter, even though he was probably asleep back home. In it, beads of water dotted our cheeks, and I looked more relaxed than I had in months.

I got an instant reply.

Carter: This makes me SO happy!!

Me: Why are you up so early??

Carter: Woke up to watch the sunrise with my dad at the Shore. I've never seen someone so excited to get up early on vacation.

Carter was close with his parents, even if they were opposites. His dad was a math professor and devout early bird, Carter a creative night owl. But my friend always dragged himself out of bed for the sake of father-son time.

Me: LOL. All in the name of love.

Carter: ☺

Carter: How are things with Forrest?

I lifted my eyes from my phone to my best friend, who lay on a towel beside me with her eyes closed. I thought of last night, how I could still feel her phantom fingers on my lower back.

Me: You know how it is…

Carter: Still down bad?

Carter was the only person I told about my summer fling with Forrest. When he met her for the first time, when she visited UNC, he said, "I can see why you were so hung up on her." Wearily, I answered, "*Were*?" Through all the long conversations and drunken tears, he listened without judgment. That was why he was so proud when I got engaged to Matthew. I was finally moving on. "Forrest is wonderful" he'd say, time and again, "but you deserve someone who wants you back. That's the bare minimum of a relationship." Of course, now that we were sharing a honeymoon suite it was clear those feelings were not as dormant as I thought. Carter was the only one who'd understand.

Me: I was engaged like a week ago idk what's wrong with me.

Carter: Nothing is wrong with you, Ally.

Carter: I'm sure it's all v confusing, but try to enjoy your honeymoon. You need a carefree vacation!

He was right, and I told him as much before he said "G2G, sun's rising," and was offline again. I slipped my phone into our tote bag and sighed as I laid back on the beach. To my relief, things were normal between Forrest and me today. The mysterious magic of the night before had stilled. Being in her presence, as a friend and nothing more, almost felt like enough. Or at least, it was enough to put my pining aside and enjoy my honeymoon. Today was only ocean and sunshine with my dearest friend, and the gentle elation of floating in the sea.

We stayed at the beach until lunch, when I rode the moped into the town of Furore to buy focaccia sandwiches before wandering aimlessly through the winding, medieval streets. The afternoon sun baked our skin but only heightened the beauty around us. The sun-bleached sandstone buildings created a maze of shops and cafés — a new delight awaited around every corner. We meandered at a slower pace; the place seemed specially designed to pay homage to lazy summer days like this.

That was where we found the fabric shop — even more spectacular that the one I shied away from in Positano. I stopped dead in my tracks, sandals skidding against the cobblestone. There were endless rolls of cloth in bright colors and patterns, geometric, floral, bohemian. There were linens, lace, and thicker fabrics, even some nylon for bathing suits. Staring in the shop window I could see material for dozens of different outfits, ones that fit to my style, Forrest's, Carter's, even Gemma's, who I could never seem to figure out. My jaw fell open as the images flooded me. After months without energy or creative vision, the sudden urge to design was overwhelming. The whole world seemed to open itself to me at once; endless possibilities lay between the folds of fabric.

"Alana," Forrest murmured beside me, and I turned to her with wide eyes. "Do you want to go inside?"

We stared at each other as I nodded, and she opened the door to usher me in.

An older woman was reading a magazine behind the counter when we walked in, perched on a stool. We exchanged *bongiorno*'s, and she returned to her reading, no questions, no skepticism on how good I really was at sewing. To my relief, she ignored us. I steered my focus back to the fabric, ogling at the colors and patterns. "I want to make something for Gemma," I said softly, like we were in a museum.

"I love that idea," Forrest whispered back. She didn't sew, but she understood the sanctity of this place and honored it unquestioningly.

"I just struggle with Gemma." I frowned, thinking of my sister's minimalist fashion, the way she's strut through a room like a runway model. "Her style is so different from mine. I don't think I've made anything for her that she genuinely liked. I've never seen her wear something I made her."

Forrest pressed her lips together as she stared at the fabric, thinking. "I think it's tough because you make this amazing, unique clothing that you can't get anywhere else, which I love, obviously, but I don't think Gemma likes to stand out. She's fashionable, of course, but her clothing always seems to blend in. The challenge for her is to make something that is unique, the way all your designs are, but at the same time, basic enough that nobody will look twice when they see her walking down the street."

It always amazed me how well Forrest seemed to instinctively understand my loved ones, especially Gemma. My little sister, who hated everyone, always liked Forrest. And Forrest kept encouraging me to fight for our relationship, no matter how many times Gemma seemed to push me away. She compelled me to hope that things could get better between us.

"You're right," I said. Most of my designs did not cater to Gemma's taste, but that could change. I bit my lip as I sifted through fabrics. Golden honeycombs, blue flowers, green stripes. None fit Gemma, until I reached an off-white linen. The fabric was simple but light, and somehow felt quintessentially Italian. "Maybe a two-piece set, with this. A long skirt or some wide-legged pants with a matching crop top. No patterns or colors thrown in, just a simple clothing set well cut to her figure. Something you'd normally pay $200 for at Abercrombie."

Forrest squeezed my shoulder. "I hate to break it to you, but a piece like that would cost a lot more than $200." She smiled. "I think Gemma will love it."

"Really?" I met her eyes, startled at how close my face was to hers. Again. It was almost like we were drawn together as we examined the linen, subconsciously compelled to be close. I remembered the velvety soft feel of her cheek against mine, of her back against my fingers. Before memories of last night's dance could overtake me, I jerked my head away.

"Really," answered Forrest. Did I imagine the breathlessness in her voice?

I nodded to myself. Of course I did. I took a few self-conscious steps away from her, returning my gaze to the fabric. "So that's settled."

We left the shop with that linen, a red hexagonal print for Carter, a geometric pattern of pinks that reminded me of the Valeri, and an intricate cotton mosaic of dyed blues that was too beautiful to leave behind. It felt like a game of Jenga, getting everything loaded onto the moped. How I'd fit all the fabrics in our suitcase was a problem for another day. For now, there was just the calm euphoria of feeling inspired, after a long creative drought.

"Do you think Nonna would let me use her sewing machine?" I asked Forrest nervously as we buckled our helmets.

Forrest studied me with tenderness in her eyes, her smile almost giddy as she answered: "Yeah." She squeezed my shoulder affectionately. "I think she will."

Nonna seemed to light up at my request, leading me to the small side table where her sewing machine sat. Forrest disappeared to wander Positano with her sketchbook, leaving me with Nonna and the reassurance that I could take as long I needed. I took her up on it. As Nonna prepared Gnocchi for her family, I sat before the machine, measuring, cutting fabric, and making stitches for the first time in a year. It felt like I never stopped. Everything came back instinctively.

I referenced an old note in my phone of friends' measurements to map out Gemma's two-piece set, and added some padding to the top so she could wear it without a bra. It was a good first project to shake off the rust. No patchwork, embroidery, or frills, just a well-fitting piece. I grew more sure of myself with each stitch. Cutting straight lines in the fabric, setting up the perfect stitches, and watching the item slowly come together felt liberating. There was nothing more exciting than turning off the machine to find a completed, perfect hem — not that anyone else would notice. I loved pouring my soul into something that only mattered to me.

Nonna's company soothed me as much as the sewing. I felt closer to her in our comfortable silence, as we each focused on our work. Here, the rigid life I led in DC was a distant memory. I could hardly fathom how I lived with so much of my time planned around others. Taking morning exercise classes, working from home, checking my phone for Melissa's texts, making Matthew's dinner as he vented about work, knitting through his favorite TV show, only to do it all again the next day. If someone asked if I was happy, I would have said yes.

I had everything I was told to want, and no words to express the deep-seeded sense that something was missing. There was no reason to complain.

Only that I didn't have sewing. Only that I didn't have Forrest.

"Forrest!" called Bianca, and I jumped out of my skin as my friend reappeared with a tote back slung over her shoulder. (How did I not notice Bianca come in?)

"Hey, Bianca! Thank you for the Positano recommendations," Forrest piped up as she swept through the kitchen, gave Nonna a kiss on the cheek, and pulled up a stool beside me, where I finished up the stitching on Gemma's top. She was sun-kissed, beaming, and talking a mile a minute. I ignored how my stomach fluttered at the sight of her. "There was this cute little used bookstore that Bianca told me to see. All the books were in Italian, but the shop had... guess how many cats."

I couldn't help but smile at her excitement. "Three?"

"*Thirteen.*"

My jaw dropped.

"Right?"

Bianca giggled. "I like to tease the owner that she's running a cat sanctuary, not a bookstore."

"All bookstores should be cat sanctuaries. That place was magical." Forrest began flipping through pages of her sketchbook, showing quick sketches of an old woman with narrow glasses writing in a notebook as cats stretched and slumbered around her. "She let me sit in there for a while and draw. I think I might turn one or two of the sketches into paintings when I get back home."

That explained her bliss. I beamed at her when I realized. "Your inspiration."

"I still have a ways to go, of course. But I had ideas." The glow of her smile was infectious. "And they're pretty good."

I stood from my stool and wrapped her in a tight hug, unable to contain my excitement for her. "Your version of 'pretty good' belongs in the MoMA. I'm sure they're fantastic." As I felt Forrest's arms start to circle my shoulders, I pulled away. "I'm so happy for you."

"Thank you." Only now she looked a touch disappointed, like maybe I shouldn't have pulled away. Before I could say anything else, her eyes snapped to the sewing machine. "Did you already finish Gemma's outfit?"

I shrugged. "Basically."

She gave an adorable, delighted wriggle and stepped toward the machine, lifting the skirt to examine it — loose, with a short, tasteful slit in the sides to make it easier for walking — and the cropped tank top that accompanied it. Forrest's advice on the design approach had paid off. It was simple, but functional and flattering. I could actually see Gemma wearing it. "She's gonna love this, Al."

"Thank you."

Nonna and Bianca emerged behind her to study the outfit, too. "Beautiful," said Nonna, gesturing to the fabric. She smiled at me kindly, her hazel eyes gleaming.

"Agreed," echoed Bianca. "Now I want to hire you to make me something once my paycheck comes through. If I can afford it."

I smiled. "You can, because it'd be free. After everything your family has done for me, it's the least I can do."

Bianca waved away the comment with her hand. "Please. All my family did was damage control after that one guest ridiculed you at dinner." She smiled. "The rest was because we like your company."

Forrest squeezed Bianca's shoulder affectionately. "That was not your family's fault."

Nonna muttered something in Italian, and Bianca nodded her head in agreement. She said to us in English: "Some people could do with a little more manners."

I was about to respond when a chipper voice interrupted us. "Hello? Oh, there you are!" Bianca flinched as Peggy Townes appeared in the kitchen, her shoulder-length blonde hair lightened from sun, with pink cheeks, a sunhat, and white capri pants. Forrest's eyes widened, and Nonna indifferently returned to preparing the pasta. "Jia told me I might find you two back here," she told me, then smiled politely at Bianca.

"Hi, Peggy," I said. "Yeah, Nonna let me use her sewing machine for something. It was very kind of her." I turned around to acknowledge my companion for the afternoon. Nonna's eyes gleamed as she smiled back.

Peggy nodded as she noticed the skirt Forrest was still holding. "Oh, that looks lovely. You made this?" When I nodded, she asked: "Where did you learn to do that?"

I shrugged, suddenly shy from the attention. "YouTube videos, when I was in high school."

"How remarkable." Peggy studied the skirt a bit longer, and I shifted my weight from one foot to the other. She lifted her gaze back to me, plastering a polite smile over her features. "Dominic and I wanted to see if we could take you girls out to dinner. It's our last night here, and we're going to a nice restaurant in town. We'd love to have you both join us."

I opened my mouth in surprise. Peggy did mention taking us to dinner, but I saw that as a Southern invitation — plans to *catch up sometime* that never materialized. I was surprised she meant it.

"We wouldn't want to impose," Forrest demurred, saving me from giving an answer.

"Oh, please do. Really." Peggy nodded earnestly. "I feel terrible about how I acted the other night. I want to make it up to you, and Dominic would love to spend some time with you both before we leave. It's the least we can do, please."

Forrest gave me a look that said what I was thinking: The mortified Reverend Townes would probably sooner give a sermon in his underwear than spend an evening with us. But it didn't seem like Peggy would take no for an answer. "I don't think we have plans tonight," I said, "but I'll have to double check." That was code for *I'm going to talk about this with Forrest when you leave, then decide.*

"Of course." Peggy clasped her hands together as she shifted her gaze from me to Forrest. "Well, a car is picking us up to take us to the restaurant. If you're free, please join us. We can meet in the lobby at seven."

"Thank you." I tucked a chunk of hair behind my ear. "It's really kind of you to invite us."

She waved me off and smiled at us, then Bianca, whose attempt at appearing pleasant only made her look slightly constipated. When Peggy left us to get ready for dinner, Forrest burst into laughter as she gave Bianca a playful shove. "Girl, we have got to work on your fake 'I like you' face."

Bianca returned her laughter, shaking her head. "How can I work on it with you, when I really do like you?"

Forrest swung her arm around her in a sideways hug. "You know what? I take it back. Please don't ever change." She turned to me. "Do you actually want to get dinner with them?"

I crossed my arms and leaned against the table, pondering. "I don't know. Do you want to?"

"All I care about is you." Her eyes bore into mine as she said it. "I'll do whatever you want."

I flushed. It was impossible to show a semblance of bravado when she looked at me like that. "I mean... I don't know." Maybe it wasn't a bad idea to spend the evening in a group, to keep myself from confusing this as more than friendship again. As much as I balked at the thought of seeing anyone who witnessed my wedding, another night alone with Forrest could torment me even more. I smiled at her, hoping I looked more confident than I felt. "Honestly, part of me thinks we should do it for the plot."

Forrest threw her head back and laughed. "You're not wrong." She shook her head, but her eyes lingered on me, like she knew my explanation was a lie. Before I could say something more, she shrugged indifferently, and her questioning expression vanished. "If it doesn't go well, we'll never see them again, anyway. How did you find Dominic for the wedding?"

"Melissa did. He's apparently well-known among DC elites; she wanted someone with an impressive reputation."

"Of course she did." Forrest smiled softly, thinking of Melissa. The memory of her carefully curated choices had become almost endearing, not that it wasn't a cause for stress. "It sounds like there's not much left of his reputation now. I hope he'll be alright, now that he's been outed as an RBG super-fan."

"A *what*?" said Bianca.

"He's a feminist." Forrest backtracked, remembering our promise to keep his secret. "Surprise, surprise, the church isn't cool with it."

"Of course they're not." Bianca frowned. Her face softened as she thought of the blushing reverend. "Maybe I misjudged him."

"I think maybe we did, too." Forrest smiled at me. "We should get ready for dinner."

We took turns with quick showers before throwing on sundresses and a swipe of mascara for dinner. In a decorative mirror over the room's wooden desk, I adjusted the straps in the burnt orange cotton dress that I bought with Forrest in New Orleans. I studied my wet hair, Sunkissed skin, and dusting of freckles, as I remembered my wedding day. The woman in a constricting white dress and tightly bound hair felt wholly at odds to the reflection that greeted me. I smiled softly at the thought.

Forrest emerged from the bathroom just then, and I watched her walk up behind me from the mirror. "What is it?" she asked when she reached me.

I turned around to face my best friend. "I just realized my wedding was exactly one week ago."

"Oh." Her face crumpled as she studied mine, looking for signs of heartbreak, looking to comfort. "I'm so sorry, Al. Do you want to talk about it?"

"That's the thing." I pursed my lips, watching her enchanting eyes. "I'm not sad, just the opposite. I haven't felt this relaxed in..." Months? Years? It was hard to pinpoint when exactly my relationship began to feel like a cage. I lowered my eyes as I confessed: "I'm having way more fun with you than I would have if Matthew were here. I know that's a completely heartless thing to say, but it's true."

"It's not," said Forrest. I lifted my gaze away from my hands her, surprised by the conviction in her reassurance. She grabbed my hands gently as she locked eyes with mine. "It's not heartless, Alana. You don't owe Matthew anything. The only person whose feelings you should be thinking about right now is your own. If being here, having fun for the first time in *months*, is helping you, you shouldn't feel guilty for that.

"When you lose something, the grief comes in waves." She rubbed her thumbs over the back of my hands. "If you don't allow yourself to cling to moments of joy, it will destroy you. Honestly, it's a miracle you're happy right now." Her eyes softened as she squeezed my hands. "Cherish it."

I pulled my friend into a tight hug, relishing the love in her voice, the reassuring warmth of her embrace. Sometimes I wondered what my life could be if I loved myself the way Forrest did.

16

"You came!" Peggy cried as we appeared in the lobby. Dominic stood beside her offering a pained smile. I couldn't tell if he dreaded dinner with us or if he was just embarrassed by the circumstances. He stood rail straight and was blushing slightly as he nodded in our direction; his white button-down shirt emphasized his pink cheeks.

"Thank you for having us," I said after giving them each a hug. Bianca pretended to study paperwork at the front desk, but I caught her watching us when I looked her way. She grinned as she dropped her eyes back to a manila folder, and I returned my gaze to Peggy.

"Of course," she said. "I'm glad we can spend some time together before Dominic and I leave tomorrow." She launched into a monologue about everything they had done on the Amalfi Coast so far, occasionally pausing to confirm that we also swam at Positano Beach, and that we had plans to see Capri, a conversation that continued throughout the cab ride into Positano. Peggy seemed ignited by the place, her blue eyes glowing as she punctuated her stories with wild hand gestures. Or maybe this was her personality everywhere — enthusiastic with a talent for appreciating the little details of her day.

They took us to La Sponda, an upscale restaurant in the middle of Positano with a stunning view of the city's basilica. A waiter seated us by the window, and we enjoyed an up-close view of basilica's ornate dome, decorated with green and yellow diamond-shaped tiles, surrounded by stacked shops and houses on the hillside. Of course, an endless ocean view was part of the deal, along with a white tablecloth and two empty wine glasses each, which the waiter filled with sparkling water and a bottle of red wine selected by Peggy. I didn't understand wine well enough to follow her choice, but the bottle she chose was perfection, a smooth, slightly smokey pinot noir from a vineyard in the mountains. We toasted the Valeri family and Positano itself as we drank.

She was a recently retired math teacher and a proud grandmother. They had three children, two who lived in the DC area, and seven grandkids, which must have been who we saw in the family photo on his desk. "I spoil them rotten," said Peggy. "Dominic does, too, but he won't admit it."

The reverend smiled shyly. "Is it spoiling if they deserve it?"

Forrest rewarded him with a burst of her musical laughter, as she took another sip of wine. "I think we might have seen a photo of your grandkids in your office," she said, smiling warmly at Dominic. "They're adorable."

Dominic flushed at the mention of his office, but Peggy grinned warmly back. "Thank you, dear," she said, placing a hand on her husband's knee under the table. "We're really the luckiest people."

"About that," said Dominic, clearing his throat. "I'm very sorry about our behavior when you two arrived here. Peggy and I came here to escape the city after... everything. We were just surprised to see you." He turned to me with guilt-filled eyes as he awkwardly ducked his head. "I hope you're having a nice vacation despite our outburst."

"Thank you, but you don't need to apologize." I held his eye contact so he could see that I meant it. "I'm having a better honeymoon than I could have ever imagined." I smiled at Forrest. The warmth in her gaze seemed strong enough to carry me through anything. "It's hard to dwell on the wedding too much when I'm in Italy with my best friend."

Forrest raised her wine glass as she returned my smile, and toasted the air before taking a sip, her eyes twinkling.

"I can tell by the way you look at her that you're crazy about her, and she clearly feels the same." My eyes widened, but Peggy smiled brightly as her eyes shifted from me to Forrest. "I wish everyone had a friendship like yours. I think the world would be a much better place."

Forrest nearly choked on her wine, and I fought a blush. "I think it would." I took a sip of my wine, attempting to bury my expression behind the glass.

"That's something I've been working on in the church, actually," Dominic added. "I created Bible study program to foster more intimate friendships between the church members. It was quite successful, too. Some young men became inseparable after our six-week study on David and Jonathan." Dominic shook his head. "Who knows where that will stand when we get home, if I'll still have a job."

"But do you even want the job, honey?" said Peggy, leaning toward her husband. "This could be God telling you it's time for a change."

"Or punishment for my deep... uh... respect for Justice Ruth Bader-Ginsberg." Dominic crossed his arms and stared down at his lap somberly. "Like the church seems to think."

"Honey, don't be ridiculous." Peggy shook her head. "God doesn't do that sort of thing."

Forrest swirled her glass as she smiled at the bickering couple. "I agree with Peggy. Besides, if God really was punishing you..." she said, gesturing toward the view outside, the basilica gleaming gold in the sunset. "He's doing a terrible job at it."

Dominic chuckled, resting a hand on his wife's shoulder. "Amen to that."

As we ate a decadent pasta dinner, Dominic told us how Marty Ginsburg came to make all the family meals for his wife and children. Originally, RBG prepared weekday dinners, and Marty weekends.

But his cooking was better than Ruth's, so their kids begged Marty to take over. It was unconventional for the time, but he embraced it. "He was her constant supporter," said Dominic. "And she was his. She's the reason he graduated Harvard Law despite his cancer diagnosis. She would helped him write his essays, then completed her own."

"That's really interesting," I said, stabbing a piece of rigatoni with my fork. "It's really impressive how much you know about her life."

Peggy nodded emphatically. "Dominic has read everything she's written, and many of her biographies. It's been eye opening to learn how much she contributed to women's rights over the course of her career. I feel like I'm always learning something new about her, thanks to Dominic."

Dominic smiled warmly at his wife. "I'm grateful that you listen. I know it can be a lot sometimes. For decades, you were the only person I could talk to about her." He twirled his pasta and stared at the night sky. "It was difficult at first, when everyone found out. I was mortified by how the church handled it, like they were waiting for the opportunity to push me out. Like everything I did for the congregation meant nothing. But now, I suppose it's kind of a relief?

"I felt so much pressure to keep my feelings a secret. I obviously never allowed anyone into my office. I held all my meetings in a different room and was careful not to mention the Justice, but that meant I didn't talk much, at all. I'd be out to dinner and something would remind me of one of her Supreme Court opinions, or of a story from her legal career, but I couldn't say anything. Sometimes I felt like Peggy was the only one who really knew me." He looked at his wife, who smiled proudly back, knowing those days of secrets were over. "It's nice to stop hiding. It feels like I can finally be myself." He laughed. "Only took me sixty-four years."

He grinned with a self-assuredness I'd never seen in the months I'd known him. The slight flush in his cheeks was from excitement, not embarrassment, and he puffed his chest out confidently in his seat as he spoke. "I'm sure it's been hard dealing with the fallout, but I'm glad some good could come from this, too." I smiled. "It's nice to meet the real you. I like you a lot better than the perfect pastor at my wedding."

"Right?" said Peggy, resting her fork on her plate. "People were so surprised that I knew about Dominic's feelings toward RBG and still supported him." Peggy shook her head. "But I don't see this part of him as a flaw. Sure, we've had the occasional argument about how much RBG memorabilia I'll allow in the house. But at the same time, he's a massive feminist. He loves to cook and knows more about the Equal Rights Amendment than I do. I can't appreciate those parts of him while trying to change what society won't accept. That's not what marriage is."

"Compromise is important, of course," Dominic added. "We didn't do the statue out back because I respected your wishes."

"Oh, yeah." Peggy huffed a laugh as she turned to us. "He wanted to commission a custom marble statue of RBG to put in our garden. We're talking *thousands* of dollars."

"There are statues of male historical figures all over the city." Dominic crossed his arms. "Why shouldn't we give Ruth Bader-Ginsberg the same respect?"

Peggy cocked an eyebrow at him. "I agree, dear. But in our *garden*?"

He raised his hands in mock surrender. "The point is, compromise is important."

"It is." Peggy laughed. "Every person has traits that are a core part of who they are; they might express those traits in ways you love, and ways that drive you crazy sometimes. The RBG stuff is part of what makes Dominic who he is. His feminism, his curiosity, his passion for social justice. Because I love all those core traits about Dominic, I can appreciate his love for RBG, even if I don't share it to that extent.

"I don't think marriage is about loving someone despite their flaws, or loving someone enough to make them 'change' for you. It's finding someone whose core traits match your own in a way that makes you both better. Dominic and I have always had that, so it's easy to love him. I mean, aren't our flaws just an expression of our true selves? When you fall in love with each other's imperfections, that's how you know your true selves match." She winked at me. "But what do I know? I'm just a math teacher."

Dominic was staring at Peggy like she hung the moon, with round eyes and soft pink cheeks. Shockingly, it mirrored the way Forrest looked at me throughout this trip. Her warm eyes and gentle smile were watching me now, and I returned a shy grin. I thought I had done so well getting over her. But when Peggy described the love she shared with Dominic, it was Forrest I thought of. With Matthew, I had to force the pieces to fit. I convinced myself that if I loved him enough, gave him enough, changed enough, we'd be happy. He would stop resenting my people pleasing, my 'vain' hobbies and anxious temperament. But with Forrest it was effortless. She was the only person who ever fit me like that, the only one whose very being seemed divinely designed to match my own. "That's beautiful," I said, and my heart answered, *She is.*

"I'm glad we did that," Forrest said when we were alone again. After we'd hugged Peggy and Dominic goodbye in the lobby, promising to see them once we were back in the States; after we debriefed with Bianca and had the girl placing a heart over her chest at Peggy's romantic confession; after we closed the door to our suite and were alone again, Forrest's mannerisms contained quiet reverence as she spoke. "Peggy and Dominic have singlehandedly restored my faith in love."

"They're really something, aren't they?" I changed into pajamas with my back to her, then followed her into the bathroom to wash my face and brush my teeth. She had taken off her makeup and wore my old Carolina t-shirt and a pair of boxers decorated with cartoon kittens. They were the same pajamas she'd worn the whole trip, but it was suddenly difficult to keep my eyes off her.

Forrest constantly scrambled to support the people around her. Attending to students at school, checking up on friends with spontaneous phone calls, making small talk with whoever looked uncomfortable at a party. Seeing her utterly relaxed at night, when she finally focused on herself, took my breath away.

Suddenly, she flicked her gaze to mine, and we locked eyes in the mirror; my eyes widened as she caught me staring. I quickly lowered my head to spit out my toothpaste and trained my eyes on the sink.

When I left the bathroom, I swore I could feel her watching me, still.

I slipped into bed and aimlessly scrolled through Instagram, past photos of friends on vacation, book memes, and DIY sewing projects. I was interrupted by a text from Carter, who replied to a photo of us dressed for dinner with: "two of my favorite people!!" I was busy selecting a flurry of emojis to send back when I heard the bathroom door open.

There was Forrest, shifting from one foot to the other, as if afraid to enter the bed. Something was different between us. The thought set my heart pounding. I couldn't be the only one feeling this. Only I thought the same thing last time.

I opened my mouth to speak, but she beat me to it. "I can't sleep yet," she said quickly, folding her hands behind her back. "Do you want to see what's on TV?"

We filled the awkwardness with an Italian soap opera, which was even more entertaining because we didn't speak the language. All we could discern was that two hot mafiosos were fighting over a woman in a red dress, who was having an affair with the gardener — until Mafioso Number Two shot him. Knowing soap operas, he would probably come back the next episode. I strained to keep my eyes on the show and not Forrest's silhouette, as she eased into the sheets and her chest began to rise and fall at the pace of slow, even breaths.

The sound of her sleeping made me brave enough to face her, with her mouth slightly open and arm curled around a pillow. Her delicate lashes fanned across her cheeks, reminding me of Renaissance art. I flicked off the TV and settled into bed beside her. I spent a while lying in the dark, Peggy's words echoing in my head, before I finally found sleep.

17

We slept in until the streaks of morning sunlight became long strips across the wooden floor. When I rolled over, I found Forrest smiling at me between the sheets. "If we don't have plans today," she said, "what if we stay here?" And that was that. We lazed in bed until the late morning and lay by the pool until lunch, reading, idly chatting, and occasionally taking a dip to cool off from the summer heat. It was like our first day here, only a sense of peace replaced my melancholy. At one point, I dozed off and woke to find Forrest drawing me; an artistic intensity flared in her eyes as she studied my face, then the sketchbook, and back. Maximo brought us espresso and focaccia sandwiches from the bar, then lingered when he saw Forrest's sketch.

He started to ask about her art, how she started, what she loved to paint, and what her old work looked like. He sat on the lounge chair with us to swipe through her art and gasped when he saw the brilliantly colored portraits. Then Maximo unlocked his phone to show us his photography. There were breathtaking landscapes of Positano and the other towns along the coast, coupled with close-up shots of a cat wandering an alleyway, Nonna rolling out pasta dough, Bianca writing on a notepad while she spoke on the phone. The photos were strikingly intimate; the soft lighting and close-up camera angle made you feel like an insider, studying a private scene. It was the Positano that only a local could capture. "I tried to draw when I was younger, but I was useless at it," he said, as Forrest swiped through the images on his phone. "But I love this. It's a good second income, too. I sell prints of the landscapes at souvenir shops in town."

I swiped back to the shot of Bianca at the Valeri's front desk. Her dark hair was clipped back, her mouth a flat line, and her polo shirt wrinkle-free as she wrote something in a notepad and cradled the phone with her cheek. "I love this one," I told him. "It's so Bianca."

"Thank you," he said, smiling down at the photo. "She's a brilliant girl, isn't she?"

I nodded.

"She seems born to run this place, almost," Forrest said casually. "She looks like such a natural behind the desk."

To my surprise, Maximo nodded. "She really is gifted. Hard worker, too. But she has a bit of growing up to do before she could take over." He crossed his arms, eyes still trained on the picture. "Besides, we already promised the hotel to Giovanni. He might be living the exciting city life in Rome, but when he's ready to settle down, I want this place to be here for him."

Forrest nodded as she tilted her head to the side. "I didn't know he wanted to go into the family business."

Maximo shrugged. "He's still young. What you want changes all the time at that age, and he'd be a natural, too. You'll see when you meet him. Gio is so charismatic; the guests always love him."

"When is he visiting?" I asked.

"Tuesday." Maximo's face brightened at the thought. "He'll stay through the weekend. His schedule is more relaxed in the summer, when he's not studying at the university, so we get to see him more."

"He sounds great," said Forrest. "Just like the rest of your family."

"Yes," Maximo said, smiling softly at the praise. "They really are." As he examined the photo of Bianca again, he spoke softly, as if he'd forgotten we were here. "I think the ideal would be if they could run it together. Giovanni would be the owner, of course — that's what Jia wants, and it's her decision. But it would be an empty title. They'd be equals in every other way."

"What do I want, exactly?" Jia emerged from behind Maximo, her arms folded, and her husband jumped.

"For Gio to run the hotel, my love," he said, smiling up at her. "We just were chatting about it since he's coming to visit."

"Of course I want that." Jia frowned. "You want that too, Maxi."

"Yes, yes. Well, of course I do. I just mean—"

"It doesn't matter." Jia waved him off and smiled at us. "What is it with my family and their passion for oversharing, huh? Between Maxi and Bianca, you girls must be sick of hearing about Valeri family politics."

"No, no, it's fine," I said, shaking my head. I wanted to tell Jia that the Valeri's felt like family at this point, that afternoons sewing beside Nonna, exchanging banter with Bianca, and laughing with Maximo made me eager to talk through this decision with them. The Valeri family brought me back to life — listening was the least I could do. But Jia's tight frown and guarded eyes told me the conversation was over.

Maximo took his phone back from Forrest and stood up. "I think it's time for me to pick up some incoming guests from Sorrento. *Ciao*, ladies." He kissed his wife and hurried away.

Jia stared down at us from where she stood, her arms still crossed as her husband slipped inside. "You know, this situation is a lot more complicated than Maximo makes it seem. It is a lot of pressure to run this place, decades of family tradition to uphold." She shook her head. "I was the first woman in the family to inherit the Valeri. Nonna might support Bianca now, but my mother gave me a very hard time. She wanted it to go to Bianca's father, and she told me the same things I'm telling Bianca now — that I wasn't charismatic enough, that it wasn't mine to inherit, that I needed to earn the job. She doubted me every step of the way. I rose to the challenge, because that's how badly I wanted it."

Forrest frowned as she looked up at Jia. "That sounds like a lot of pressure."

Jia shrugged. "It is what it is. I'm happy with where I am now. Bianca reminds me of myself at that age, which is why I push her. But that doesn't mean I'm going to name her the successor. This is Gio's birthright. He helped with the hotel his entire childhood. We both worked hard so he could inherit this. I'm not going to give that up just because Bianca is the so-called 'better' choice. Gio worked for this, too, and he'd do a fantastic job in his own right."

Jia spoke calmly, but there was fire behind her eyes. I clasped my hands together and smiled softly up at her. "I'm sure he would."

Jia shook off the thought as she stared across the pool to Positano below. "Anyways, it doesn't matter all that much right now. Bianca and Gio are both still young. It will be another five years, at least, before Maximo and I retire. This is an ongoing conversation."

Forrest and I nodded. It wasn't our place to tell Jia about Bianca's job applications, about the decision she was grappling with. We could only hope Giovanni's visit would clear things up. It seemed that every person had a different opinion about what he really wanted.

Then, Jia smiled at us again, as if remembering we were there. "What am I doing? Scolding Maximo for oversharing with the guests and then doing the exact same thing. I'm so sorry, girls."

"Don't be." I shook my head and smiled reassuringly. "I'm glad you could get it off your chest. It's a lot to sit with, especially as the decision maker for the family."

"It is." She smiled softly back at me. "But if this is the price I pay for having a close family, I will pay it gladly. You know, for all her frustration over wanting to run the hotel, Bianca adores Giovanni. She always put her love for her family first, the way each of us do. This won't change any of that."

She left us to attend to something at the front desk, and I bit into my focaccia sandwich, unsure what to make of it all.

In the afternoon, we retreated to the suite to change, and I spent the rest of the day sewing while Forrest sat beside me, finetuning her drawings. Nonna was nowhere to be found, taking a rare day off. Maximo said she spent her Sundays at the local Catholic church in the morning, then ate lunch with a few old friends in the afternoon. We had the whole kitchen to ourselves. I measured fabric for Carter's shorts and worked on a surprise I was planning for the Valeri's, while Forrest focused on her sketchbook. I assumed she was polishing the sketches she wanted to turn into paintings for the gallery exhibition, but I couldn't be sure. Oddly, she wouldn't show me.

I loved these comfortable silences with her. Matthew never respected my work enough to grant me quiet, and if he was silently brooding, I'd grow too nervous to focus on anything else. He never lost his temper but was easily annoyed. If there were dirty dishes in the sink, if Netflix didn't have the show he wanted, if I put too many exclamation points in a text, he'd make his displeasure known. I walked on eggshells without realizing, because I thought it was my fault. But if Forrest could join my honeymoon without getting sick of me, if Carter could move heaven and earth back home so I could relax, maybe…

Maybe I wasn't the problem.

Maybe we were just two incompatible people, trying to make uneven pieces fit.

"Ow!" I hissed, and Forrest dropped her sketchbook.

"Are you ok?" She asked, eyes falling on my outstretched middle finger, where a small blood droplet blossomed on my fingertip.

"Yeah, my finger just got caught in the needle." I shook my head. "I guess I'm just rusty, and Nonna's sewing machine is a bit old."

"Well, if you are rusty, you wouldn't know it from the stitches. These?" She pointed to what I was making for the Valeri's. "Gorgeous. Here, let me get you bandaged up." She left the kitchen and returned moments later with a small First-Aid kit, which she clutched in both hands. She slid onto a high stool by the kitchen counter, and I joined her, reaching for the kit. "No, let me," she said, smiling softly, her dimples a subtle accent on her cheeks. "Bianca sends her love, by the way."

Forrest picked my hand up gently, her palm cupping the joints, and gingerly wiped away the circle of blood that had gathered there. Our knees touched as she bandaged the small wound, her long, narrow fingers working delicately., I studied her lowered eyelids and swooping lashes. She pressed her lips together the way she always did when she was deeply focused, as she wrapped my finger meticulously, without any folds in the bandage that would hinder my sewing. As she finished, I fought the urge to close my hand into a fist, to trap her fingers, just to keep her there a minute more.

It was like she heard me. She didn't let go, even as she clumsily closed the First Aid Kit with her one free hand, our knees still touching. She held my hand like it was made of porcelain, like setting it down would break me. Maybe she was right.

"All better," she said, forcing a bright smile as looked up at me. But her face fell when she met my eyes. My wide gaze, flushed cheeks, and parted lips betrayed me. She could see my every thought; I knew it by the way her pupils dilated in recognition and... was that hunger in her eyes? Only my thoughts went blank as she tightened her grip on my hand, swiping my knuckles with her thumb. She leaned forward, close enough that her eyes ran together in my vision.

My breath hitched as she leaned in and kissed me on the cheek.

It was a quick, soft kiss, her lips barely brushing my skin. The gentleness of the gesture put my stomach in knots. We had always been careful to keep a physical separation between us, to avoid repeating the night that almost ended our friendship. I never let our hugs linger, never let my hands wander too far past her shoulders. But something about Positano seemed to unravel all the unspoken rules that we maintained so carefully, for so long. Her hands seemed to mold into my back when we danced last night, and now, this kiss. More intimate than we'd been since we were teenagers, but somehow...

Somehow it felt like we spent our whole lives touching each other like this. It was so natural, yet insatiable. I wanted more of her lips on my cheek, my neck; wherever she kissed me I'd welcome it. I wanted—

"Come on," she said, pulling away suddenly. My hand hovered awkwardly in the air, where she held it moments before. I lowered it to my knees as a blush bloomed across my face where she kissed me. "Let's get out of here. I think we could both use a break."

Was that hesitation in her voice? Regret? Or was I grasping at straws? "Yeah," I said with a scratchy voice. "A break would be nice."

The second we got back to the honeymoon suite, it felt like a bad idea to be alone with her, here. That was how we decided to hurriedly pack a picnic for a casual dinner by the beach. We brought a towel, rosé, and snacks we picked up at a cheese shop to an open space on the public side of Positano Beach. The beach was packed with groups watching the sunset on blankets, as tourists strolled down the promenade behind us. We listened to the rhythm of the waves combing through the pebbly beach, water trickling like rain on the rocks. It mingled with the sound of warm conversations in Italian, French, English, and a few languages I couldn't place. As the sun slowly dropped behind the city, the light shifted from gold to orange. The sky became denim blue, and a rim of pale pink separated Positano from the rest of the sky.

It was a slow, quiet shift from day to night that took hours of beautiful, subtle changes you could only notice by paying close attention. How pink now rippled across the water, how the blues changed from light denim to cobalt, how the orange streaks grew even more brilliant until they suddenly, slowly faded away. The sky accentuated the warm tones in Forrest's skin, and her eyes widened with awe as she watched the shifting colors around her — like she was looking at art.

I sighed. This was a terrible idea. The beach was way more romantic than our hotel room. Her animated eyes left me speechless, and her lips looked pinker in the evening light, calling to mind how soft they felt on my cheek.

So much for clearing my head.

We drank wine from plastic cups as we indulged in our picnic spread: focaccia, prosciutto, cheese, olives, and grapes. The meal was simple but delicious, each ingredient fresh and bursting with flavor. I had to stifle a moan when I tried the flaky, paper-thin prosciutto. "Oh, wow," said Forrest, as the crumbly aged parmigiana melted on her tongue. She nodded as she chewed, then leaned back on her elbows, watching the waves crash.

Something was wrong. I could tell by the way she ran her fingers through the rocky sand as she sipped her wine, suddenly disinterested in the food. There was a wet sheen over her eyes that replaced her earlier awe. She lowered her gaze from the water, as if the beauty were too much for her.

"Penny for your thoughts?" I said gently, searching her face for clues. It was an effort to keep myself from touching her, from offering some sort of physical reassurance.

She brushed the sand off her hand as she looked up at me, her round eyes shiny with melancholy. "My parents never saw Italy," she said. "They always talked about visiting. My mom wanted to try real Italian pesto, and you should have seen the way my dad lost his mind over a good piece of lasagna. They went to some other places, closer to home, but never here. They were so focused on taking care of us."

"Oh, Forrest." I wrapped my arm around her, pulling her into me. "I'm so sorry."

"Don't be." She shook her head. "I'm having the best time with you. I wouldn't trade it for anything. It's just, part of me that hates doing things they never could, either because of the accident or because they were too busy raising me and Monique."

She placed a hand on my knee, leaning into me as she stared at the water. "They were so convinced I could do anything I put my mind to. They framed a drawing I made in kindergarten and hung it in the house, right next to an A+ essay Monique wrote about *The Odyssey* in ninth grade. They wanted me to have the world, but the thing is, I wanted the same for them. I wish that they could eat food like this and have memories like this, watch sunsets like this. I wish I could bottle up everything good I ever experienced and give it to them, the way they did for me. At the very least, I wish I could have told them that."

I thought of the photo of her parents that Forrest showed me in college — sitting on the front porch of their New Orleans home, when her mother was newly pregnant with Monique. Her mother had long locs, a delicate nose, and kind, round eyes that were a mirror image of Forrest's. But my best friend had her father's wide, dimpled smile — the kind that conquered her face. I knew that by her father's grin in the picture as he wrapped a lean arm around her mother's shoulder. They looked perfectly in love and content with each other. The kind of happiness people spend a lifetime chasing, and most never live to see.

"They know," I murmured, rubbing reassuring circles into her shoulder. "Trust me, they know. You've been bottling up beautiful things for them your entire life. Isn't that the whole point of your art?"

Tears rimmed her eyes as she nodded, looking up at me. "You're right," she choked.

"They were happy, Forrest." I watched the waves as I spoke. "I never met them, but I know that much. You and Monique... you made them very happy."

"You're right." She sniffled loudly as she squeezed my knee. "It's been so long since I lost them. Sometimes, I think maybe I'm okay again, and others, I feel like I'm sixteen again." She shook her head. "I can't believe I've gone this long without them."

I nodded as I squeezed Forrest's shoulder. Her grief was older than our friendship. I knew she'd always carry it. All I could do was help shoulder the weight. "I think it's safe to say that even though they never got to come here, they wouldn't change a thing."

"You're right," said Forrest, wiping her eyes. "I know they wouldn't." She rested her head on my shoulder as we watched the waves crash.

My legs were just beginning to cramp from sitting on the ground when I whispered: "I wish I got to meet them."

"Me, too." Forrest smiled at me. Sadness lingered on her features, but her tears had dried. "They would have loved you, Al."

I nudged her shoulder playfully. "How do you know that?" I teased.

"I just do." There was a softness in her eyes when she looked at me. "There are some things in life you just know, like breathing."

18

"Let me tell you something you don't know," the man began in an exaggerated Australian accent, gesturing wildly at the ruins behind him, "about the wondrous city of Pompeii."

Forrest snorted back laughter, and I grinned wickedly at her, wiggling my eyebrows. Touring Pompeii was a spontaneous decision we made last night. I originally left it off the itinerary because Matthew never would have agreed to go (history lectures bored him, as did long walks in the heat). But when I casually mentioned it to Forrest, she sprung into action. I tried to tell her it was okay, we didn't have to do it, but she just showed me pictures of the frescoes on a Pompeii mansion and said, "Alana, yes we *do*." That decided it. Our Google search yielded only one available tour guide who didn't cost a fortune — this middle-aged Australian man who seemed to be the love child of an archeologist and a high school theater kid, with his flair for the dramatic. He dressed like he stepped off the set of an Indiana Jones movie, in a short-sleeved khaki button-down and matching shorts that revealed an ambitious stretch of thigh. One look at him, and we agreed: This was one of the best choices we made on the trip, so far.

"I grew up in the heart of the Outback, a long way from here," he continued, taking off his wide-brimmed hat to wipe sweat from his nonexistent hairline. "But when I first saw these ruins at nineteen years old, I knew it was my calling to dedicate my life to uncovering the stories buried here, beneath the rubble."

We entered the ancient city in the morning at Porta Marina, the seaside entry point. Though we were far inland, our guide said this used to be the shore, making Pompeii a hub for trade and travel in the ancient world. We arrived before the crowds and the sun's full heat — not that either inconvenience would have kept us from coming. Not with the city's rich history, culture, and art, waiting to be explored. Not with its tragic end. The place was a siren call for romantic hearts like ours.

"That," our guide said dramatically, pointing to the tall, stocky volcano beyond the ruins, an indigo shadow against the clear sky, "is Mount Vesuvius, the most dangerous volcano in the world."

"As we say in America," Forrest muttered, "No shit, Sherlock."

It was my turn to snort back laughter.

The guide launched into some lengthy explanation of what makes Vesuvius so dangerous, something about the volcano's unpredictability and proximity to Naples. Most active volcanoes weren't located this close to large cities. "Of course, locals now know the risk. The citizens of Pompeii had no idea they even lived by a volcano, let alone such a dangerous one. Before the blast that decimated this city, Vesuvius hadn't erupted in over 1,800 years. In fact, Pompeii was one of the most prosperous cities in the ancient world. Locals believed the place was blessed by the gods."

He started by leading us into a bathhouse that was the first stop for merchants who arrived by boat. An impressive network of plumbing rimmed the floor, while the walls overhead featured intricate, ancient paintings of orgies. Yes, orgies. "Think of it as a menu," said our guide. "A lot of sex workers came here to service the merchants, and since most of them didn't speak Latin, they used this."

He walked our group through more of the ancient city, past ancient homes, storefronts, crumbling columns and archways. Pompeii was a vibrant Roman city and a popular tourist destination, thanks to the stunning beaches nearby. There were raised stone crosswalks that elevated pedestrians above the trash-filled streets, with space for carriages to pass between the stones. Spacious plazas served as gathering places for citizens. Roman aqueducts and fertile volcanic soil brought prosperity, while booming trade allowed for abundant wealth, and entertainment awaited on nearly every street corner — from theaters, to carriage races, to gladiator arenas. Theirs was an advanced, progressive society. "Not so different," our guide added, "from our own."

It was easy to imagine daily life here, dining at fast food restaurants, rushing over the raised crosswalks to catch the latest play at the theater, writing jokes in graffiti on the walls, all while Mt. Vesuvius loomed on the horizon. Our guide showed us the ruins of temples to several gods and a bathhouse for Roman soldiers, decorated with intricate mosaics of angels flying into battle. There were shops, hotels, and government buildings in between the city's private homes. On one, our guide pointed out the entryway's ornate mosaic of a pet, with a Latin warning to "beware the dog."

We walked through two of the city's mansions and beheld the breathtaking architecture. Each home sported a shallow pool in the entryway that collected rainwater for visitors to wash their feet. There were rooms for eating, dining, cooking, and entertaining guests. Courtyards sported well-curated gardens with statues of figurines. Intricate mosaic patterns blanketed the floor, while the walls featured stunning frescoes in vibrant colors, depicting portraits of Romans, the gods, and historical scenes. Each design was intended to flaunt the family's education and wealth.

It was hard to believe the paintings, with their brilliant colors and realistic depictions, were two thousand years old. It delighted Forrest. She drifted through the rooms several paces behind the tour group, leaning into the walls to glimpse the details of the frescoes, figures dining and dancing against vibrant backdrops. As usual, I spent more time admiring her awestruck eyes than the art.

We left many streets unexplored as we continued; there was too much to see in one week, let alone in one day. Our guide said only a third of the city had been excavated; archeologists were torn about digging up the whole thing, since the city only remained well preserved because it was buried. Even the uncovered portion was too vast for one person to see everything.

But somehow, it only took one day to wipe the whole city out.

Our guide was in the middle of an elaborate re-telling of Spartacus's last stand against the Romans, which apparently took place on the summit of Mount Vesuvius. His army of ex-gladiators was sustained by the natural springs there before he finally escaped to freedom. We were in one of the city's amphitheaters when stories of the people forced to fight here somehow turned into our guide shouting "I am Spartacus!" at the top of his lungs. He scared the shit out of a passing tour group. Complete with reenactments, dramatic pauses, and a few removals of his hat to wipe away sweat, the guide put everything he had into the retelling — his face bright red from exertion.

"I share this story, because of the contrast it presents," he said. "For Spartacus, and for everyone living in Pompeii before 79 AD, Vesuvius was a source of life, the reason for the city's prosperity... Then one day, it wasn't."

Most of Pompeii's residents remained in the city even after the eruption began. With ash raining from the sky, they thought they'd be safer indoors, shielded from the rock that seared their skin. By the time ash buried the streets, and buildings started to collapse, it was too late. Wading through the scalding rock was impossible, and Tsunami-like waves brought on by the eruption made Naples Bay its own death trap. Everyone still inside the city perished. A day after the eruption began, one final blast of sulfuric ash incinerated them. Those who were still alive died instantly.

The city was frozen in time ever since.

"Which is great for historians," said our guide, smiling brightly. "Pompeii has been perfectly preserved since 79 AD. It offers even more insight into the Roman Empire than Rome itself, in my opinion, because nothing about the city has changed."

I crossed my arms as I leaned into Forrest and muttered: "I don't think I've ever heard mass death described as 'great for historians' before."

Forrest smirked. "Definitely makes me feel better about the whole thing." We giggled together as we walked, and our guide stopped in front of a museum.

"This part can be a little disturbing, so it's not a formal part of the tour," he said. As the volcano incinerated the citizens of Pompeii, he explained, it froze them with the city. Scientists used the outline of their skeletons to create casts of the dying in their final moments. The museum before us housed many of those restored remains. This was where he left us.

"Whether you go inside or not, it was an honor to show you the mystic, tragic ruins of Pompeii. Remember, your tips are what make it possible for me to continue providing these tours to visitors of the city. If you had fun today, show your appreciation with that spare change!"

He was focused a couple asking questions about the eruption when Forrest and I dropped a few euro coins in his outstretched hat and slipped away. As we stepped inside, we were glad to leave his theatrics at the door. This place was meant for silence.

They stretched across the floor all around us, housed in glass cases. We passed by each person slowly as we took in their expressions. A woman hiding her face with her hands, a man attempting to crawl to safety, a child curling into their mother, others lying on their backs, hands blocking their faces, perhaps resigned to their fate. Here, past and present bled together like watercolors. It was stunning to glimpse their intimate, immortalized final moments. So many people perished at once, and each reacted differently, with fear, horror, acceptance, lingering hope, even love.

Eventually, we came upon the two lovers, perhaps the most famous of the Pompeii remains. Two men lay on the ground holding each other, one with his head pressed into the other's stomach. They could have been lovers, relatives, close friends, or even strangers who wanted someone to hold through the apocalypse. Everything about them was a mystery except their last moment. We only knew that they did not die alone.

Wasn't that what we all wanted, in the end?

When confronted with catastrophe, everyone wants to believe they'd be among the lucky few to survive. But I knew as I wandered the ruins that my body would have been ash alongside the thousands who stayed in Pompeii. The rock raining down would have compelled me to stay in the place where I felt safest, even as that impulse doomed me to death. I would have been like these two, clinging to love, to home, with my final breath. Clinging to Forrest, really.

That was what she always was to me, from the moment we met.

Home.

We took the train to Sorrento for a lunch and rode back to Positano by ferry, watching the coastline lazily roll by as we approached the city. After stopping by a souvenir shop to buy a gift for Monique — an apron covered in lemons for her baking — we spent the rest of the day lying by the Valeri's pool. I read the romance novel Forrest just finished, while she alternated between filling the pages of her sketchbook and cooling off in the pool. She leaning against the edge of the pool with her eyes closed, hair piled in a bun on top of her head, looking ravishingly content, when I texted Carter.

Me: SOS. This trip is wayyy more romantic than I thought it would be.

Carter: You mean your honeymoon on the Amalfi Coast with the girl you've been in love with since you were a teenager feels… romantic? I'm shook to my core.

Me: Ha, ha.

Me: I thought I was over this. I was engaged like a week ago…

Carter: You can't get over something without getting closure, and your story with Forrest never had a real ending.

Carter: That means what you're feeling is NORMAL!

Carter: And you shouldn't feel bad about it!!

Carter: You know that right??

Carter: ANSWER ME, ALLY.

Me: Hahaha you know me too well!!

Me: Don't worry, I'm fine, and I know… Thank you. <3

I thought of our dance after dinner by the water, of her soft kiss against my cheek, how her eyes were warm enough to melt butter when she looked at me. There were the compliments she dropped into conversations like Easter eggs, the electricity on my fingers when our hands brushed. Either I was crazy, or something was different. I couldn't bear to keep it to myself.

Me: I know what I'm about to say sounds crazy…

Me: But I feel like she might be sending signals back?? Maybe? Like, just how we've been interacting and stuff. Idk, it sounds insane when I type it. Am I delusional?

There was a conversation bubble with three blinking dots that came and went for what felt like an eternity.

Carter: You're not crazy. Honestly, there were a couple times before the wedding when I thought… Idk. Just be careful, Ally. You're going through a lot rn. Forrest is lovely, but make sure you're taking care of yourself!

Carter was the one I cried to for months after Forrest abruptly ended things that summer. He came to love her once he got to know her, but he never forgot the drunken nights mascara ran down my cheeks, leaving black stains on his pillow in the morning. He still remembered the long text messages he kept me from sending, begging for answers. I never experienced a heartbreak like that since, either because I was nineteen and irrational, or because there was no one whose absence ached like Forrest's. It hurt less to lose a lover than a friend, and she was both.

Together on this honeymoon, we were closer than we'd ever been. I was being pulled closer into her orbit, falling all over again, but too afraid to do anything about it. But maybe that was a good thing. Carter was right. I was fresh off a botched wedding, my life in tatters. I was in no place to risk losing Forrest again.

Even if it felt like something had to give.

Me: You're right, love. I will. I love you sooo much!

Speaking my thoughts to him made them feel real, like I set something in motion. As I leaned back in the lounge chair and closed my eyes, I tried to ignore the fluttering anticipation that emerged in my chest. I tried to tell myself that I was imagining things, that I could keep this a honeymoon between friends.

I almost could.

19

I was drifting in and out of sleep when Forrest's wet footsteps on the terrace brought me back to reality. I could hear pool water dripping at her feet, the sound as soft as a kiss. My eyes fluttered open just as she sat on the lounge chair beside me. She returned a faint smile as she bit her bottom lip. Her sudden proximity was disorienting. I spent the last half-hour fending off dreams of those eyes. I sat up in the chair, curling my knees toward my chest. "What's up?"

Forrest folded her hands in front of her, silver rings flashing in the sunlight. "So," she said, leaning toward me, then sitting up straight. She clasped and unclasped her hands, then placed them on her knees — like she was trying to keep herself from twisting her rings.

Was she... nervous?

"I have a surprise for you," she said.

I raised my eyebrows as I sat up in the chair. "A surprise?"

Forrest dropped her gaze to the trail of her wet footprints on the terrace, leading back to the pool. Before I could say anything more, she looked at me an intensity that flustered me. I could sink to the bottom of those eyes. "It's just... you put so much work into planning the honeymoon. I want to contribute something, too. So, I made a plan for tonight." She shrugged, feigning nonchalance, but her eyes flit over my face hesitantly. She crossed and uncrossed her ankles, then twirled the ring on her middle finger. Heat rushed to my face. She *was* nervous, almost like—

No. Not a date. This was *not* a date.

"That's really sweet of you, Forrest." She rewarded me with a radiant grin; dimples and sunshine eyes replaced her nervous ticks. If only I could bottle up that smile. I'd get drunk on it. "What are we doing?" I hoped she didn't notice the breathlessness in my voice.

Her grin became a smirk as she leaned back in her chair and closed her eyes, crossing one leg over the other. "You'll see," she said. "We should start getting ready in..." She picked up her phone to check the time. "An hour? Forty-five minutes?"

I nodded as I stood from my chair to jump in the pool, my bones humming in anticipation. I strained to remain rational. There was no way this meant anything, even if my hands shook underwater. Even if I could feel Forrest's eyes on me as I swam the entire length of the pool.

The only thing Forrest told me about this evening was to wear comfortable shoes. "You can dress up if you want to," she said, sliding long, thin gold hoops into her ears as she sat on the bed. We were freshly showered and back in the honeymoon suite, my hair in a towel as I applied mascara in front of the bathroom mirror. "But it's not necessary."

Necessary, my ass. I wanted to impress her, even if it didn't mean anything. If she only rewarded me with a pair of awestruck eyes, it would be worth it. I chose a blush pink satin midi skirt that hugged my figure, a white, backless halter top, and Birkenstocks. After pairing it with carefully done makeup and a pair of silver dangling earrings that I bought in Positano, I was satisfied. Forrest borrowed a simple sleeveless t-shirt dress in powder blue that felt like pajamas. The hem danced around her legs as she walked from the bed to the bathroom mirror, revealing taunting glimpses of her upper thigh.

I dropped my eyes to my phone as she touched up her make-up. It wasn't my place to stare. This was not a date. After all these years, I couldn't forget that now. I scrolled through Instagram instead, flicking past photos of friends until creaking floorboards, a growing shadow, and my own fluttering chest signaled Forrest's approach. My nerves tracked her movements like a sixth sense, blood racing the closer she got. Carefully, I lifted my gaze.

"You always look amazing in my clothes," I said. It awed me to see how the fabric changed against her figure, how the skirt flowed around her long legs, and the V-neck fell lower on her chest.

She smiled absentmindedly as she studied my outfit and murmured, "You always look amazing." Her eyes widened for a moment, breaking her trance. She turned away to grab her purse, and her composure returned when she faced me again. "Shall we?"

My throat was dry as I nodded, following her out the door.

Bianca met us in the lobby with a picnic basket looped under her arm. "Good evening, ladies," she said with a soft smile. She dangled the family car keys in her outstretched hand as she informed me that she would give us a ride to dinner. Forrest kissed Bianca on the cheek in greeting as she took the picnic basket. "Don't wait up for us, though. I know Giovanni gets in tonight."

"You're in on this?" I shifted my eyes from Forrest to Bianca, at the shared laughter in their eyes. "When did y'all plan this?"

Bianca shrugged while Forrest smiled coyly and held the hotel door open for me. Our feet shuffled against the cobblestone driveway, offsetting the awkward silence as I fought a blush. There was a bag of hotel towels in the shotgun seat, so I sat in the back of the car beside Forrest. Our thighs brushed together as she whispered, "Wait until you see where we're going."

The car wound down the mountain, offering glimpses of greenery and seaside cliffs as we descended into Positano. The seatbelt rubbed against my shoulder with every turn, and I strained to keep my posture straight. The air felt heavy, the way it does before a thunderstorm. Every inch that separated Forrest and me hummed like the city. The tension in my shoulders persisted as the car slid to a halt in front of the dock, as we waved goodbye to Bianca and Forrest led me to the water. We were alone, and somehow that felt dangerous — like we were on the cusp of crossing a point of no return. I tucked my hair behind my ear.

If Forrest felt the same, she didn't show it. She walked down the dock with the picnic basket hooked under her arm, long hair swishing behind her. When we reached the end, where a row of small motorboats was docked, she grinned and said: "Did you know you can rent these and take them out into the bay?"

She got the keys from a boat rental shack and helped me into our boat, fingers flexing around my palm. I sat on the narrow tan bench, and Forrest slid behind the steering wheel, to my right. I watched her as she drove us out to sea, her delicate fingers gliding over the wheel. Only — I didn't answer her question. No, I was gaping at her like lovestruck idiot, watching light flicker in her dark eyes as she scanned the waves, lips pressed together in concentration. I cleared my throat. "When did you get this idea, anyway?"

She smirked back, eyes glinting, before facing the bay. "Details, details," she teased with a wave of her hand. "Don't worry about it, just let me do something nice for you, because I want to."

I leaned back in the seat and studied the houses stacked against the cliffs, behind cerulean water that shimmered with golden light. Forrest was right. The scenery could have been plucked from a fairytale, and no matter my feelings, I was with my best friend. Nobody made me feel safer than Forrest. For once, I let myself enjoy it.

There was a glass Tupperware of the tortellini we folded with Nonna, a large helping of focaccia, Caesar salad, and cannolis, all packed neatly into the basket around a bottle of rosé. Forrest dropped anchor in the middle of the bay, and we bobbed lazily alongside other little boats and yachts, out to enjoy the sunset. We clinked our plastic cups and dug into the feast. The focaccia was light, with the subtle tang of fresh olive oil, while the taste of fresh parmesan and black pepper made the salad feel decadent. The tortellini burst on my tongue like feathers in a pillow fight; the lemon-ricotta flavor was sharp and soothing at once. Between bites, Forrest kept me laughing. We made up outlandish backstories for our Pompeii tour guide, ranked the shops and galleries we visited, decided which was our favorite meal of the trip. (This one.) A deep peace settled between us, an effect of the vacation and our mutual contentment at being together. My nerves from earlier all but dissipated. Being with Forrest felt like stepping into sunshine and curling up with a book on a rainy day. Like I was flying down a rollercoaster while dozing off in a spa. She left me dizzy, giddy, and perfectly calm, all at once. This night was no different.

Just then, she turned to face me, her eyes piercing mine. The flickering shades of brown reminded me of a campfire; her stare seemed to reach my soul. "So," she said.

"So," I echoed, sipping my wine.

"How are you doing, Al, really?" Forrest searched my face, and I must have imagined her eyes dropping to my lips, as her gaze combed through my faux nonchalance.

I leaned back, my elbows on the boat's edge. "What do you mean?"

She shrugged. "I guess I'm worried about you. You seem happier than you've been in a long time, and it's amazing. But..." she rested her hand gently on my arm, raising goosebumps. "I know it will be stressful, going back. Dealing with your parents, moving out of Matthew's place, getting caught up on work."

"I've been trying to forget about all that." I forced a light, breathless laugh.

Forrest shook her head, running her thumb over my forearm. "Ugh, you're right. I'm sorry. I didn't mean to stress you out by asking about it."

I squeezed her arm back, intertwining our limbs. "You're not. I've been thinking about it, anyway." My eyes dropped to the artful curve in her knees, a hair away from touching my own. "I'm sure this will change, but I'm not worried about all that right now. Carter has been collecting my stuff from Matthew, and he said I could live with him in Philly until I figure out what to do. Honestly, I owe him a kidney for that. The one thing that scared me was seeing Matthew again."

"Do you still love him?"

I flushed at the question. *If only she knew.* I forced a smile as I shook my head. "No." The Positano cityscape turned rosy as I spoke; window lights flickered on, and the sky grew deep pink. It was easier to study the shifting colors than return her gaze. "I'm obviously hurt by what he did, but the relief outweighs the hurt." I looked at her, then down at her knees again. "I'm lucky I didn't marry him." I confessed where only Forrest and the ocean could hear. "I must have stopped loving him a long time ago."

When I finally looked up, Forrest's face was free of the judgment I expected to see. Instead, there was only softness, like she understood. It suddenly occurred to me how close we were sitting, as her eyes dropped to my lips again. She nodded. "I'm glad you didn't marry him," she whispered.

"Me too." My voice was feather light and not quite my own. "I mean..." *When did my throat become cotton?* "I guess I already said that."

She laughed; the sound was a salve for my nerves. She brushed her thumb over my forearm again, and I shivered at the contact. For years, she only ever touched me casually, the way friends do. This felt charged. Her thumb pressed into my skin with an intention that reminded me of crickets and the soft wood grain of a dock, of feet dangling over water. My thoughts went blank, consumed by a desperate craving for more. For her.

"I liked dancing with you," I whispered as Forrest ran her fingertips down my arm, painting me with goosebumps. My body arched toward her, pulled by a force I couldn't control.

"Alana," Forrest breathed, her voice low as she continued her caress. Her stare intensified, drinking me in as she offered a helpless, sighing smile. "You have no idea what that did to me."

My lips parted at her words. It felt impossible, but she was leaning toward me, too, soft lips falling open — and when I dared to brush my hand over her knee, she shivered. Her eyes were so wide, I could fall into them. Maybe I already did. She was only inches away, so close I could feel her breath on my cheeks, and—

HONK! Honkhonkhonk! Forrest flinched back from me, flying so fast to the other side of the boat, I thought she'd fall in the bay. A small yacht appeared behind us; an older woman in a striped shirt stood at the bow, waving her hand. "Excuse me," she called. "Can you move your boat, just a bit toward the sea? You're blocking the way to our dock."

Forrest nodded awkwardly. "Uh, yeah, ok." She forced a laugh, but her hands shook as she reached for the wheel. I could hardly move, still tingling where she touched me. It felt like a dream, what she said, the hunger in her eyes that was gone now, as she surveyed the water and steered us toward less crowded water. I clasped and unclasped my hands, waiting for her to break the silence.

When the yacht passed, she finally met my eyes. Whatever she glimpsed there compelled her to do the exact opposite of what I really wanted. She jerked the wheel, turning us away from the horizon, back to shore. "Um," she said, eyes on the water again. "Since we're done eating, do you want to head back?"

The crashing waves masked my sigh as I nodded. "Sure."

Just like that, the spell was broken. Forrest's smile was terse as she steered us home over the darkening waves.

20

Silence weighed heavy between us as our cab slowly wound up the cliffside coastal roads, and the bustle of Positano faded away. Forrest and I stared out opposite windows of the cab, while a jazz singer drawled in scratchy Italian on the rundown radio. My mind was racing as I combed through my memory. *You have no idea what that did to me.* She couldn't have meant what I thought — not when she turned the boat around. I shuddered to think how I embarrassed myself, my yearning so blatant she ended the night early. Now, we'd return to our honeymoon suite, to the bed we shared for the past week and a half. Only everything was different. How could I have been such an idiot?

"The nights here are so beautiful," said Forrest as we pulled up to the hotel. The Valeri's windows glowed invitingly, while the moonlight cast flickering shadows over the driveway. I paid the cab driver in cash, and he left us alone with the cozy view and the faint sound of ocean waves. Forrest was right — the nights were ethereal. But was that really all she was thinking about?

"I know." I crossed my arms, shifting my weight. "It feels like we're in a movie."

"It really does."

Just as the weird silence began to resettle between us, Forrest said, "Shall we?" and lead the way inside. The lobby was eerily quiet. Bianca sat at the desk alone with the lights off and her head in her hands. She lifted her gaze when she saw us. Her smile would have been laughably fake, if she weren't so distressed. With a flat voice, she asked: "How was your night?"

"Great," I answered quickly. "Thank you for helping plan it."

She waved me off nonchalantly as Forrest propped her elbows against the front desk. "Bianca," she said firmly, leaning down to meet our friend at eye level. "What's going on?"

Bianca looked from Forrest, to me, and back again. "I got the job."

Forrest's jaw dropped. "The apprenticeship?" she beamed at Bianca's melancholy nod. "That's amazing!"

But Bianca hardly looked celebratory; loose hair fell out of her normally pristine bun, her chin propped against her elbows on the front desk. She raised her eyebrows doubtfully at Forrest. "Are you going to take it?" I asked.

She sighed. "It will be hard to give this up," she shrugged, "to really accept that I'm never going to run the Valeri."

"Isn't there still hope that you'd inherit it, though?" asked Forrest. "If Giovanni doesn't want it."

Bianca frowned as she began clicking a pen with her right hand, in and out. Her lip quivered. "I used to think Giovanni would tell Jia the truth, but now I don't know." A single tear streamed down her cheek, and Bianca quickly brushed it away. "You should've seen when he got here. Maxi said something about how the hotel would be ready for him when he came home, and he just smiled. He didn't say anything to correct him; he didn't even look at me. It wouldn't surprise me if he took over just to please his parents. He's never been able to say no to Jia." She looked up at us, her eyes bright with anger. "But this is *my* dream, not his. This is everything I worked for." She shook her head, resigned again. "It's stupid. I should be grateful. So many people would kill for this apprenticeship."

"I'm so sorry, Bianca," I said. There was nothing else we could say, no clean resolution to her dreams for the Valeri. "I will say — you don't have to be grateful for the job offer just because other people want it. That doesn't mean it's right for you."

Forrest nodded. "You should never beat yourself up over your feelings." Then, she smiled, stepping back from the desk. "But we can drink to them."

We stole away to the kitchen to find a celebratory bottle of Prosecco, tiptoeing past the sound of her family's welcome dinner for Giovanni. The awkwardness between Forrest and me was muted, with Bianca between us, her family's laughter filling the silence. There was the gentle hum of conversation, laughter, and clinking glasses of her relatives and neighbors filling the pool terrace outside, as Bianca grabbed a bottle of Prosecco from the fridge. I opened random cabinets until I found three glasses, and Forrest told Bianca about the picnic, the sunset, and the woman who made us move for her yacht. It would have felt normal if not for the details Forrest left out, the unusually quick pace of her voice, and the way she carefully avoided brushing hands as she took a glass from me.

Bianca popped the Prosecco bottle and started filling glasses, pausing to let the bubbles fizz away, when a man's voice interrupted us. "Bianca! I've been looking everywhere. What are you doing back here?"

I turned toward the sound to find the most beautiful man I'd ever seen.

Giovanni Valeri.

He was tall and tan with toned muscles, artfully precise stubble, and dark brown hair that was carefully styled to look like he just rolled out of bed. He wore a pale blue button-down French tucked into white linen shorts, a gold chain and hint of chest hair visible through the top of his shirt, which he left unbuttoned. His piercing blue eyes were the color of the Mediterranean, and he flashed a pair of dimples when he smirked at his cousin. "You can't leave me alone with the grown-ups," he scolded, placing his hands on his hips. "In case you forgot, we made a spit oath when you were eight."

"In case you forgot, Gio, you *are* a grown-up," Bianca said. She glared at him, but there was laughter in her eyes. "You're thirty-one."

Giovanni clutched his chest like he'd been shot. "Well, you better call the nursing home to see if they have room for me, since I'm so ancient."

Bianca flicked him off, and he laughed. Then she turned to me. "Can you get Gio a glass, too?"

"Breaking into Mom's Prosecco?" He raised an eyebrow. "What's this about?"

Bianca shrugged, hiding a smile. "Nothing special. I just got a job offer."

"The apprenticeship?" A grin overtook his face as she nodded, revealing perfect teeth. "Congratulations! That's amazing!" After wrapping his cousin in a bear hug, he nodded at Forrest and me. "Who are you celebrating with?"

"This is Forrest and Alana. They're guests, here until Friday on a honeymoon... gone wrong, I guess."

"Oh, yes. I know about you two. Mom told me." He smiled at me apologetically. "There are no secrets in our family. I'm sorry for what you went through."

"Thank you." Somehow, I did not feel self-conscious that a stranger knew about my debacle. Maybe it was the matter-of-fact way Giovanni offered condolences, like the wedding was no different from any other blame-free bout of misfortune. Or maybe it was the way empathy softened his eyes as he spoke. He seemed to understand how I felt without saying a word. I could see why his father called him a charmer. "Honestly, the trip has been healing." I nodded in Forrest's direction. "Your family was so welcoming to both of us."

"I'm glad to hear it. They usually are." He grinned as he shoved his hands in his pockets. "I'm sure they'd love it if you join us. So would Bianca and I. It's a lot of older neighbors, mostly their friends. We need some fresh faces for them to interrogate."

I laughed. "Ah, yes. The 'how's your life?' and 'why are you single?' family function."

"So they have those in America, too?" Giovanni laughed. "I never realized how many people care about my dating life until tonight."

"Well, I definitely have a good enough story to keep them occupied, and I finally feel comfortable telling it." Plus, it was an excuse to delay the inevitable — going to the honeymoon suite with Forrest, sharing a bed, only for her to brush off what happened and fracture my heart again. I shrugged and turned back to Bianca and my best friend. "I don't know. What do you guys think?"

Forrest shrugged as she leaned against the counter with her arms crossed, a slight frown on her lips. As her eyes locked with mine, it felt like she could see right through me, like her gaze contained multitudes. "I'll do whatever you want, Alana," she said.

My face flushed. I opened my mouth to reply when Bianca said: "Perfect! I've been hiding away from my family for suspiciously long. Can you guys be my alibi? I don't want them to know about the job offer. I'm not ready for that conversation yet."

She looped her elbows through mine and Forrest's as she led us to the patio, Giovanni trailing behind with the Prosecco. Maximo was telling a story in Italian to a group on the other side of the pool, who were howling at whatever he said. Jia was closer; she paused her conversation to greet each of us with kisses on both cheeks. "Bianca, where were you?" she asked. "You disappeared completely; I was starting to worry. I sent Gio to find you."

Bianca smiled back at her aunt. "I ran into Forrest and Alana coming back from their girls' night. I wanted to hear how it was."

Jia nodded. "I'm so glad you two did that. The bay is such a lovely place to watch the sunset, so romantic. Did you enjoy yourselves?"

"Yes," we answered at the same time, too quickly. Forrest flashed her wide, dimpled smile at Jia. But it felt forced, tonight. Or was I imagining that? "Thank you for everything you did to help me reserve a boat. I'm so glad we could do it."

Jia waved off her gratitude as she sipped a glass of red wine. We were quickly interrupted by new faces who wanted to meet the American girls from the honeymoon suite. I retold the story at their urging — which was met with gasps, signs of the cross, and an exclamation of "Mamma Mia." They adamantly agreed that Matthew was an asshole, that his ex must be crazy, and that he had to be an idiot to let me go. At least, they concluded, his mother had some sense. Somebody had to. What a pity. Clearly, her brains didn't run in the family.

At that, they clinked their glasses in Melissa's honor. For the first time, I actually enjoyed revisiting what happened, if only to fill the terrace with laughter. On nights like this, the worst moments are the best stories. We were the life of the party.

The terrace was filled with the Valeri family's oldest friends. People Jia and Maximo grew up with, along with some parents of Giovanni's school friends. They were farmers, chefs, shop owners and artists who made a living on Positano's summer tourism. For our benefit, they spoke in English. The only people missing were Bianca's parents, who were stuck working late in Naples. "They're always working late," said Bianca, shaking her head. "But they told me to send Gio their love."

I could scarcely get a word in with Forrest, as we each parried questions about our work, life in the U.S., and our uneventful dating lives. Still, one look at her and I'd remember her fingers brushing my forearm. *You had no idea what that did to me.* But she turned the boat around — I had to remember that. If she wanted me, she could have taken me right there in the middle of the bay. That she didn't was its own answer. Not that my heart would listen. The corner of my eye followed her all night, searching for the right words to say when were finally alone.

"Alana," said Maximo, nudging my shoulder.

"Sorry?" I snapped my head away from Forrest.

"I was wondering when you're going to start dating again," said the woman I was talking to, a lemon farmer named Donna who lived in the hills nearby.

"Oh, um... I don't know. I guess I haven't thought about it."

"I think it's a bit soon to ask that, Donna," Giovanni said. He'd been chatting with Forrest but swooped in now, to my rescue. "Alana's break-up is still fresh. She probably needs more time, no?" He turned to me, questioning.

Before I could answer, Donna said: "Don't be so dramatic, Gio," shaking her head. She waved her hand dismissively. "Life is short. She shouldn't let some man keep her from enjoying herself."

Giovanni cocked an eyebrow at Maximo, but his father only shrugged. "It might be a little soon, but Donna has a point. The girl has to move on, and," he turned to me, "you're in the most romantic part of Italy, on a honeymoon. Might as well go out with a nice Italian boy while you're here."

How? How did the conversation end up here? I still had a faint tan from my engagement ring, not to mention the crippling crush on my best friend. Though I couldn't exactly tell them *why* a nice Italian boy was the last thing on my mind. "I'll think about it," I said carefully.

"Your generation and your thinking." Donna shook her head distastefully. "If you're not careful, life will pass you by. Giovanni is the same. We find all these women to set him up with. He always says he will 'think about it,' and never calls, never does anything, and look at him, single as can be. Trust me, thinking is no way to find happiness. In fact, I'd say it's the dumbest thing you can do."

"Now, now, Donna," said Giovanni, holding his hands up to show his innocence. "If I'm not interested in someone you want to set me up with, why should I go out with them? That would be unkind."

"Well, you're not interested because you're thinking too much." Donna waved her hands at him for emphasis. "That's my whole point."

"That's not the problem, Donna."

"Then what is?"

"I—" Giovanni ran a hand through his hair. "I don't know. But if you introduce me to someone I like, I promise to go out with them. Okay?"

"How about Alana?"

Giovanni blinked at her, then me, his blue eyes wide with surprise. "What?"

"It's perfect!" Donna took my arm, pulling me closer to her and Gio. "Here is a beautiful woman who just had her heart broken. Why don't you take her out on a date and show her what a real gentleman is like. And don't say you're not interested, because I know for a fact that is not true. She's gorgeous."

"You are very beautiful," Giovanni said to me, smiling softly. He turned back to Donna. "But it's like you said, she just had her heart broken. The last thing she needs is another man bothering her with a date."

"How do you know that?" Donna crossed her arms. "Did you ask her out?"

Giovanni flashed his father a look I couldn't read, but Maximo just shrugged. Gio shoved his hands in his pockets as he turned to me. Was he… blushing? He smiled softly. "Would you like to go on a date with me, Alana?"

Immediately, my eyes found Forrest. "Um, I don't know," I said. One word from her, and I'd never date again. But if she knew what I felt on the boat, if she was embarrassed, maybe clearing the air with a date wasn't a bad idea. "What do you think?" I asked her.

My best friend shrugged indifferently; her soft smile carved a faint dimple on her cheek. "I think you should go, if you want to." She fiddled with her rings as she spoke. "I think you should do what you want."

My heart fell. Why did I always forget she wasn't interested? A failed engagement later, and I was back where I started — hoping the next date would be the one to finally end my pining, the way I hoped before every date for the past eight years. "Sure," I told Gio. "I'll go out with you."

Maximo clapped his hand on his son's back. "Hell must have frozen over," he teased. "My son, the shameless player, is finally going on a proper date."

Giovanni groaned, pressing a hand to his forehead. "*Papa*, I am not a player."

"That," he tapped his son's chest, "is what players always say."

"What's all this about?" A voice interrupted.

"Giovanni and Alana are going on a date."

"Gio? A date?"

The news rippled through the party, and the rest of my conversations were interrupted by congratulatory pats on the back. I tried to share their excitement, if only to be polite, but the whole thing felt hollow. Gio was the most beautiful man I'd ever seen, let alone gone out with, but he wasn't Forrest. The corner of my eye stuck to her like glue, desperate to know what she made of all this. If what she said on the boat was true, if there was an explanation for everything that came after, if she really —

Who was I kidding? I couldn't keep living like this. It was the same with Matthew. Months into dating him, I still clung to the hope of Forrest. I tried not to appear too in love, too over her, just in case. I studied her smile when I talked about him, searching for some sign that she was... Jealous? Forlorn? Hoping I'd break up with him? I would have left Matthew in an instant if I saw even a trace of whatever I searched for so desperately. I never did.

Two phrases followed me into my dreams that night. *You should go, if you want to*, and *you have no idea what that did to me.* Opposing words from the honeycomb voice that was slowly driving me insane.

They were all right. I needed to move on, just not from Matthew.

I met Giovanni in the lobby the next day promptly at 7:30. His hands were stuffed in the pockets of his linen pants as he leaned against the front desk and spoke softly to Bianca in Italian. I couldn't understand the words, but Bianca's tone was comforting. Gio bit his lip apprehensively — almost as if he were nervous.

Bianca cleared her throat when she saw me; Giovanni turned around and smiled. "*Ciao*, Alana," he said, kissing both cheeks. His gold chain hung over a fitted black t-shirt that showed off his muscles.

"*Ciao*, Giovanni." I crossed my arms over the crochet tank that I knitted for stress relief in the spring, powder blue with orange and white diamond shapes. Forrest smiled approvingly when I put it on with loose-fitting jeans, before she left for dinner in downtown Positano. She told me she hoped the date went well before disappearing with her sketchbook.

Today we took the ferry to Sorrento to wander the city and swim at Bagni Regina Giovanna — a quiet beach secluded by cliffs and woods, with inviting turquoise water. The day felt like many of the others we'd spent here. We ogled over art galleries, smelled the soaps and candles that lined the souvenir shops, ate focaccia sandwiches for lunch, then shed our clothing to swim in the afternoon. I supposed I really did imagine that moment in the boat, when I was almost absorbed by her orbit. There was no trace of last night's hunger in her eyes.

In other words, there was no reason for me to cancel the date.

I tried not to be down about it.

"So, there's this beautiful little restaurant up in the hills with the best ravioli you've ever tasted," he said. "Plus, the view is amazing. Mountains everywhere, ocean in the distance. I was thinking we could go there if you'd like."

I nodded, ignoring the sinking feeling in my chest. "That sounds perfect."

I clung to Giovanni on the back of the Vespa as he drove us to the restaurant, trying not to think about Forrest's hands on my waist when I was the driver, steering us around the coast. The restaurant was a low-level stone building near the top of a mountain, with a large patio shaded by a vine-covered canopy. The hostess was a childhood friend of Giovanni's, and she led us to a table in the corner of the patio, with a prime view of the ocean, framed by cliffs. We started with burrata and two glasses of red wine as we studied the gold-tinted landscape surrounding us.

Giovanni told me about the Galleria Borghese, the art museum where he worked as a tour guide to pay bills as he earned his PhD in art history. I told him about my work as a web designer, and the passion for clothing that I reawakened on this trip. He called me "impressive," and I said the same about him. We ordered two different types of ravioli, and the waiter refilled our wine. The conversation was pleasant, if a little awkward. I smiled at him as I swirled my glass and tried not to wonder where Forrest had gone for dinner. I tucked a loose hair behind my ear as he thrummed his fingers against the table. We locked eyes, and he smiled at me warmly.

It was when our conversation lapsed that I realized couldn't do this. Gio was as kind as his family. I couldn't string him along — not when my heart was somewhere in Positano, wherever Forrest had gone with her sketchbook.

He blurted, "So, I'm gay," right as I said, "I think I'm in love with my best friend."

We stared at each other, dumbfounded. "Wait, what?" We said in unison.

Giovanni burst into laughter, and I joined, giddy with relief. He tilted his head to the sky, flashing his teeth. I opened my mouth speak, but he shook his head. "No, no," he said, "you first."

I told him everything. Our night on the lake, the years of pining, my complicated feelings before the wedding, the charged energy between us that emerged here, our maybe-almost-kiss last night. I told him how sometimes she was so beautiful I forgot to breathe, how I felt that way even at my wedding. Like I was being killed and reborn all at once. How I knew in my heart she didn't feel the same, even if that very heart fluttered wickedly whenever she said my name. I told him it felt like a cage sometimes, wanting her so much my chest could split open, feeling my desire rot inside me. I told him that was why I said yes to this date, how dating always felt like a chore. The people were nice enough, but they weren't Forrest. No one could be. Still, I had to find some way to move on. Wanting her was the best, worst feeling in the world — and if I didn't stop it would eat me alive.

Giovanni gaped at me. When I finished, he muttered "Mamma Mia," under his breath, shaking his head. "I think," he said, "we're going to need more wine."

We ordered a bottle to share, and he tapped off my glass as our ravioli arrived. It was just as heavenly as Gio described. Mine had a lemon, spinach and ricotta filling, topped with lemon butter sauce, while Giovanni chose mushroom ravioli in truffle sauce; both were topped with a generous helping of parmesan. The lemon sauce creamy and comforting, while the ravioli filling was as light as a cloud. It was easily one of the best meals I had in Amalfi.

I said, "So, I'm assuming your family doesn't know you're gay, and I obviously won't say anything, but... Do you want to talk about it?"

"Bianca knows," he said matter-of-factly, as he sipped his wine. "I'm not out to my parents yet. They'd still accept me. It's just... I've been a disappointment to my parents in many areas of my life. Studying art, moving to Rome, waiting to start a family. None of it was what they wanted, and I don't want to see them disappointed about this, too." He shrugged. "I'm proud of who I am."

"I get it." I nodded as I cut into a ravioli. "The lukewarm acceptance still hurts... you feel like everyone is wishing you will grow out of who you are, but no one is brave enough to say it. That's how my parents are. I think that's why they were so excited about my wedding — marrying a man and all that." I frowned into my pasta. "It's obviously better than being rejected outright, but sometimes I wonder, why do I have to settle for that? Why can't I wish for a world where I don't have to earn their love?"

Giovanni nodded solemnly. "My mom has always wanted me to get married, have children, and take over the Valeri. If I had a Euro every time she mentioned 'my future wife...'" He shook his head. "They're already in denial about how I don't want to run the hotel. I do not want to hear them regret another part of me. Maybe I'm not doing right by the gay community, to still be in the closet at my age. I know it's important to come out, but I can't bring myself to do it."

"Gio." I propped my elbows on the table as I spoke. "You don't 'owe' coming out to anyone. Coming out should never be expected, not when there's so much at stake for doing it. It's a privilege, not an obligation. The whole point of being Queer is to be true to yourself. If waiting to come out is what's best for you, then you *are* being true to yourself. That's my opinion, anyway."

Gio nodded, smiling softly. "I never thought of it that way, probably because I hang out with too many academics." He sipped his wine and smiled. "You're so wise, Alana!"

I waved my hand dismissively. "Not really. I'm a big idiot in my own life, clearly."

"Maybe you need to be gentler on yourself." Giovanni smiled as he swirled his wine glass, eyeing me thoughtfully. "So, when are you going to tell Forrest you're in love with her?"

I choked on my wine at the question, starting a coughing fit that drew curious looks from the other diners. I felt like Peggy that first dinner at the Valeri's, struggling for breath as I fought my shock. Giovanni laughed until he had tears in his eyes.

"I can't," I said when I finally regained composure, my voice hoarse.

"Ah, ah." He wagged his finger at me. "Never say 'can't.' What if she feels the same way?"

The thought was laughable. "She doesn't, trust me."

"How do you know that?"

"I just do."

"Well, with evidence that compelling—"

"Shut *up*!" My face flushed at the mirth in his eyes.

Giovanni giggled — actually giggled – at me. "So feisty, Alana. Do you kiss Forrest with that mouth?"

I groaned and lightly smacked his shoulder with my napkin.

"Okay, okay! I'm just kidding. Have mercy!"

I smiled through my blush, and folded my hands in my lap civilly. "I know."

He grinned, leaning back in his chair as he folded his arms. "In all seriousness, I don't think the situation is what you think. I mean, I obviously wasn't there, but it sounds like you almost kissed last night. Just because she wasn't into you when she was nineteen doesn't mean she still feels that way." He shrugged. "Either way, you won't know until you tell her."

Damn him for being so convincing. He was right. Telling her was rational, but after all our years of friendship, I couldn't bear the thought. "I told you I can't." I shuddered as I cut into another piece of ravioli. "I don't want to lose her."

"If some silly feelings are enough to drive her away, she's not a true friend." His eyes were gentle as he spoke. "But something tells me it will be alright." His smile fell as he leaned forward; his eyes flared as dark as the ocean at this hour. "Isn't it better to take the risk and fail than to say nothing and always regret it?"

I frowned, tilting my head to the side. "What if I regret telling her?"

"People never regret saying how they feel." He swirled his wine glass; the cloud in his eyes lifted. "But a wise woman told me that if you're not ready yet, it's okay."

I imagined it — telling her. Her brow furrowing in discomfort at the confession, her voice exuding composure, refusing me. Her hands studiously avoiding mine thereafter. Her awareness would inflict awkwardness on every interaction. It could take months for us to go back to normal, maybe even years.

Maybe we never would.

But I also saw the freedom in being honest, in knowing I wasn't keeping secrets from her. Not anymore. Maybe Forrest deserved to know. If my feelings could change our friendship, she had a right to make that choice, even if it meant losing her. The thought was terrifying, but Giovanni was right. It was the only real path forward. Waiting wouldn't make it any easier. "I am ready," I told him. "I'm just scared."

"Of course you are." His eyes softened. "You've been scared for eight years. But it's never too late to take your power back. I, for one, am proud of you.”

I smiled shakily. “It will be a relief, to be done with secrets.”

Giovanni tilted his wine glass toward me, and I toasted him in return. “I can't wait to hear how it goes.”

We relaxed on that patio well into the darkness, lethargic from the pasta and the bottle of wine. My head was light, my limbs heavy, but my nerves surrounding Forrest finally subsided. Nothing could break the peaceful spell I'd fallen into, as I watched the stars glimmer over the moon.

We had just ordered a Torta Caprese to share for dessert when Giovanni clapped his hands and said, “Okay, I have offered my opinion on your life, it's only fair if you do the same.” He smiled as he leaned forward in his seat. “What do you think, Alana?”

I stroked my chin like a mock intellectual. “About what?”

“Anything, everything.” He shrugged.

I smiled playfully. "Well, if *anything* is on the table... I think you should tell your parents that you don't want the Valeri before Bianca accepts the apprenticeship."

Gio raised his eyebrows. "You think she'd take it?"

I shrugged. "She thinks your parents will let her run the hotel."

"But she's worked her whole life for it." Gio waved his hands in the air for emphasis. "She's perfect for the job."

"According to her, they don't think she's charismatic enough? I don't know." I shook my head. "It doesn't make sense to me."

Gio frowned. "Isn't that a thing in the U.S.?" he asked. "People didn't vote for Hilary Clinton because they wouldn't want to have beer with her?"

I nodded.

"I read that in an article. Absolutely moronic." Gio shuddered. "Who would want to get beer with a politician? That sounds like the dullest evening ever."

I laughed as I shook my head.

"I hate all that 'charisma' talk." Gio stared at me intently. "My father tells me I have charisma, but that doesn't mean I should run the Valeri." He shook his head. "I always helped with the hotel growing up, and I hated it. I wasn't good at keeping track of the reservations, the complaints, the *laundry*." He frowned as he flicked his gaze toward the sea, watching the water's flickering pathway to the moon. "I hated having to act cheerful for the guests all the time. They would insult me, hit on me, demand ridiculous errands, and I just had to take it." He shuddered. "Now, I spend the days talking and writing about art. I work at one of the best museums in Rome, I am one year away from completing my PhD, and they still think my career is just a phase. Why would I put myself through all that hard work if it wasn't my dream?"

He looked down at his hands; his eyelashes cast shadows on his cheeks. "It's even worse because the hotel is Bianca's dream, and she's perfect for the job. She's organized and hard-working, sets boundaries with the guests, and has the vision to grow the business. I don't get how they don't see her potential."

As he spoke, the waiter presented us with a Torta Caprese, a flourless chocolate cake that is the region's specialty. After we nodded our thanks to the waiter, I said: "Maybe you should tell your parents that. I know it's scary because you're keeping a lot from them right now, but you can tell the truth in pieces. Start with the hotel, because that affects Bianca. Save coming out for when you feel ready."

He nodded thoughtfully. "That is a good point." He frowned as he folded his arms. "I really don't want to be in the closet forever."

"You won't be."

He smirked at me, a dimple denting his left cheek. "I'll tell them the truth if you tell Forrest." He cocked an eyebrow. "Tomorrow."

Maybe it was the wine, or the vast, tranquil scenery, or perhaps Giovanni's unwavering faith emboldened me. Maybe I was just crazy. But for some reason, I met his stare and smiled as I said, "Deal."

Giovanni's friend gave us a ride back to the hotel, since we were both too drunk for the Vespa. She said

I was the first girl Gio had taken out since he was a teenager, to which he added: "and the best beard I've ever worn, including the one on my face." We erupted into giggles as the landscape whizzed by on the winding roads. She dropped us off at the Valeri, and Gio promised to collect the Vespa in the morning.

As we walked up the cobblestone driveway to the hotel's entrance, I told him: "You know, I think this might have been the best date I've ever been on."

He cocked an eyebrow at me. "Not last night with Forrest?"

I frowned. "That wasn't a date."

Giovanni chuckled, then winked at me. "Sure, Alana." Warmth filled his eyes as he smiled at me. "This is one of the best dates I've been on, too. There will not be a second one, for obvious reasons, but I would love to be your friend."

I beamed at him, suddenly giddy. I always found friendships to be the most romantic of all. "I would love that, Gio."

We hugged as we parted ways in the empty lobby, bound for opposite sides of the inn. Before he disappeared down the hall, Giovanni pointed at me and said, "Tomorrow."

"Tomorrow," I promised.

Forrest was asleep when I got back. I lay awake for a while, listening to her steady breaths. My promise to Giovanni rang with each heartbeat. *Tomorrow, tomorrow, tomorrow.* I knew he was right. I also knew telling her would change everything.

I just didn't have a choice.

22

"Alana, you have to choose," said Forrest, standing in the middle of the narrow street. "This café, or this one."

She wore loose jean shorts and a blue tank top over her bathing suit, while I'd opted for a sleeveless cotton dress to cover mine. We were about to spend the day touring Capri. The boat left at nine, and Forrest and I hardly said two words to each other as we scrambled out of bed and rushed to the water on foot. The lack of a Vespa made us later than we hoped, but we had enough time for a to-go cappuccino.

"This one's fine," I said, pointing to the one that was about three steps closer to where she stood. Forrest nodded and didn't say another word to me as we bought our cappuccinos and headed to the dock. We found a small group of tourists and joined them in waiting for our guide. I tried to make small talk, but Forrest, the extrovert between us, was silent. I told the only other American in the group that I was traveling with my best friend; Forrest stayed silent as she sipped her coffee.

An older man in jean shorts and a striped t-shirt introduced himself as Leo, our guide. "We will spend the day touring one of the most beautiful places in the world, the island of Capri," he said. "Prepare to have your life forever changed."

It took about forty minutes to reach the island. Forrest and I sat together toward the front of the boat. "So, what did you end up doing last night?" I asked her.

She shrugged. "Drawing, dinner, hung out with Bianca."

"Nice. What did you draw?"

"Nothing special. Just some experimental stuff."

I nudged her playfully. "You always say that about your drawings, then end up painting something that belongs in the Louvre."

Forrest's smile rang like tin between us. Something about her was hollow.

I nodded and studied the glimmer on the water. Capri's outline grew larger, until we could distinguish the limestone cliffs and the dots of bushes topping them. The cliffs towered overhead as spots of greenery sprung implausibly along the edge.

It contrasted beautifully with the deep blue water and clear sky. Forrest and I gaped in silence; thankfully, the island's splendor engulfed the awkwardness between us.

If any place could make me brave enough to confess my feelings, this was it.

Our guide slowed the boat as it rounded the cliffs, and hurried through a recap of the island's history, which was settled by the Greeks but changed hands to the Romans, the medieval Italians, and even Napoleon, before becoming a modern haven for tourists, artists, and celebrities on vacation. Capri seemed permanently engulfed by the tranquility of a quiet summer afternoon, glamorous and understated at once. The imposing limestone cliffs only heightened the mystique. We approached one that formed an archway in the middle that was large enough for our boat to pass through. The arch was tiny in comparison to the rock itself, which made the boat feel miniature.

"This is Faraglione di Mezzo," said Leo. "Couples, get ready. Local legend says if you kiss as we pass under the arch, your love will last forever."

Instinctively, Forrest and I locked eyes. Her dark eyes widened slightly, lips parting; then she turned away, facing the rock. My heartbeat rang in my ears as our boat passed through. A few couples kissed around us as Forrest looked up and studied the limestone. She positioned her legs so we wouldn't touch.

We passed through, and I could have sworn I saw Forrest sigh in relief.

This was going to be a long day.

After guiding our boat past the green and white grottos, Leo left us at the Marina Piccolo with caprese sandwiches to pass a few hours wandering the island. While most of the group waited for the crowded bus to take them into town, Forrest and I walked uphill, through winding one-way streets toward the town of Capri, Capri's mountains looming to our left.

Neat white buildings fit together against the hillside as we approached the island's largest town, following the narrow stone streets. There were shops selling expensive clothing, fabrics, and postcards, places where the hill dropped and the street became a tunnel beneath buildings. The occasional iron gate separated us from pathways to private residences, where dogs and cats sprawled in the sun. Aside from the busier roads where tourists crowded around the Basilica, designer stores and restaurants, the town was surprisingly desolate. It was clean in the way that made it hard to imagine people living here, despite the many homes we passed.

We stopped for gelato at a tiny storefront along a hilly street away from the center of town, toward the mountain. The strawberry gelato was creamy, tangy and refreshing, and the light, thin cone tasted homemade. We ate it quickly to keep the heat from sending the gelato dripping down our fingers, which at least removed the awkwardness from our silence — staring at the view of town, cliffs, and sea, the Sorrento Coast a thin strip of land in the distance.

Forrest turned to me as she pointed at the mountain. "Want to go up there after this?" she asked.

I nodded. I would have said yes to anything she asked, anything to get her talking to me. "There's got to be some cool hiking trails, here. Right?"

She nodded and smiled softly back, flashing one dimple, as she looked up Capri's hiking trails on her phone. After some scrolling, we hailed a cab to reach the trail's entrance, a long stone staircase at the base of the mountain, that led into the woods. The white houses that clustered to form the town of Capri stretched across the greenery behind us, the sea to our right. The woods were soothing in the summer heat, and beyond it, the colors of the landscape were as vibrant as gemstones. Somehow the view grew more breathtaking with each step, as the stairs led us from the woods to a cliffside, offering sweeping views of the ocean. Several times, we stopped in our tracks, awestruck by the beauty of it.

I could almost forget Forrest was ignoring me.

In all our years of friendship, she'd only been upset with me twice. Once, when I forgot to text her I made it home safe after a night out in DC, after she'd gone home with her then-girlfriend. And another when I put a mug on the bottom rack of the dishwasher (Forrest had a very specific way of washing dishes, learned from her aunt and uncle.) Each time it went something like this: A brief silent treatment before she confronted me in a firm but gentle tone, where she explained her feelings and asked for my perspective. It felt more like a therapy session than a fight.

This silence was sharper than the others. It didn't sit right.

Maybe she knew what I told Giovanni. I reminded myself that she turned the boat around. Maybe I made her uncomfortable. Maybe if I could prove to her that I was her friend first, that my feelings were irrelevant, maybe she'd look past it.

It was a terrible plan, but it was the only plan I had.

I would just play it cool.

"I'm glad we're doing this together," I said as Forrest stopped on the steps to take a photo, sliding to the right so a couple descending the stairs could pass.

Forrest pocketed her phone and smiled politely back. "Me, too."

"You're such a good friend," I added. Another olive branch.

She just nodded, her eyes disinterested, and continued up.

The trail led us to the Villa San Michele, a 19th-century mansion with halls of statues, sweeping gardens, and breathtaking seaside overlooks. We wandered the gardens under a canopy of vines rimmed by Roman-style columns, past magenta and violet flowers, but skipped the home, too enchanted by the natural beauty surrounding us to spend even a minute indoors — no matter how beautiful those indoors might be.

Then we crossed the mountain to the other side of the island, to Anacapri, where tourist-centered pizza parlors and tacky souvenir shops reigned supreme, not a designer store in sight. We were here for the funicular, a chair lift that carried tourists over the terrain to very top of the island, to the best views on Capri.

Turns out, so was every other tourist.

"This line is insane," Forrest grumbled as we walked toward the back of it, past couples, families, and friend groups carrying cameras and backpacks, filling the narrow street.

We didn't even reach the back before I said, "Are you sure you want to do this?"

She turned back to me with a blank expression. "I'll do whatever you want."

But I saw the droop in her smile. "I bet we can walk to the top."

She looked up the mountain doubtfully, where the funicular churned chairs toward a point we couldn't see. "You think so?"

"Yeah, why not?" I smiled at her, turning away from the line, walking the other direction. "It's worth a try, and it'd be better than waiting in line all day."

Forrest smiled softly and nodded as she followed me. "Yeah, waiting is the worst," she muttered, kicking a rock with her shoe.

I didn't know what to say to that, so I pretended not to hear.

We made our way up a winding gravel road past the outskirts of Anacapri, up a dirt trail full of hairpin turns, barely saying two words to each other. The whole way I agonized over what to say. To ask what was wrong, or to let her be. I didn't want to foist my anxiety onto her, if this was all in my head, but I couldn't bear the thought of letting her anger fester, unresolved. Every time I opened my mouth, I stopped myself. There was no room for my words. The only sound to break the silence was wind combing grass.

We kept walking, and I pretended to lose myself the view. I pretended the sea breeze, white cliffs and endless ocean were enough to drown the emotion raging inside me. When we reached the top, it almost was. A grassy meadow stretched out ahead, ringed by cliffs, water, and a cloudless sky. The town of Capri was a cluster of white dots; the thin strip of Italian coast seemed bare at this distance. It felt like 'The Sound of Music,' like the world was nothing but possibility, unfurling its infinite self before us. Forrest's jaw dropped at the sight of it, her lips forming the delighted 'O' she always made when admiring art. Her joy stung because I couldn't share it. I was watching her behind glass.

She rested her hands behind her head, revealing a sliver of stomach underneath her blue tank top as she scanned the horizon panting. Her lively eyes meticulously avoided mine as she retrieved her water bottle from her purse and took a long sip.

I crossed and uncrossed my arms, then drank my water. "What a view." It was the only think I could think to say.

She nodded, her eyes grazing mine for only a second before facing the scenery once again, pointedly distracted from me.

I decided to mirror her. I looked away.

We took a cab back to Marina Piccola to rejoin the tour group, finding a spot at the front of the boat to sit in prickly silence, unchanged since the hike. After pulling away from the dock, Leo dropped anchor so we could swim in the sea, a refreshing change from our trek in the heat. I could see it on Forrest's face, the way she closed her eyes treading water and tilted her face to the sun. My jitters eased, too, as my body bobbed with the current. Maybe Forrest was tired. Maybe floating in saltwater would mend whatever ruptured between us.

I was about to say something, to test that theory, when Leo called: "Back in the boat! We are going to the Blue Grotto."

We huddled together under our towels as Leo described the most famous site on Capri, where ethereal blue light glimmered along the walls of a narrow cave beneath the island. The grotto was only accessible through long, narrow wooden boats. A local guide would yank us through the little gap in the rock by rope, and we'd be surrounded by blue waves of light.

The island of Capri charges an 18-euro tax to enter the grotto, but tourists end up paying much more than that. The guides charge extra to sit in their boat, to cut the hours-long line that winds up the cliffside steps to the Grotto. A tourist could pay hundreds of euros to enter it, only to stay there for a few minutes. It cheapens the magic, Leo said, because beauty shouldn't be priced.

"You're lucky," he continued. "We'll get in at a fair price and cut the line. My daughter is dating one of these scam guides, and he wants me to like him."

Forrest chuckled. "Is it working?"

Leo faced her with a flat expression. "No. But at least I can get my tour groups into the Grotto until she leaves him for someone worth her time." He smiled at her. "The thing about dating is, it matters how they treat strangers. The way a partner treats people who don't matter to them is how they will one day treat you, when the sparks go away. You can't let romantic gestures distract you from that — not even the Blue Grotto." He began walking back inside the boat, to the steering wheel. "My daughter is smart," he called over his shoulder. "She'll see that eventually."

Sure enough, a guide with a nervous smile greeted us when we arrived at the Grotto, his gaze flickering to Leo with every other word as he welcomed us. After handing over 18 euros each, the guide directed us to enter the long boats in pairs. We jumped back into the water and swam toward the entrance to board the boats.

When it was our turn, Forrest and I lay side by side in the boat as our guide prepared to pull the us through the low tunnel. My breaths grew short as I stared at the cliffs and felt all the places Forrest and I were touching. Forearms, shoulders, the side of our legs. Out of the corner of my eye, I noticed her head turn toward mine, but when I looked back at her, she snapped her gaze to the sky.

Then, the boat jerked forward, and the sky disappeared.

Darkness filled my vision as we passed through the mouth of the cave, close enough to touch the rock's rough edges. My stomach dropped at the speed of our movement, as the walls closed in, the darkness constricting as we passed through the Grotto's entrance. In a flash, we were inside.

Waves of electric blue light flickered across the ceiling, as the sound of sloshing waves echoed off the cave walls, against the glowing sea and ribbons of light. Below us, the water was so bright it looked alien; the light seemed to take a life of its own as it danced across the cave to the rhythm of the current. Forrest gasped lightly at the sight, and the Grotto amplified the noise. We were still touching. As I sat up, I turned my head to look at her. The blue light illuminated her skin, and her eyes wide with wonder. To my delight, she turned back.

"This is insane," I whispered as I stared into her eyes. The darkness made them feel infinite, like I could see to her soul. Traces of the Grotto's light sparkled in them, as her gaze dropped to where our hands touched.

"It is," she whispered back. She pulled her quickly hand away quickly, then grabbed a waterproof disposable camera that she'd bought for the trip. "Smile, Alana."

I grinned softly as she snapped a photo, then grabbed the camera to take one of her. In her blue bikini with her wet hair spilling down her shoulders, bathed in cerulean light, Forrest looked radiant. She smiled widely, both dimples flashing brilliantly, as if her morning moodiness were a fever dream. The camera clicked, and I was grateful to capture her looking like this, looking at me.

Our guide motioned at the two of us and reached for the camera. "I take for you?" he said.

We nodded and scooted next to each other as he pointed the camera at us, our arms wrapped around the other's shoulders. Though she smiled for the picture, I could feel Forrest's body tense next to mine, as if she were holding her breath. My heart fluttered, and I tried not to squeeze her shoulder too tight, to respect the distance she put between us.

The camera clicked. *"Bellisimo,"* he said, handing it back.

Forrest smiled politely, but the joy from before vanished. Her fingertips grazed her shoulder where I touched her, then she extended her hand to take the camera back from the guide. She didn't say another word to me in the Grotto. We studied the cave wordlessly for a few minutes more, until we had to lie down again, and our guide yanked us back into the daylight.

The cool sea water was a refreshing reprieve as we swam back to the boat.

The sky shifted from sunny to gray as we road back to Positano. Dark smudges of rain grew larger on the horizon, inching toward the shore as we rode back. Sitting in wet bathing suits made us restless, despite the day of adventure. By the time we returned, it was pouring. Water seemed to fall down and up at once, as raindrops ricocheted off the streets. When we got off the boat, I had to squint to make out the Positano buildings, as we thanked Leo and began the trek back to the Valeri. We took a hard left in the main plaza and walked up a narrow alley that held a staircase up the cliffs. The quiet between us rang louder than the thundering rain.

I started speed walking through it, to escape the water, even though I was already soaked to the bone. But Forrest lagged behind, walking slowly, her eyes glued to the ground. I stopped when I realized I'd left her.

"There's no point running," she said, her pace steady. "It's too far."

I crossed my arms as I waited for her to catch up. "I don't think we could have driven the Vespa in this, anyway. The visibility is awful."

She nodded but didn't say anything.

We were halfway up the steps when I had enough. This was my best friend. I couldn't imagine what I possibly did to warrant her anger, but I would make her tell me what I did. I would make us work this out, because there was no other way forward. I needed her too much.

I stopped at the top of the stairs, between two houses with closed shutters and water streaming off the roof. Forrest halted behind me, rain streaking between us.

"Forrest, what's going on?" I said, crossing my arms. "Are you mad at me?"

Her expression stayed flat as she locked eyes with mine. So she was mad, then. I took a shaky breath as she shifted her hips from one side to the other and sighed in frustration. Finally, she said: "How was your date?"

"My what?" I blinked at her in surprise. "He's gay."

Forrest's mouth opened, then shut; her eyes never left mine. "Oh."

"It was fun, though." I crossed my arms. "I think we'll be friends."

"Oh."

We stood like that for a moment, staring dumbly at each other. She didn't look any less angry.

Cautiously, I took one step toward her. "Is this about the Vespa? Look, I'm sorry. I wasn't thinking, I didn't mean to mess up our plan."

Forrest dropped her crossed arms to her side. "Of course it's not the Vespa." Forrest frowned at me, as if offended. "Come on, Alana. You know how I feel about you."

I studied her guarded gait, the hurt in her brown eyes, the way her breath seemed caught between her lips, and glowered at her. "What the hell is that supposed to mean?"

Forrest flinched at my reply. "You know what it means." Her eyes narrowed as she studied my face. "You're mad at me? Really, Alana?"

My voice trembled as I snapped: "How would I know how you feel, Forrest? You never told me! I pined after you for *years*. You gave me no indication that you could ever want me back. I would have known if you did, because I hung onto your every word like my life depended on it. For years, I waited for you, because what else could I do? You're *Forrest*." The rain slapped my hands as I gestured wildly at her. "You know exactly how I feel about you. You've known since we were nineteen, and you didn't say anything. So don't go blaming me now."

Forrest stepped toward me defiantly. "When was I going to tell you, Alana? When we were in college and I almost destroyed our friendship by hurting you? When we were living together, and my life was in shambles, and I would have only dragged you down? When I started grad school and we were living in different states? When you were dating Matthew? In case you forgot, you were *engaged*. I thought I was going to lose you forever, but I didn't say anything. I didn't *do* anything because you finally had what you wanted. I care about you way too much to stand in the way of what you want. But my mistake, Alana. I should have just read your mind."

"Oh, please." I said, meeting her glare. "I want *you*. There never would have been a Matthew if I thought, even once, that I had a chance with you."

At once, the anger melted off Forrest's face, replaced with wide-eyed shock. The roaring rain was the only sound between us as we gaped at each other. I longed to take back what I said, to apologize, but I couldn't.

Because then she kissed me.

23

It was everything I wanted faster than I could process. Forrest's lips parting my mine as her fingers found their way behind my head, tangling my hair. Her delicate, earnest movements pulling my body into her orbit. She tasted like the rain. When she started to pull away, I wrapped my hands around her lower back, a silent plea that she answered by pressing her hips into mine as she tightened her grip. I gasped, letting air and rain and Forrest fill my throat as she cut off my breath with her kiss. Or maybe she was the air, the water. I needed her too much to know the difference.

I rubbed her hip with my thumb, and she sighed into my mouth. She was everything and nothing like I remembered at nineteen, because we were adults now. Now, I knew her like the back of my hand. I could feel how badly she wanted this by the frantic movement of her fingertips. I could tell by the confidence in her kiss, the way she took control once she felt my encouragement, that she had matured from the uncertain teenager she once was. We both had.

I pulled away just enough to say: "You can't say that about yourself."

She simply moved her kiss to my neck, and my knees almost buckled as her lips traced my throat, gentle as butterfly wings. "Hm?"

"You'd never drag me down, Forrest. You didn't then, and you won't now. I—" I stifled a breathless sigh at her kiss. It was an effort to form words. "I — I'm always better off with you, even when you're at your worst." I sighed as she grazed my nipple with her thumb, over my bathing suit.

"Hm?" I could feel her smile on my neck.

It took all my willpower to pull away, just an inch. "I'm serious."

"And you're a beautiful orator." Forrest smiled as her eyes dropped to my lips. Her expression was electric, her eyes brimming with mischief and unfettered joy. "But maybe we can talk later."

"But—"

"*Fuck*, Al. I take it back." She grabbed my hips and pulled me back, closing the distance between us. "Please just kiss me."

I pressed my forehead into hers and beamed. "Well, because you said 'please.'"

I christened her lips with long, slow kisses. How did I go eight years without this? The more I kissed her, the more it wasn't enough. I yearned to touch every part of her, to peel her wet clothes from her skin, to hear her beg for me, and give her everything she wanted. "I've waited too long," I whispered into her lips, "to not do this in a bed."

Forrest laughed. "Agreed." She smirked as she wound her fingers through my soaking hair, dark eyes scanning my face. "This time, I want to make you scream my name, and we can't do that here."

Only Forrest could make me blush while shivering in the rain. "Okay," I said.

"Okay." We spent a breathless moment staring at each other, Forrest watching me with eyes that could melt butter. "Oh, and Al?"

"Hm?"

"I don't care if there's a fucking fleet of yachts between us and the Valeri," she said, kissing my lips softly before pulling away. "We're not stopping."

We practically ran the rest of the way to the honeymoon suite, giddy with the rush of whatever finally clicked between us. It took longer to get back than we would have liked. We kept pulling each other into alleyways, behind trees and fences to steal kisses, hungry and full of promise, before continuing.

When we finally made it to the honeymoon suite, as Forrest unlocked the door and ushered me in, I grew nervous. I didn't expect to fear what I've always wanted — to feel unsettled by the sense déjà vu that came with living out my dreams. I wrung my hands as she closed the door behind me, her hand resting on the small of my back. This felt impossible. This would change everything.

Just as the doubt sent my hands shaking, as I began to pick apart the nuances of Forrest's confession in the street, I turned around to find her leaning against the door, watching me. A wisp of a smile lifted her lips; her dark eyes drew me in like magnets.

"What?" I asked.

"You're so beautiful." Forrest grinned, flashing her teeth, and I flushed at the tenderness in her eyes. Then, she let out a sudden burst of laughter, like she couldn't help herself. "You went on a date yesterday."

I smiled back. Her giddiness was infectious, easing my nerves. "Well, I was strong-armed into it by some very persistent middle-aged Italians."

"Still, though." She pushed herself off the door and stalked toward me. "It drove me crazy. I thought I had no chance with you, obviously. But then, you almost kissed me on the boat, and I started to think maybe I was wrong... Only to see you go out with a guy who looks like he stepped off a magazine cover." She grabbed my hand and rubbed the top of my wrist with her thumb. "But you're not into him."

"No."

She raised her gaze to mine; her brown eyes were spellbinding. "Even before you knew he was gay?"

"Even before." I stared at her in disbelief. How could she not see how enthralled I was by her? "I've always wanted you, Forrest. Even when I knew — or, um, *thought* I knew — that you'd never feel the same. I just learned to hide it, I guess."

Forrest stepped closer and gently kissed my cheek. She leaned into my ear as she whispered: "I know the feeling."

She kissed down the line of my jaw to my neck, as her hands found their way to the hem of my drenched dress. Gingerly, she grabbed fistfuls of the fabric and lifted it over my head, the dress brushing my lips as she did. The garment smacked the ground as she tossed it aside, and I stood before her in my wet bathing suit.

Forrest fondled the back strap of my bikini until it sprung loose, and she peeled the top away, leaving my breasts bare in front of her. She stared brazenly, running her thumbs gently over my nipples, and I shuddered at her touch. "So you're saying," she murmured, as she tortured me with caresses. "That all those times we lived together, and I wanted you so bad it hurt, Alana." She flicked her eyes to mine as she said my name. "All those times, I could have done this." Her lips enclosed my left breast as she began to tease my nipple with her tongue.

"Forrest," I moaned; between my thighs, I throbbed with need.

As if sensing that, her fingers tugged at the hem of my bathing suit bottoms. "You're so fucking hot, Alana," she whispered as she pulled the bottoms down, and my skin tingled with freedom from the bathing suit. I flushed as I realized I was completely naked. "You want to know something terribly cruel about that night on the lake?"

"You still think about that?" We never talked about this. In eight years, not once.

"Come on, Alana. You're too smart for that." She tucked my hair behind my ear. "I always think about how I never got to taste you. You went down on me, and it was wonderful." She kissed me softly and ran her hands down my sides, to the wet spot between my thighs. "But I was too shy to return the favor."

"You did other things, though." My voice was not my own, hoarse and light.

"But it tortured me," she purred. "Not knowing how you taste." Her hand reached my folds, running fingers through my wetness. "You make the same face," she whispered, slipping her hand inside me. I gasped, struggling to stand upright. Her fingers were delicate, but precise, as if she remembered exactly how I liked to be touched. Then, she took her fingers away too quickly, and I moaned, yearning to feel her inside me again.

Instead, she raised her wet fingers to her lips and sucked, holding my eye contact as she moaned softly at the taste. "You're sensational, Alana," she murmured. "Now sit on the bed."

I obeyed her. There was scarcely time to sit before Forrest was upon me again. She dropped to her knees and tauntingly kissed my inner thighs, drawing closer and closer to my center. She ran her tongue through the heart of me, and my legs quaked at her touch. My body arched to the current of her tongue as she explored me; my pleasure grew with each movement. I could tell by her commanding touch that she relished this — knowing me in this way, slowly unraveling me — so she took her time. Matthew had treated eating me out like a chore, but Forrest seemed thankful to be on her knees. I didn't have to worry that I was taking too long to finish, that she wasn't enjoying this. She was in complete control, and I gladly surrendered myself to her.

I looked down to find her watching me. Her round eyes were darker than I'd ever seen them, studying my expressions with laser focus as she continued, like she was committing every curve of my body, every strained sigh, to memory. She saw through my soul with that look. It was electrifying, to lay myself bare before someone who knew me completely. I'd never felt so vulnerable and safe at once. I wanted to tell her — but instead, I said, "Forrest," and her name became my breath.

I could see the smile in her eyes as she thrust two fingers inside me, working alongside her tongue. I tilted my head back as my muscles tensed, and all I could do was gasp for air and cling to Forrest, utterly at her mercy.

"I love feeling you hold me like this," she whispered, pressing her hand even deeper inside me. "Keep going, Alana. I won't let you go."

My vision went blank as my orgasm reverberated through me, and I cried out the name that made me weak in the knees. Forrest drew out my pleasure with her fingers, and I spasmed at the sensation or waves breaking through my body. Forrest squeezed my hip with her free hand, anchoring me through the ecstasy.

When she removed her fingers and smiled up at me, my wetness coating her lips and cheeks, I was lightheaded and covered in sweat.

"Holy hell, Forrest," I panted as I collapsed on the duvet. Forrest giggled as she grabbed the dress I wore earlier to wipe her face, watching me with laughter in her eyes.

"Alana," she said, shaking her head. "You're divine."

"Me?" I placed a hand against my chest. "I can barely walk because of you."

We laughed together, giddy from the sex and our disbelief that this was real. Then Forrest threw herself on the duvet next to me. She ran her fingertips over my forearm, eliciting goosebumps as she grinned at me.

"What are you doing?" I asked, turning to face her.

"Just looking at you." She smiled bashfully, and I flushed to be the subject of her awe. I kissed her, running my hands down her back, and she shuddered against me.

"Don't get too comfortable," I whispered into her mouth. "We're not done."

"Oh? What did you have in mind?"

"I want you to sit on my face." I brushed my fingers across her lower back. "If you'd be into that."

She ground her hips into mine as she kissed me again. "Is that a trick question?" she teased.

I laughed as I kissed my way from her jawline to her collarbone, down her neck. My touch was reverent; I handled her skin like Renaissance art. "Ride my face until you come, Forrest."

She sat up and straddled me, resting her rear against my chest so I could feel the wetness pooling at her center. Now it was my turn to watch her in wonder. I held eye contact as I massaged her breasts, running my fingers tauntingly over her nipples. Forrest tilted her head back and sighed.

Her wet heat amplified beneath my chest, making me impatient for a taste. So I slid underneath her and parted her with my tongue, catching her by surprise.

"Oh," she gasped before sinking into me, welcoming my lips to hers. Her low moan was honey to my ears. "Oh, Alana."

I rose to meet her, bathing myself in her heat as I carefully uncovered all the places that would make her moan for me again. She jerked her hips, and I pulled her closer to heighten her pleasure. It was a wonder to watch her writhe on top of me, rendered helpless by my touch. Forrest was louder in bed than I was, and I relished the symphony of her groaning, cursing, and crying my name like a plea. Gradually, I quickened the pace, hastening her undoing. Her mouth hung open as her fingernails scratched my head, her eyes glassy as she looked down at me, full of hunger and awe.

It was everything I wanted — pleasing her. So I shifted my fingers deeper, drawing cries from Forrest as an orgasm overcame her. Her inside pulsed against me as she cried my name, sinking deeper into me as I stretched out her undoing, relishing each weighted gasp.

It wasn't until she collapsed on top of me, covering my face with her stomach, that I finally removed my fingers.

She rolled off me, laying on her side as she faced me, sweaty and panting. For a while, she didn't say anything. Just stared like I was the most beautiful art she'd ever seen, like she couldn't believe this was real, like I'd just shattered and remade her completely.

I could tell, because I looked at her the same way.

"Al?" She bit her lip.

"Yes?"

"You're incredible."

My lips parted in disbelief. Of course, I wondered over the years what it would be like to make love to Forrest, but I never imagined this. I never dared to dream that she'd share my devotion. "Look in the mirror, Forrest."

She bit her lip again, then laughed. Her dimples were stunning up close. "I'm so sorry," she said. "I totally messed up your hair."

I laughed because she did. Between our swim in the Mediterranean, the rain, and her wild hands, my hair was a rat's nest. Not that I minded. "Trust me, I don't care. That was..." I looked past her to the ceiling, searching for a sufficient word. "Magic." I smiled at her. "Better than any dream."

She wrapped her arm around my waist and pressed herself against me. "So you've been dreaming about me, huh?"

I laughed at her bashful banter. "For almost a decade, now." I kissed her gently, unhurried. She seemed to melt into me, and I shuddered when she ran her hands down my back. Somehow, my hunger for her grew with every touch. I parted her legs with my knee to find her wetness returned. I smiled as she moaned into my mouth.

This was heaven.

We explored each other, reveled in our pleasure, cried each other's names, until our muscles ached too much to go on. At that point, we slipped under the duvet with drooping eyelids and laced fingers. I lay on my back while Forrest tucked her head against my shoulder and slung an arm over my chest, our legs intertwined. The musky, cozy smell of her sweat filled my nose as she breathed softly against my chest, lulling me into perfect serenity.

Before I fully surrendered to sleep, I heard her whisper: "We should have been doing this the whole time."

24

I woke to Forrest's arm draped across my waist, her light snore sending tiny ripples across the pillowcase. I remembered that I didn't have to turn away from her; what we had just done was far more intimate than watching her sleep. So for once, I stared unabashedly at the freckle under her collarbone that moved slightly with each breath, at her long eyelashes that cast feathery shadows under her eyes. The soft sunset light streaking into the room only heightened her beauty. The rain must have stopped when we fell asleep.

Her eyes fluttered open, and she beamed as she saw me, a wide, lazy grin with dimples that carved grooves down her cheeks.

Were it possible to die from happiness, this moment would have taken me.

"What is it?" she said, her voice scratchy from sleep.

I returned her radiant smile. "You're very beautiful."

She smiled as she kissed me slowly, cupping my cheek with her hand. "You are, too, Al."

As I kissed her back, I didn't think about leaving tomorrow, what this meant for our friendship, or what we'd do when we got home. All that mattered was whatever I could do to keep her kissing me, to keep my body melting at her touch, to keep her laughing in bed when she said, "We should go downstairs," and I said, "Should we?"

We slipped into the shower instead, picking up where we left off. Forrest's hands roamed my skin under the steam, slow and determined. We had nothing but time, now.

There was a family dinner awaiting us on the back patio. The Valeri's were serving a large pan of Nonna's homemade lasagna and a few bottles of red wine from a vineyard up the road. Bianca greeted each of us with a kiss on the cheek and a warm smile; only the faint smudges under her eyes betrayed the weight of the decision she had to make tomorrow. Giovanni was uncharacteristically quiet when he greeted us. Still, he offered Forrest a crooked grin as he said, "You two look like you had a nice talk."

"We did," said Forrest, smirking back. "Alana was very expressive."

I coughed, cheeks flushing as Forrest squeezed my arm.

Gio laughed. "It's too bad you couldn't join us for dinner last night, Forrest. I think you and I would have a lot to talk about."

"I bet," she answered, her eyes shining. It took everything I had not to kiss her right there.

"We're so happy you girls could be here," said Maximo, swooping in behind his son. "Our plan to fix you up with Gio might not have worked, but we still consider both of you like family." He ran a hand through his dark, wavy hair.

"We're honored," I said. "And we will definitely come back to visit, once we save up some money for flights."

"Good." He winked, eyes twinkling like we shared an inside joke. Then he placed a hand on his son's shoulder. "Let's eat!"

We ate bread dipped in balsamic and olive oil, passed around a plate of caprese, stuffed ourselves with lasagna, finished and re-filled our glasses of wine. The Valeris didn't ask me about going home, about what I'd do once I got back. Instead, we talked about our favorite spots on the coast, the souvenirs we got our families, how Italy compared to the U.S.

"I feel much more relaxed here," I said, "and not just because I'm on vacation. People seem to be in less of a hurry. DC can feel very intense, as a place, very career focused. I want to take this way of living back with me, when I start my life over. I want to slow down and appreciate things." I shrugged as I took another sip of wine. "At least, I hope I can. I think it will be easier now that I'm not planning a wedding."

The thought unnerved me for a moment, the void in my time that Matthew used to fill. You always want to believe you could turn your life around, if given the chance, but that wasn't a guarantee. I could re-launch my clothing business and fail. I could fall back into the same habits that got me here. There was no way to know. Only now, Forrest squeezed my knee under the table. "You will," she said.

"It is important, though," said Maximo, "to keep your motivation." He turned to his wife, and his expression softened. "Like Jia, running the Valeri. She works hard, she moves faster than I do, and look at what she's built for our family." He gestured around us, at the hotel, lit up by patio string lights and the moon, at Positano, rising against the cliff, and at the vast indigo sea, stretching endlessly below. "The key is balance. She works hard, but she also makes time for nights like this." He smiled at her as he tucked some hair behind her ear. "She amazes me."

Jia raised an eyebrow, but her cheeks warmed, and gaze softened. "Maxi," she scolded. "No talk of the business, please."

"Actually," said Gio, cautiously laying his silverware on his plate. "There's something I wanted to talk to you two about. It's about the business." He locked eyes with me from across the table. His expression seemed to say, *If you can do it, so will I.*

"Actually," said Bianca. "I have something I need to say, too."

Jia shifted her eyes from her niece to her son, and sighed. "If we have to talk about this now," she said, laying her napkin beside her plate. "I would like to speak first."

Bianca and her cousin shared a nervous look, and Gio nodded to his mother.

But it was Jia who took a deep breath and pressed her lips together, wringing her hands in her lap. "I owe you both an apology," she said, and their jaws dropped in unison. "Before I took over the Valeri," she said, "the hotel always passed to the oldest son, every generation. As you know, I am oldest, but Bianca's father was the son. So where did that leave us? Running the hotel was the only dream I had, and I worked very hard to get your grandfather to see that I could do it. I skipped parties to do night shifts at the front desk, spent summers attending the guests and winters redoing our budget so we could renovate the terrace. This hotel was my life. I had only one boyfriend before Maximo, and he dumped me because I spent all my time here.

"Alfredo never put in the work like I did. He partied, spent too much money, always seemed to have a girl on his arm. At the time, I thought he acted entitled to the Valeri, because he didn't have to work to inherit it. Of course, now I see he didn't want to.

His dream was to be in the city, to live more than he worked, and he did it. My father didn't see it that way. Giving the hotel to me was perhaps more about punishing Fredo for that choice. For a long time, I hated my brother for it — because I never knew, did I finally gain my father's trust, or did Fredo just lose it?

She smiled at her son affectionately. "I wanted Gio to run the hotel ever since he was a boy. In truth, it was not just about what I wanted for you. I think some part of me still felt that the hotel was not completely mine. I thought passing the Valeri to my own child would prove that I earned it. It would give me a legacy. Only now I realize that by tying my legacy to Gio, I was doing the very thing that hurt me in the first place: Passing the hotel to the person who fits tradition over the one who fits the job."

She stood from the table and walked to her son, grabbed his hand. "Gio, I've known since you were a boy that this wasn't your dream. I just wouldn't let myself see it. But you are much too accomplished of an art historian to do anything else. I don't say it nearly enough, but I am so proud of you, my future doctor."

Gio brushed a tear off his cheek as he smiled at her. "Thanks, Ma." He squeezed her hand back. "But I'm not a real doctor."

Jia waved her free hand dismissively. "The only time you say you are not a doctor is if someone asks for one on an airplane. Otherwise, you're the best doctor I know."

Gio laughed. "Thanks, Ma."

"And Bianca," she said, turning to the girls sitting at Gio's side. Bianca blinked at her wide-eyed, frozen at the mention of her name. Jia placed her free hand on her niece's shoulder. "I hope you can one day forgive me for how I've treated you. You are the perfect person to run this hotel. I was hard on you because I see myself in you. Your passion, your work ethic. You earned the Valeri, just like I did. If you even want it. I suppose I'm getting ahead of myself. I don't even know if—"

"I do!" she cried, choking back a sob. She sprung from the table, then froze when she met her aunt's eye. As she straightened her posture and took a hesitant breath, she held her hands tightly to her chest — as if any sudden movement would break this moment. She stood like she was in a museum or a dream. "I do want to run the hotel, *Tía*, more than anything." Her tone was solemn, almost reverent. "I accept your apology, but is that really what you want? Truly?"

Jia's eyes reddened as she studied her prodigy. She nodded once.

Bianca beamed as she moved her hands from her chest to her mouth, covering her crumpled face as her eyes swelled with tears. "I won't let you down, I swear."

"You never have," answered Jia, "and you never will." She wrapped her niece in a tight hug, and when Bianca pulled away, Jia rubbed as tears that left a sheen on her cheeks. She shifted her gaze from her niece to Giovanni. "So, what was it that you wanted to say?"

Gio smiled as he shook his head. "Nothing, Ma."

Bianca grinned. "Me, neither. Though, I do have to send an email tonight."

Jia gently pinched Bianca's cheek, then turned to me and Forrest apologetically. "You two really are part of the family now, huh?"

Forrest smiled reassuringly. "We wouldn't have it any other way."

Gio leaned back in his chair as he rested his hands behind his head, facing Forrest and me. "My father told me this is your last night staying with us," he said. "Where are you going next?"

"Home," I answered.

He dropped his relaxed posture as he leaned into the table, toward us. "You're not spending one last weekend in Italy?"

I shook my head. "When I planned this with my ex, he wanted a few days to adjust to the jet lag before work. Our flight is out of Naples tomorrow."

"Americans and their work." Gio thrummed his fingers on the table. "You haven't even been to Rome."

I shook my head again. "But we'll come back."

"No, no." Maximo's furrowed brow and pursed lips mirrored his son. "You have to see Rome. Gio has a place there. Just move your flight and stay with him."

"We can't do that," said Forrest.

"Why not?"

"We can't intrude on Giovanni."

"I won't even be there," said Gio. "I go back Sunday. You guys could stay for the weekend. I don't mind, as long as you clean up after yourselves."

"But we—"

"I'll make the question easier." Gio clapped his hands together. "Do either of you have somewhere you urgently need to be this weekend, back in the U.S.?"

Forrest and I shared a hesitant glance, then shook our heads.

"Then *go*." Gio seemed to stare into my soul as he spoke, blue eyes flashing. "You're my friend, Alana. It's not an inconvenience. Don't push away something good because you are afraid to accept it. You won't regret saying yes, I promise."

I blinked at him, a lump forming in my throat, then turned to Forrest. She squeezed my knee encouragingly, her wide, dark eyes absorbing my every expression. I knew she'd do whatever I chose. She would follow me to the end of the earth, if I asked.

I turned back to Gio and smiled, my voice slightly hoarse as I said, "I guess we're going to Rome."

After everyone was full on lasagna and lemon cake, a couple empty bottles of wine behind us, I stood up and faced the Valeri family. "I just wanted to say thank you, for everything these past two weeks," I said. "I obviously came into this trip feeling very..." I thought back to my first day here, how miserable and embarrassed I felt, how I couldn't bear to leave the room. "Unhappy. But you guys welcomed us into your family and made this honeymoon better than I ever could have imagined." I turned to Forrest, who smiled proudly as she handed me the tote bag that she'd stashed under her seat. "I just wanted to give you something to say thank you."

For each member of the family, I presented a white handkerchief with their initials embroidered in magenta, framed by stitches of flowers that mimicked the ones outside the hotel. I gave matching neck scarves to Jia and Bianca, a head scarf for Nonna, and ties for Maximo and Giovanni

— made with the pink geometric pattern I found at the clothing shop, to complement their blue uniforms.

"I know you don't technically work here, Gio," I said, "but I thought you'd like a tie to remind you of home as you're giving your brilliant art lectures in Rome."

"I love it," he said, beaming at me.

"You shouldn't have, Alana," said Jia, brushing the embroidered handkerchief with her fingertips. "This is too much."

"It was nothing compared to everything your family did for me," I answered.

As I spoke, Bianca stood up and wrapped me in a sudden, tight hug. "You did more than you know, Alana." She turned to Forrest. "You both did."

Forrest walked over and wrapped her arms around both of us. "We're gonna miss you, B." She smiled proudly at me after she said it, squeezing my shoulder.

"Ok, I need to get in on this," said Gio, joining our hug. One by one, the rest of the Valeri family followed, and soon we were one laughing, tangled mass. Somehow, sandwiched between the Valeris, my eyes found Forrest's. When they did, her dimples deepened, and her eyes shined proudly, as infinite as the night itself.

We said our goodbyes to each family member then. Jia thanked both of us, while Maximo made me promise not to give up on love. Nonna smiled wordlessly as she planted kisses on both of my cheeks, and Bianca made each of us promise three times to visit. "I'll even give you a discount," she said, "since I will get to make that call."

Gio gave me the key to his apartment and told me to leave it with the neighbor when we left. He folded me into a strong hug, rocking slightly as he said: "You and Forrest are made for each other, huh?"

I grinned up at him. "It definitely feels that way."

Gio laughed as he let me go. "I can't believe you thought she was just your friend. I mean, have you seen the way she looks at you?"

I flushed. "Apparently not."

He nudged me playfully with an elbow. "You better invite me to the wedding."

My jaw dropped, but before I could say anything, he squeezed my shoulder. "When the time comes," he added, "and you've gone on a few more proper dates."

I smiled at the thought. I couldn't help myself. When I said yes to Matthew's proposal, it felt like the ground was being swept from under my feet. I twisted myself in knots to ignore the anxious waves that accompanied the image of forever with him. But when I pictured the same with Forrest, I felt calm. Like no other future would do but the one at her side.

For the first time in a while, I was excited for tomorrow.

We picked up where we left off when we were alone again. Kissing between the bedsheets, touching like we had all the time in the world, stopping only to call the airline and change our flight. As we lay in bed together, we Googled things to do and Rome and talked over our weekend. We had to try Carbonara, of course, and the tiramisu bar Forrest found on TikTok. We'd leave some time unplanned, too. I insisted.

"I can't keep my hands off you for that long," I breathed into her neck. "We need intermissions."

Forrest giggled as she wrapped her hands around my waist. "What kinds of intermissions?"

I ran my hands down her back as I planted a kiss below her ear. "I can give you a preview, if you'd like."

"I'd love that." She arched into me, melting at my touch. "I need to know exactly what you have in mind."

Planning the trip was quickly forgotten, when Forrest kissed me like I was salvation. There was nothing we'd see in Rome that could be better than this.

"This is so kind of Giovanni," I breathed, my arms twined behind her neck. "I have no idea how we can ever pay him back."

Forrest rubbed circles on my back with her hands. "We'll figure out a way to thank him," she said. "Maybe we can leave a nice bottle of wine in the apartment, or I can make him a painting. We should definitely invite him to stay with us in the U.S."

Us. The word rolled off her tongue so naturally, it was music. pressed my forehead into hers and smiled. "We definitely will."

When we finally lay down for bed, I checked my phone to find a new text from Carter.

Carter: Home tomorrow! Can't wait to see you love!!!

Me: Just had a last-minute change of plans… We're going to Rome! The Valeri's son has a place there. We'll be home Sunday night.<3

Carter: Aw, that's so fun! I'm SO happy you're doing this!!

I smiled at the screen, thinking of all the nights I'd cried to Carter about Forrest our sophomore year, how fast my fortune changed on this honeymoon. After everything we'd been through together, Carter was the person I wanted most know. I started typing.

Me: Also… I think Forrest and I might be dating now? I'll fill you in when I'm back. Life is a dream!!

Giovanni lived in a one-bedroom apartment above a café in Testaccio, a bustling neighborhood near the Tiber River. It was small but well decorated with vintage furniture and a collection of sculptures and paintings by his artist friends. We arrived in the afternoon following a train ride from Naples. Forrest scarcely spent five minutes studying an abstract painting by the window before I interrupted her with hands on her waist and a kiss on the cheek — what I longed to do whenever I caught a glimpse of her face awed by art. When she turned around to kiss me back, she looked at me with more wonder than I'd seen her bestow on any painting. I smiled as she kissed me, and it was better than my dreams.

She pulled me into the bedroom. It felt like we were teenagers again, only now age freed us from any hesitation, any impulse to pick apart what our desire could mean. My longing for Forrest grew stronger the more I touched her, our physical connection deepened by our emotional one. That night on the lake was nothing to what sparked between us now, each touch guided by years of deciphering Forrest. I was fluent in the subtleties of her face, so I brought her to ecstasy with confidence. If her eyes were wide and slightly glassy, she liked it, and I'd keep going. If she bit her lip, she was feeling unsure, and I'd make a point to call her beautiful. Knowing her deeply made her moans of pleasure irresistible. I would have moved heaven and earth to make her cry my name. I did, more or less.

It was dinner by the time we left the bed.

"I love Rome," said Forrest, as we slid back into our pants.

"Well, we haven't seen any of it yet."

She smirked, flashing a dimple on one cheek. "I'm seeing everything I want to see. Trust me."

We wandered Gio's neighborhood in search of a restaurant and settled on the one that, at 6:30 pm, had already formed a line. We drank beer cans from a convenience store while we waited, then at dinner, split a bottle of rosé and feasted on carbonara and cacio e pepe. We were lulled into a quiet content by our wine and the creamy comfort of parmesan and pecorino, as we talked into the night. Things between us were natural as ever but entirely different. I didn't avert my eyes if Forrest caught me staring at her. She smiled knowingly when our feet brushed, dimples flashing, and even reached across the table to squeeze my fingers.

Once we finished and paid the bill, we took the long way home, with detours to see the river and steal kisses in quiet alleyways. I kept finding her hand or the small of her back just to assure myself this was real. I could almost forget I'd been engaged to Matthew at all, that this trip was supposed to be a honeymoon with someone else. My world began and ended with Forrest. Everything else could wait.

Even the text I woke up to this morning felt unimportant now. The hesitation from Carter that twisted my stomach in knots until Forrest kissed them away.

Carter: I'm happy for you, obvi. I love Forrest. But please be careful, Ally... You're going through a lot right now, and I don't want you to face any more heartbreak!

Rome is not the kind of city you can see in only one day. But that was all the time we had — lessened by our decision to sleep in, by how easily we could convince each other, with only a touch, to stay in bed. By ten, I finally mustered the will to shove Forrest out. My best friend would not spend a day in Rome without taking in the art. I was adamant, no matter how much she giggled and said, "I *am* taking in the art."

I frowned at her. "I don't count."

She stuck out her lower lip as she said: "But you're half Italian."

I laughed at her pouting face as she traced my thigh with her middle finger. "Forrest, seriously."

"No you're right. I'll hate myself if I go to Rome and don't see anything from the Renaissance. That would be blasphemous." She rose and planted a chaste kiss on my lips. "Let's go!"

We decided to start at the Trevi Fountain, as an homage to Lizzie McGuire, and let the day unfold from there.

It was way more crowded than we expected, with eager tourists posing for photos and digging out coins in the crowded piazza. We held hands to keep from losing each other in the crowd, and when we reached the fountain Forrest produced two coins from her front pocket. She turned from the structure to face me. "The proper way to do it is with your right hand, over your left shoulder, according to Wikipedia" she said before tossing hers nonchalantly into the fountain. It plunked in the aquamarine water behind her as she slid the second coin into my palm. "I'm telling you my wish," she added, with a taunting lift to her eyebrows. "I want it to come true."

I smiled slowly as I turned around shoulder-to-shoulder with her, and tossed my coin in, too. I had nothing to wish for but a lame, earnest plea to the universe for more. More days waking up to Forrest and share deep talks at night. More exploring her, kissing her, navigating life beside her. Whatever started between us in Positano, I didn't want it to end. That was all I knew, and two weeks after my failed wedding, all I could stomach asking for.

I leaned into her ear and whispered: "I'm not telling you mine either."

We walked through whatever we could see without reserving tickets in advance. The outside of the Coliseum, Roman Forum, and Pantheon. A chapel with a flat ceiling painted with a breathtaking illusion to look like a dome, since their budget ran out before they could build a rounded ceiling. We walked at a meandering pace with laced fingers, engrossed in conversation. We stopped to eat face-sized focaccia sandwiches for lunch, then continued to the Spanish steps.

Rome reminded me of New York City, only stuffed to the brim with ancient ruins and Italian restaurants. There were crowds of tourists blocking the sidewalk, tacky souvenir shops, scammers and pickpockets. There were hole-in-the-wall café's, trash bags on the curb, and locals cutting around everyone in a huff. The pace wasn't my taste, but I could enjoy anything with Forrest.

We were taking photos on the Spanish steps, sandwiched between crowds of tourists doing the same, avoiding eye contact with a man selling overpriced roses, when a voice made me jump. "Are you two together?"

An older woman with short auburn hair and light green eyes studied us. She had a kind face, with rosy cheeks and a calming smile. Judging by her accent, she was also American. "Together?"

"You know, like an item?" She smiled. "I'm sorry to pry. You just seem so happy; it reminds me of my wife. She couldn't be here because of her job. Reporter." She rolled her eyes. "Of course she uncovered a sex scandal with the governor right before our big vacation."

"How rude of the governor to do that to you," said Forrest, swinging her arm around my shoulder.

"I know." The woman chuckled softly. "Thank you. I hate doing these things without her."

"I bet."

"Well, you two enjoy your vacation. You make a lovely couple."

"Thank you." Forrest waved as the woman passed us to continue up the steps. It was not lost on me that we did not answer her question. Then again, I couldn't. Forrest and I had been friends too long for this to be casual, but neither of us dared to broach the conversation of what this meant, and what would happen when we came home. This was too precious, too fragile, to risk ruining with questions. I decided I could make do with the uncertainty until it felt safe to ask. We continued down the steps, and I hoped Carter was wrong.

We picked up pizza from a restaurant in Testaccio and wolfed it down as soon as we stepped through Giovanni's front door. I jumped in the shower while Forrest scrolled through her phone. When I turned the water off, I barely had time to reach for a towel when she slipped into the bathroom to kiss me, wet and naked. "Let's watch a movie and cuddle tonight," she said. "And maybe do other stuff."

I smiled into her kiss. "What kinds of stuff?"

"I'll let you know after I shower."

I brushed my hair and slipped into an old t-shirt to sleep, soothed by the faint sound of running water. I sent Carter a selfie of Forrest and me under the Trevi Fountain then put my phone face-down on the bedside table. I studied the bedroom, the packed bookshelves with pothos vines, the colorful art covering the walls, the glass doors opening to a small balcony overlooking the street. There were only a couple feet of floor between the bookshelves and Gio's bed, which was low to the floor and covered in a plush white duvet, where I sat at the head, across from Forrest's purse. The bag was open, and some of the contents spilled onto the duvet, near my feet. A stick of strawberry lip balm, a corner of her wallet, a couple pencils and a white eraser, a folded-up piece of notebook paper labeled 'MOH speech.'

Wait a minute.

I scoot to the foot of the bed and gingerly unfolded the thin piece of notebook paper. There it was. In Forrest's rounded, dainty script, the speech she planned to give at my wedding reception.

For those of you who don't know me, I'm Forrest Manning, and Alana is my best friend. I've known Alana and I would be close ever since we survived a summer wrangling 11-year-olds together at Camp Darby. We became friends when I rescued her from a bat that got into our cabin. If I remember correctly, we got out by hiding under a blanket together and running for our lives, like a life-sized Pac-Man ghost. For those wondering, yes, we looked as ridiculous as it sounds. It's ironic that our friendship started that way, when Alana has rescued me so many times since then. She has been there for me through everything — my college graduation, my career change, every single breakup since I was nineteen. Our friendship means the world to me.

I have always wondered who could be good enough to deserve Alana. I stopped wondering when I met Matthew. He is exactly the type of man I always thought Alana would end up with — brilliant, gentle, kind. I have loved every minute of watching you two build a life together. He is perfect for you. I can say without a shadow of a doubt that you belong together. It makes me so happy that Alana has found that kind of love. Cheers to the beautiful couple!

I read it several times before Forrest came out of the bathroom wearing an oversized Carolina t-shirt with no pants. My t-shirt. It hung loosely over her, the hem curving around her upper thighs, revealing her long, toned legs. Her hair was covered by a lavender satin bonnet, and she tilted her head slightly as she leaned against the doorframe, watching me with a playful smile. She was so achingly beautiful, just like she had been when I first saw those dimples at nineteen. Her smile disappeared as she studied my expression. "What's up?"

I stared at her, not bothering to hide the paper unfolded in front of me. "Did you really think Matthew and I belonged together?" I asked.

Forrest sighed as she took a seat on the bed, the note between us. "It was your wedding, Al. What was I supposed to say?"

I looked at the note, then back at her. The writing on the paper was careful and confident, no eraser marks, crossed out words, or slanted script. Her face was equally calm, like believing the girl who shared her bed belonged with someone else, *without a shadow of a doubt*, was the sensible thing to say. I supposed it wasn't so different from typical wedding speeches. Her point was painfully rational. But if Forrest meant what she wrote... My heart splintered at the thought.

"Do you really want to be with me?" I asked, flipping the speech over. I couldn't bear to look at it any longer.

"What?" Forrest's eyes widened slightly.

I crossed my arms, folding myself in a protective hug. "My wedding was the most humiliating experience of my life. It's still hard to think about, that everyone I know saw that, what they must think of me. Now, I'm going to come home in a new relationship, two weeks after my fiancé left me, and everyone's going to judge me for it. My parents, Matthew's parents, my friends…"

"Why do you care what Matthew's parents think?" Her eyes on me were razor sharp, studying my every breath.

"I don't. I'm just saying—"

"If you didn't care, you wouldn't say it. Are you not over Matthew?"

I sighed. "I let them down, ok?"

"You didn't. Matthew did." She crossed her arms. "Is that really what matters to you, Alana? What all these people think?" Her eyes dropped to the duvet. "It doesn't matter, anyway. We're not in a relationship."

"Oh." It was so clinical, the way she laid everything out. Her tone was calm and detached, while I felt like my world was collapsing. "Then what are we?"

Forrest cocked her head to the side as she studied me. She whispered so softly, I strained to hear. "This was a mistake, wasn't it?"

I flinched at the words. What a hideous trick of Deja vu. *This was a mistake.* I recognized the shame in her eyes from when she uttered that same phrase on the dock eight years ago, eyes downcast as she fidgeted with her rings. I told her what I said then. "It wasn't to me."

Forrest stood suddenly, her face expressionless. "You're going through a lot, and it was unfair of me to do... this, right after your wedding. I'm sorry."

My eyes filled with tears. I dropped my gaze so she wouldn't see. I spoke slowly, trying to keep my voice from cracking. "You're saying you're not serious about us?"

"There isn't an us, Alana. Not like that." She was so achingly calm. "I'm saying we both need time. I'll sleep on the couch tonight, then when we go home, we can both take space from each other like —

like last time." She refused to look at me. "Then we can go back to being friends."

"Oh." My face grew hot as my tears threatened to spill down my cheeks. "Okay."

"Okay." Silently, she grabbed a sweatshirt, a blanket, and her phone, and I prayed that she'd change her mind, that she'd tell me she wanted this, too. "Alana?" she said, standing by the door, and my breath caught in my throat. "Goodnight."

I nodded knowingly at the familiar guilt in her eyes. "Goodnight, Forrest."

We didn't talk. Not on the train to the airport, not on the flight, not in line for U.S. Customs. Not when Carter picked us up from Dulles and dropped Forrest off at Union Station. The last and only thing she said to me was "Take care, Alana," as she slammed the car door and hurried to catch her train.

The last of my things arrived in a box that was too neatly packed to be done by Matthew. My French press, dish towels, a few books, the tan sweater I knit him, a small watercolor Forrest painted me in college, and some ceramic dishes wrapped in old newspaper. Things that Carter didn't recognize as mine when he collected my stuff from Matthew's over the honeymoon. There was no note inside, but what would Jessica have to say to me, anyway?

I never heard from Matthew again — not that it surprised me. He was lost in the business of work and the bliss of a new relationship. He would never think to apologize. Melissa, though, said she was happy I enjoyed Positano, when I texted her some pictures of Forrest and me. Of course, we didn't make plans to meet up.

I now realized how naïve I was to think Matthew loved me enough to marry me. Our connection was not the kind to build a lifetime on. We loved each other the way you love college after graduation. As much as you might romanticize the long nights out and lazy afternoons in the quad, you know that life would never suit you as an adult. I'd have to remember to thank him, if I ever saw him again.

Maybe I was meant to be a metaphor. The one that got away. A story for daydreams to assuage his discontent, on the odd afternoon he felt nostalgic. Maybe that was my problem. Maybe I was only an attractive *what* when you added an *if*. Matthew had no choice but to leave, because he fell in love with an enigma, not me. Maybe Forrest felt the same way. All my magic lied in being lost.

The reality of my life certainly wasn't romantic. It was restless nights on the pullout couch in Carter's living room, watching headlights cast moving shadows on the ceiling, living out of the same suitcase I brought home from Italy.

Not that I wasn't grateful. I thanked Carter and his two roommates just about daily for letting me take up temporary residence in their brownstone in Rittenhouse. They waved me off every time, probably because I helped with the rent and random chores. Cooking Sunday dinners, sweeping the foyer, cleaning the dust bunnies behind the refrigerator. Whenever Carter caught me, he'd try to rip the dustpan out of my hands, but the work relaxed me. It was nice to focus on something I could control, besides the gaping hole in my chest left in Forrest's wake. I learned in Italy that moping wouldn't do me any good.

When I texted Carter what happened, he drove from Philadelphia to Dulles to pick me up from the airport. I nearly cried at the sight of him there, leaning against his station wagon with his arms crossed. As soon as Forrest left us, he wrapped me in a comfortingly suffocating hug outside the train station.

"Oh, Ally," he said. "I'm so sorry."

"I didn't want you to be right," I muttered, my voice breaking.

"Me neither," he mumbled into my shoulder. "I hate being right."

The tears were less frequent now, but the hole in my chest was the same. At night, the absence of her arms around me ached like a phantom limb. I dreamed of her and came to loathe my alarm clock for taking her away again, each morning. More than anything, I missed my best friend. I imagined myself telling her about Philadelphia, Carter's rowhouse and the two roommates he met through a roundabout trail of mutual friends, the routine I built working remotely from their kitchen table and taking lunchtime walks to Rittenhouse Square. I wanted to know how she spent the rest of the summer and how her art show was coming along. I hated being in the dark on her life. It felt like my favorite TV show ended on a cliffhanger only to get canceled.

I wondered if she'd be proud of me, if she'd sympathize with me deflecting calls from my mother to give Matthew another chance. But I knew Forrest didn't want to talk. If she wanted me the way I wanted her, she would never have walked away. I had to finally accept that.

I threw myself into my sewing, determined to rebuild the business I neglected when dating Matthew. To my surprise, orders came flooding in. A viral TikTok video of an influencer in one of my dresses sparked a flurry of purchases. Slow workdays that I once spent scrolling Instagram were now filled with design work. On weekends, I scoured thrift shops for cheap clothing to tinker with and sold more items in person at a Sunday flea market.

If this continued, I could quit my day job by the end of the year.

Maybe, by the time I saw Forrest again, I would. If she even wanted to be friends.

"What's that?" said Carter, nodding at the box as he slid past me in the kitchen to grab a banana.

"The last bit of my things from Matthew's," I answered, frowning at the box.

Carter studied the box more closely, holding the plates up like he was inspecting them for damage. "Clearly packed by Jessica," he said, setting a plate down on the counter. "No way Matthew would have the awareness to wrap your ceramics."

I laughed. "That's what I thought, too."

"Did they leave a note, or anything?"

I shook my head.

Carter grunted. "What a little shit."

I barked out a laugh in surprise. "Carter!"

"Am I wrong?"

"Well, no." I smiled at my oldest friend. "I'm just trying to be the bigger person."

"Well, stop trying. He's a full foot taller than you anyway." He stepped closer and squeezed my shoulder. "Seriously, Ally, are you ok?"

I studied the concern in his furrowed brow and smiled back. No matter what life through at me, he'd always be there to pick up the pieces, as I would for him. These days, that knowledge was all I had. "Yeah, I am."

"Good." He smiled. "I still think we should get wine drunk and watch *Mamma Mia* tonight, just in case."

I nodded very seriously. "Good idea. You can never be too careful." Carter laughed and texted our group chat with his roommates about a movie night. Then, we found space for the box in the hall closet as Carter told me a story about a crazy client of his, who wanted them to consult a medium before launching their marketing campaign, to make sure their late grandfather approved of the social media strategy. By the time he finished, I was laughing so hard my stomach ached, my box of things and even Forrest temporarily forgotten.

Carter kept me sane, most days.

There was an unread email from the wedding videographer, sandwiched between a newsletter from Washingtonian and a coupon from the Thai restaurant where Matthew and I used to get takeout. I read it in bed after waking up, and Carter came inside from a morning run just as I finished it, gaping at the screen. "What is it?" he asked between sips from his water bottle. He was panting, face flushed and sweaty from the heat.

"Dude," I said, shaking my head. "You're not gonna believe this." I handed him the phone so he could read it. The tone was comically perky, the way someone my age would write when composing the message felt like a form of psychological torture. I didn't blame her. Hopefully she had a good therapist.

Hi Alana,

I hope this email finds you well! As summer is winding down, I've been cleaning out my files from this wedding season and stumbled across the footage from your ceremony back in May. You were the most beautiful bride!

I know that day wasn't the most pleasant memory for you, but I don't want to delete footage you paid for without consulting you first. I'd be happy to send you the video if you're interested. But if not, I completely understand!

Thanks so much!

Carter read the email while sitting on the arm of the couch, wearing nothing but purple spandex, as the color in his cheeks faded from red to pink. He pursed his lips as he studied me. "What are you gonna do?"

I thought of that day, my stark dress and trembling voice, Matthew's indifferent departure, Forrest in her bridesmaid dress. I leaned against the back of the couch and sighed, running a hand through my tangled hair.

Forrest in her bridesmaid dress.

Damnit.

"Somehow, watching myself be humiliated on camera is worth it if I can see her in that dress again." I groaned as I threw my head back. "Ugh! Why am I such a simp?"

"Being a simp isn't a bad thing." He squeezed my shoulder. "It means you care, which is what makes you human. I'm a simp for Claude." He gestured at the bird of paradise in the corner, which he bought after graduating college and was now the size of a tree, its leaves brushing the ceiling.

That coaxed a smile out of me. "I'm also a simp for Claude."

He grinned as he pulled me into a sweaty, one-armed hug. "Let's watch it together. We'll make it fun" His green eyes lit up with mischief. "It has so much potential — can you imagine? We could create the greatest drinking game of all time."

I huffed a surprised laugh. "Play a drinking game to me getting left at the altar?"

"Don't lie, Ally. You see the vision." Carter started counting ideas on his fingers. "Drink whenever your dad clears his throat to hide that he's crying, drink when the pastor quotes RBG, drink whenever your mom motions at Gemma to fix her hair, drink when Matthew's hands looked freakishly sweaty."

I giggled. "We'd get blackout on Matthew's hands alone."

Carter raised his eyebrows. "I think your mom would get us drunker."

I snorted. "Hold on, say all that again. I'm gonna write this down."

And so the drinking game of the century began. Carter and I spent the morning making a list of rules based on what we remembered from the wedding: a groomsman who flashed the shaka sign at everyone as he walked down the aisle, the flower girl who picked her nose twice while dropping petals, Carter's embarrassing almost-fall, when he tripped on his own feet near the altar. We finished by the time Carter left for work, and he promised to pick up a bottle of prosecco on the way home.

"And now, for our feature presentation..." Carter proclaimed, standing before me with a mug of prosecco as he gestured at the TV, which he connected to his laptop so we could view the video on the big screen. "What would we even call this?"

"The Dumping of Alana?" I said.

"The Worst Mistake Of Matthew's Life?"

"Self-Induced Schadenfreude?"

"We'll workshop it." Carter stepped back from the TV and plopped on the couch next to me. He squeezed my shoulder reassuringly, then pressed play. "It's showtime!"

Immediately, the camera cut to Forrest. Walking toward the bridal suite in a bathrobe. So much time passed since I last saw her, her radiant grin took my breath away. She held a finger to her lips, signaling the camera to keep quiet, a portable speaker in one hand and the hair comb she gifted me in the other, eyes twinkling as she suppressed her smile. Then, the door opened and the music started. I watched my own eyes widen with surprise, then crinkle with delight as I realized what Forrest and Carter had done. A sudden burst of genuine laughter broke through my made-up facade.

From there, the camera followed us as we got ready, ending on Forrest fastening the satin buttons on the back of my dress. There were close-up shots of the dress, then of my face, my mother, Forrest, and Carter blinking back tears. With the comb fastened in my hair, I'd schooled my face into a neutral expression that could rival a runway model. I looked beautiful but emotionless, and perhaps a little bit terrified. It was wild to me now that I couldn't see how unhappy I was, that I didn't think those feelings mattered.

Matthew's smile was fake, too, in the church. It was obvious now. Every muscle in his body looked tense as he stood at the altar, his posture unusually rigid and his face almost pained. When his groomsmen made it down the aisle, Matthew stopped smiling altogether. He didn't even laugh at the Shaka-flashing frat bro. He only wrung his hands.

"Sweaty hands, drink!" Carter ordered as he clinked my mug of Prosecco.

Between the flower girl, Carter's near-fall at the altar, and my mother's dagger eyes at Gemma, we finished and re-filled our drinks before the bridesmaids even reached the altar. "You were right," I told Carter. "This really is the greatest drinking game of all time." I smiled. I loved that I could finally begin to laugh at what happened. It felt like healing. But when I looked back at the screen, my mind went blank.

Because Forrest appeared in her bridesmaid dress.

Her expression stayed flat as she walked down the aisle — eerily similar to the calm look she possessed the last time I saw her, when she said goodbye at Dulles Airport. She took slow breaths through her nose and looked almost somber as she took her position by the altar, eyes trained on the bouquet in front of her. She stood a little in front of Matthew, to the right. I could tell by the way her eyes welled with tears, and his widened in fear, that I must have entered the church.

There I was, in my crisp white dress, carrying white roses, with a long white veil trailing behind me, my father to my right. The camera cut between my poised smile, Matthew's obvious dread, and Forrest's tears, which silently streaked her cheeks with every step I took. What was it she said to me that day? *I'm happy for you.* Only her tears looked nothing like that. As she brushed at her tears the back of her hand and took my bouquet, all I saw was sorrow. She looked like her world was collapsing.

"Holy shit." I stood from the couch to get closer to the screen. "Holy shit!"

"What?" Carter snapped his head away the screen, his eyes imploring me for an answer. "What is it?"

"R-rewind that last part. Play it again. Just the flowers." My hands were shaking as I pointed at the screen.

I remembered my fight with Forrest in the Positano rain, my anger at her confession. *You know how I feel about you.* It didn't make sense how she could expect me to know, when I spent years in anguish at her silence. Only now it made sense, because now I remembered. How she whispered *I love you* as she took my flowers, then watched me with melancholy, moonstruck eyes as I misunderstood her completely and proceeded to the altar to marry someone else.

"Holy shit," said Carter.

"She loves me?" The words felt as delicate as old parchment, my voice cracking as I spoke to them.

"She loves you."

My vision blurred. "I thought she wasn't serious about me. I thought that's why she left." I blinked away my tears. When did I start crying?

Carter smirked at me with laughter in his eyes. "Just curious," he said, "what did you think she was doing when she confessed her love to you at the altar?"

My hands shook as I turned to him. "I thought it was a friend thing."

Carter burst out laughing, and I joined him, delighted at being so, ridiculously wrong. "Alana, she's looking at you like you're the moon." He was almost giddy as he wiped his own tears away. "It's not a friend thing."

I shook my head. "But why did she end things in Rome? I don't understand."

He ran a hand through his hair as he pondered it, Forrest's tear-stained face frozen on the TV. "Is it possible that she thinks *you* aren't serious about her? I mean, you guys got together two weeks after your wedding. Or maybe she thinks she doesn't deserve you?"

I shook my head. "Both of those ideas sound insane to me. I mean, it's Forrest. I've been in love with her since I was nineteen. Even when I loved Matthew, I still loved her. If anything, *I'm* the one who doesn't deserve *her*."

"I don't know, Al," he sighed. "She feels really bad about what happened when you were teenagers, even now. I feel like I give her a pep talk on forgiving herself every time we're drunk together, if you're not around."

"What?" I clasped and unclasped my hands. "Why didn't she tell me?"

"She didn't want to burden you with her guilt. Every time we talked about it, she made me swear not to say anything."

"It doesn't make sense." But then I remembered her maid of honor toast. I was so slighted by her insistence that Matthew belonged with me, I overlooked another line: *I have always wondered who could be good enough to deserve Alana.* I shook my head. "She was just a scared kid. One mistake isn't enough for me to give up on her. I mean, she's the fucking love of my life." The blurted confession surprised me, but it was true. Nobody ever had, or ever would, capture my heart like Forrest. My entire adult life, my days started and ended with thoughts of her. I laughed for her, cried for her, breathed for her. I wrote stories in my head for only her to see. There was no one else. I was hers.

"Maybe you should tell her that."

Instinctively, I opened my mouth to protest but stopped myself. He had a point. If she really loved me, if she *still* loved me, it was the only way. If I had even a tiny chance of being with Forrest, I would do anything to make that happen. Just... "What if I'm wrong?"

"Then you can move on." Carter placed a hand on my knee as his gaze bore into mine. "If I'm being honest, I suspected for a while that Forrest might have feelings for you. But aside from looking at you like you were water in a desert, she never did anything. I couldn't be sure until now, otherwise I would have said something. She loves you, Ally, and you love her. But even if she doesn't, you'll never move on until you hear that from her. Best case, you'll be with the person who makes you happier than I've ever seen you. Worst case, you go on living like this, in limbo with your feelings. You deserve to be happy, Alana, and happiness takes work. It takes risking everything, making a mess of your life, and making something happen for yourself, even if that goes against the good, quiet girl your parents raised you to be."

Carter barely blinked as he watched me, then crossed his arms. He'd been like this since we were in college, brimming with a seemingly bottomless well of faith in me. In moments like this, it was the only thing that sustained me, the feeling that maybe Carter was right. Maybe my happiness could be more than a daydream. Maybe I even deserved it. Seeing the truth laid bare in Forrest's tear-filled eyes hardened my resolve.

"You're right." I squeezed Carter's hand and smiled gratefully at my friend. "I know what I need to do."

27

I had five days to plan what I wanted to tell Forrest, buy a train ticket to DC, and keep myself from chickening out. Carter's steady insistence kept me brave, even on nights when the thought of telling her was so nerve-wracking, I lay awake for hours. Now, I walked from my room at The Mayflower through Dupont Circle, past the street that housed Matthew's apartment, to the art gallery hosting Forrest's first solo exhibition.

I couldn't just send her a text saying, "Hey, I'm in love with you, in case that changes anything." It had to be in person, and because we hadn't spoken in three months, this was the only place I knew she'd be. I wore a midi skirt I made earlier this summer, cream colored with two large, geometric-shaped hibiscus flowers on the sides, which I paired with a black shirt and a leather jacket. I carried a bouquet with white lilies, blue hydrangeas, and lavenders, pickings from Trader Joe's that I carefully arranged together. I carried the bouquet in one arm like a baby and shoved the other hand in my jacket pocket to keep it from shaking. I could barely put on mascara, earlier, I was so nervous.

Once a month, Dupont Circle's art galleries opened their doors for free to show off new exhibitions. This gallery was part of that event, located in the basement of a brownstone on a quiet side street with ginkgo trees. The door was open, and yellow light shined against the brick pathway leading to the door, where a steady stream of people flowed in and out. It contrasted beautifully with the cobalt evening sky.

Forrest was inside. She probably thanked each of these people for coming. Shook their hands.

I took a deep breath to calm my nerves.

I would never stop loving Forrest. I knew that from the moment we first kissed on the lake. I knew that since the morning I lay watching her sleep, vowing to never let her go. Since I was nineteen, the only certainty in my life was her place in it, the way being with her seamlessly fit, and how parting seemed to strip me bare. What I was about to do put me the precipice of losing her forever, if she didn't feel the same. The thought was overwhelming, but I knew I'd regret it if I didn't try. After everything we'd been through, I owed her that much.

I clutched the bouquet with both hands as I stepped forward, eyes locked on the door as I walked inside.

Forrest wasn't here. There were multiple rooms to the exhibition, and this first one was filled only with a greeter handing out pamphlets and strangers admiring the art. Eight large canvases spanned the walls, with detailed, close-up features and unconventional colors that were characteristic of Forrest's style. Their beauty trapped my breath in my throat, then set my heart racing, blood humming in my ears.

Because I recognized them.

My hand laced with hers, pinning it to the bed, a view of European apartment buildings out the window, all in shades of yellow-gold. *Mornings in Rome.* My smiling face, in sunset colors, floating beside ripples of Amalfi blue water as my hair fanned out beneath me. *Her Laugh.* In red, my fingers running fabric through a sewing machine. *Art In*

Motion. Forrest in indigo with pink-flushed cheeks, leaning backward into a midnight background, her eyes on my magenta silhouette. *Swept Away.*

I was surrounded by scenes from our honeymoon. These must have been the sketches she didn't let me see.

"The resemblance is uncanny." I flinched, startled by an older man who approached me. "Sorry, just, the one of you in the water is so clearly *you.* I love it. Are you friends with the artist?"

I smiled politely back. "Something like that." My trembling voice sounded nothing like my own. "Have you seen her, here?"

"Yes. Her work is spread across the three rooms of the gallery: She's in the back. Are you surprising her?"

"Yeah."

"Oh, how sweet! Well, I'll let you get to it." He smiled as he backed away. "You're a great friend."

I forced a smile in return. "Thanks."

If the first room filled me with hope, the second dashed it completely. There were some paintings I recognized, like my pointer finger and thumb holding my engagement ring, all in a somber indigo. *Promise.* Others were new. Fingers fastening the satin buttons on the back of my wedding dress, all in a pale, washed out blue-gray. *Dressing.* Forrest crying in her bridesmaid dress, the colors of fire. *Confessional.* A figure under a blanket, sleeping on the couch in Giovanni's apartment, all in shades of dark turquoise. *Left Behind.*

The Forrest who painted me laughing in the ocean could take me back, but this melancholy artist might not. I wouldn't blame her. I never realized how much my wedding must have tortured her. The dress shopping, cake tasting, and band performances she joined me for, the countless times she helped iron out details just to give me a reprieve from Melissa. All the while haunted by the same feelings I struggled to bury before the ceremony — the dread at giving up the hope of her by tethering myself to someone else.

I would spend the rest of my life making it up to her if she let me.

There was only one way to find out.

The art was just a blur of color. Everything in that final room was a blur, except Forrest. I froze in the doorway as soon as I saw her. Her dark, lively eyes shined as she spoke, gesturing at the painting behind her, surrounded by a cluster of mesmerized gallery goers. She wore the dress I made her, based on La Sagrada Familia, with a black blazer; her long twists flowed freely behind her and swung slightly as her body moved. Someone asked her a question, and as she laughed, her dimples flashed so brilliantly it hurt. To her right stood Monique, and her aunt and uncle weren't far behind, watching Forrest proudly.

Maybe it was a mistake to come.

But then her sister saw me, and Monique's eyes lit up when they locked with mine. She flashed a grin with dimples that mirrored her sister's as she gestured for me to come closer. I smiled shyly as I obeyed, relieved at the greeting. Forrest told Monique everything. If her sister didn't hate me, maybe she didn't, either.

I found a spot in the crowd and listened. "I like using colors to represent emotion," said Forrest. Her voice was the sweetest music after so much time apart. "I think each color carries its own tone and feeling, and how we interpret a color can change depending on the scene. Blue can be calming or sad, red is angry, or romantic. I love seeing how far I can push color to tell a story."

Someone asked: "I'm guessing the one behind you is love?"

Her face froze at the question, and her smile fell. She turned back to the painting. "Yes," she answered softly. "But not just any love." Surprised by her shyness, I finally mustered the willpower to take my eyes off her and study the art. When I did, I couldn't help but gasp.

It was us, at nineteen. The painting looked down at the dock where we peacefully slept, surrounded by water, with Forrest's arm draped across my waist. The water was the same subdued blue-gray from *Dressing,* only here it felt comfortingly soft. The dock and our bodies were done in brilliant shades of yellow, pink, orange and gold that reminded me of the sunrise that greeted us that morning. When the world felt euphorically serene and lush with possibility. I never thought she'd remember that sunrise like I did, but the colors were identical to my memory. It was one of the most beautiful things I'd ever seen.

I Will Always Love You.

I raised my hand without thinking. Forrest turned at the movement, and her mouth fell open when she saw me.

"Is this one for sale?" I blurted. I couldn't think of what else to say. I saw the prices of her art and already knew I couldn't afford it.

"No," she said, shaking her head as if snapping from a trance. "It's the only one that isn't. But," she added shyly, "I could be persuaded to give it as a gift, to the right person."

I nodded, a blush coloring my cheeks. "I'm hoping I could convince you."

"Me, too." Forrest nodded, then turned to the rest of the crowd. "The Q&A portion is done for now. Could you all give us a moment?"

As the crowd dispersed, I stepped closer to Forrest. Monique squeezed my shoulder reassuringly, then pretended to study a nearby painting with Aunt Pat and Uncle Artie, who were clearly eavesdropping. Forrest seemed to know, by the soft smile she flashed in their direction. Her expression was blank when she turned back to me. I handed her the flowers. "These are for you."

She took the bouquet, then raised her eyes to meet mine. "They're beautiful," she said, and I could see it. All the vulnerability, hurt, and hope of the last three months lay bare before me.

I smiled shyly back. "Thanks."

We watched each other quietly for a moment, unsure what to say. I clasped and unclasped my hands, unsure what to do with them now that I wasn't holding flowers. Forrest finally broke the silence. "I didn't think you'd come."

I blinked at her in surprise. "Why not?"

She shrugged. "I thought you hated me."

I huffed a surprised laugh at the thought. "Why would I?"

"Maybe because I picked the honeymoon after your would-be wedding to pursue the relationship that I've wanted with you since I first fucked it up at nineteen. Then when you, understandably, couldn't say you were over your fiancé, I cut and ran without even trying to talk to you about it. Like I did at nineteen."

My breath caught at her honesty, at the shame in her eyes. "I was always over Matthew, Forrest. You're the one I'll never forget." She said nothing, and I smiled at her. "I'm surprised you don't hate me, either."

It was her turn to blink in surprise. "How come?"

"Maybe because I've been pining for you our entire friendship but didn't have the guts to say it. Then, I almost fucked it up by getting married, tortured you by making you my maid of honor. Worst of all, I didn't come to my senses at the altar, when you told me you loved me." Forrest gasped lightly at my revelation. "In my defense, I thought you loved me as a friend."

Her mouth twitched, like she was holding back a laugh. "It's a common mix-up."

"Sure." I smiled, then continued. "Then, against all odds, we finally got a real shot. But I fucked that up, too, by getting insecure over a speech you wrote weeks before, when you didn't know how I felt. Then, instead of telling you, I word vomited over some petty anxiety about what people would think, I don't even care about all that. Really, all I care about is you." My eyes dropped to the floor. "You had every right to leave."

Gently, she lifted my chin with her finger. My skin tingled at her touch. "I was wrong to stop fighting for you." She searched my eyes with an earnest, soul-bearing gaze. "You're being too hard on yourself, Alana."

I smiled softly. "I could say the same about you."

"Touché." She gingerly removed her hand. "If you came to apologize, there's no need. I was never mad. I never blamed you for any of it."

"I didn't come to apologize," I said. "I came here because I'm in love with you."

Forrest's jaw dropped.

"I am sorry, of course," I continued, "but that's not why I came. I came because you're my best friend." My eyes welled when I looked at her, at the love leaking out of me. "When I feel joy you're the first person I want to share it with, and when my life feels too big to carry alone, you're the only person I trust with the weight. I go through my day collecting stories to tell you later, wondering what you're doing, and if I'll get to hear about it. I fall asleep dreaming of your arms around me. I'm here because, sometimes, when I look at you, I forget to breathe, and yet I can't breathe without you, either. I'm here because when we're apart, it feels like a piece of my soul is missing. I'm here because I love you, Forrest.

"The only reason I never told you is because I never thought it was possible that you could love me back. But then I remembered what you said in the church, and I realized how wrong I was." I dared another step toward her. "I know I might be too late. I know I don't deserve you. But I am tired of pretending that you're not everything to me. I had to tell you. You deserve that."

Forrest wiped a tear away as it slid down her cheek; her hands were shaking. "I lied in that speech, you know."

I blinked at her. "What?"

"I never thought Matthew deserved you. I just thought he deserved you more than I did." She spun the ring on her thumb like she always did when she was nervous. "I had a chance to be with you, and instead I broke your heart. I hated myself for years."

Tears ran down my cheeks when she confirmed what Carter told me. "Forrest, you were a kid."

"A kid who lost the best thing that ever happened to me. Or… almost did." She studied me shyly. "You should know that I reacted the way I did that morning out of guilt. The truth is, I loved you, even then. I'll never forget how it felt waking up next to you on the lake. Nothing in my life had ever felt so right.

"When we didn't speak, that first time, most days I didn't want to get out of bed. I made elaborate, multi-tiered promises to God, if only you'd talk to me again. One of them was that I would be the best friend you'd ever have, that I'd never do anything again that could risk hurting you. I knew I couldn't live if I lost you forever.

"Then, by some miracle, you came back to me. So I folded my feelings up really small and buried them deeper than I've buried anything, even though they grew every day. Even though I've spent every day of my adult life falling more in love with the person you've become, Alana. Your kindness, your gentle reassurance, your patience with people…

you awe me in ways I never imagined back then. Sometimes, when we were kids, my feelings for you felt larger than my very being, like loving you this core piece of who I am, inseparable from the rest. But what I felt then is nothing compared to what I feel for you now." Forrest smiled, her dimples casting small shadows on her cheeks. Her gaze flickered between my eyes and my lips. "You really love me?"

"Desperately." I stepped closer to her.

"What a coincidence." She sighed like I just relieved her of the weight of the sky. She pressed her forehead against mine and whispered, "I love you so much, Alana."

My arms circled her waist, her brown eyes glowing as they bored into mine. "I will do everything I can to be the best partner to you," I vowed. "To make you happy."

Forrest rubbed the small of my back. "You don't need to be perfect to be worthy love, Alana."

I raised my eyebrows in challenge. "Neither do you."

"Yes." She cradled my cheek with her hand. "I see that now."

"I love you, Forrest."

She echoed the words back as I kissed her, pulling her into me. She tasted like home, like cheap wine and rain. I was about to open my lips further, to deepen the kiss, when the room around us erupted into cheers. That's when I realized we had an audience. I started to pull away, to see where her aunt and uncle, Monique, and a few clusters of strangers awaited.

"Uh, uh." Forrest gently pulled my chin back to her. "No interruptions."

The cheers were mixed with laughter as she kissed me again. This time, I kissed her deeply, and she smiled into it. We stood directly beneath the painting of us on the dock, under the years-old memory that started it all.

"So," said Forrest, nodding toward the painting. "I'd say you were very convincing, Alana. The painting is yours."

I answered her with a kiss on the cheek. "I actually don't want it."

"What?"

She flinched away from me, but I held her close. "What I mean is, I want it to be yours. I want you to hang it somewhere special in your apartment, and I want to stay with you so often that it feels like mine. I just want to stay with you, really. If you'd have me."

Forrest beamed at me with melted butter in her eyes. "I think I can make that happen." She nudged her nose against mine. "But I'm still going to consider it yours."

"How about ours?"

"Deal."

I kissed her again because I could. For every past self that lay awake at night yearning for her, wondering if these feelings would kill me. For the part of my soul that came alive when I looked at her, that I no longer had to hide. I kissed her with an unspoken commitment to make her as happy as she made me. I vowed to never forget how lucky I was to love and be loved by her.

It was an easy promise to keep.

28

One Year Later...

This was nothing like my last wedding. For starters, I wasn't wearing white. The pale, blue-gray chiffon hugged my torso, parted by a deep V, while the skirt fanned out loosely all around me. I covered the bodice with embroidered flowers in silver thread, with some subtler embroidery on the tulle skirt. It was difficult to hide my design from Forrest, but that made the day even more special, knowing the dress I created would be a complete surprise.

"Wow," said Bianca as she slipped into the room. "You're stunning."

"Right?" Gemma smiled slightly but stayed focused as she touched up the powder on my eyelids, white-silver with a subtle blue accent, to complement the dress. "Alana, close your eyes."

"Thanks, Bianca," I said, obeying my sister.

"Ok, you're good." Gemma stepped away. She smiled. "Carter, where's my drink?"

"Your drink? That was my drink?" Carter frowned down at an empty champagne flute. He wore a sleeveless jumpsuit with a V-neck and wide-leg pants that was a vibrant shade of cobalt blue, the same color as Gemma's bridesmaid dress. I made both pieces, choosing a style that matched their taste and a color to complement the ocean, which would serve as the backdrop of our ceremony. Now that I made Gemma's clothing to her taste instead of mine, she loved everything I made.

We flew to Positano for the wedding. Forrest and I agreed it was the best place to start our life together, back at the Valeri with our families and closest friends for an intimate celebration.

There was no wedding planner, no grand, orchestrated ceremony. The Valeri's decorated the terrace with bouquets of lilies and hibiscus for the reception and set up chairs in a neighbor's backyard for the ceremony, overlooking the sea. Bianca took care of everything. She negotiated with a neighboring vineyard for discounted Prosecco, found catering help who agreed to make Nonna's tortellini recipe, and convinced one of Giovanni's friends to DJ the reception. She was starting to take on more responsibility at the hotel, as Jia and Maximo prepared for retirement, and viewed the wedding as a chance to expand business. "Who knows?" she told me over the phone. "Maybe the Valeri could become an official wedding venue one day."

Now, she laughed at Carter. "Don't worry," she told Gemma. "There will be plenty of Prosecco at the reception."

She was already making the changes she'd dreamed about in the kitchen with Nonna. The Ristaurante Valeri opened for dinner last month, with a team of two cooks preparing Nonna's recipes. Her goal was to earn enough to hire another worker or two for the hotel, to step in so Jia and Maximo could get a break. Thanks to Bianca's work, they visited Sicily in July, Jia's first vacation in decades.

"Well, in that case," said Gemma, "let's get this show on the road."

My sister carried the train of my dress as we left the hotel and walked through the pathway to the neighbor's garden. We stood out of view as we waited for the ceremony to start.

"You should start selling wedding dresses when you open your store," said Gemma. "This is seriously gorgeous."

I smiled back at my sister. "I think I will." A couple months after Forrest and I moved into our Capitol Hill apartment together — a basement unit with tall ceilings and exposed brick walls that we filled with art — a neighbor tipped us off to a storefront around the block that was available to rent. Since I quit my job last fall to focus on my clothing business, I'd been selling pieces online and at outdoor markets faster than I could sew them. Expanding was not a pipe dream, but a logical next step. So I did.

The store would open in three months. Not that I was focused on that now.

The only thing on my mind was seeing Forrest walk down the aisle, then spending two more weeks with her here on our honeymoon here, back in the place the brought us together.

We started dating after her solo exhibition, which was an immediately, wild success. Forrest quit her job once the fall semester ended and moved to DC. Now, she created paintings to display at galleries in Dupont Circle and New York while I spent my days sewing. The small second bedroom in our apartment was a makeshift studio, for now; once my store opened, we'd save a room in the back for her to paint. Maybe we'd even sell some of her art alongside my clothes.

There were still details to iron out, but we had time.

As we sat together on the flight over, Forrest asked if I was nervous for the wedding. "I thought I would be," I told her. How could I not? After my last wedding ended in disaster, I was convinced I'd never walk down an aisle again. Turns out, none of that mattered. No painful memory was stronger than my elation at spending forever with Forrest. I told her that when I proposed over a candlelit dinner at home, a week after moving in together. "I'm not nervous. I'm too excited to start my life with you."

I studied her silhouette in the dim light, her long eyelashes and delicately curved nose. "Are you nervous?"

Forrest laughed; her smile was almost giddy. "Honey, I've never been so sure of anything in my life." She squeezed my hand, her eyes twinkling. "I cannot wait."

It is important to fall in love someone who makes you fall in love with yourself, who reminds you that you deserve love as much as they do. I did not realize this until I surrendered my heart completely to Forrest, and in this act of giving, found myself, too. I was easy to love when I saw myself through her eyes.

I couldn't wait to see her.

The music began, and Gemma gave me one last smile before she left Carter and me to walk down the aisle. After the humiliation at my last wedding, Gemma had my back in the way only family can and quickly became one of my closest friends. If I had known disappointing our parents would restore our relationship so completely, I would have fucked up more as a kid. I beamed at her as I squeezed her hand, and she left us.

"I would kiss your cheek, but you look way to beautiful to risk smudging your makeup, so I'll wait for the reception." Carter took both my hands and stared into my eyes as he squeezed them, blinking back tears. "I am so, so happy for you. I love you so much, Ally." He grinned wickedly. "Just not like that."

We laughed together, thinking of the last time someone told me they loved me on my wedding day. "Last year was one of the hardest times of my life, and you were by my side every step of the way, like you always are. I can't even tell you how grateful I am. You're the best friend I could ever ask for." I sniffled as tears sprung to my eyes. "I just love you so much."

"Shh." He kissed my hands. "Save your tears for Forrest."

He followed Gemma down the aisle, and my father appeared at my side in a tuxedo he rented for the wedding. He looked even more polished than he did last time, with his gray-brown hair combed back and his outfit freshly ironed. I smiled softly as I looped my arm through his.

"You look beautiful, Bun," he said with a trembling voice; he didn't bother coughing to hide it. It was more feeling than I'd heard from him in years.

I squeezed his arm as I looked up at him. "Thanks, Dad." I smiled. "You look great, too."

Then it was time.

I studied the faces of my family and friends as I appeared at the aisle. There were few enough people here that I actually could study their faces, the watery smiles of my aunts, uncles and cousins, the tears Jia Valeri hastily brushed away. There was no crowd to impress, nothing to fake, just genuine joy from the people who loved me.

I began to walk.

At the altar stood Carter, Gemma, and Dominic. The paster swapped his usual attire for a suit, his black tie patterned with small line drawings of Ruth Bader-Ginsberg's portrait. He came out of retirement to perform our wedding ceremony. These days, he filled his time petitioning Congress to erect an RBG statue in DC and discussing her judicial career with the friends he made through his activism. Peggy told me he was happier than she'd seen him in awhile, now that he was no longer hiding. When she told us how he heeded the church's push to retire, she said, "He's not sad about it anymore. He can now see it was for the best. Plus, he's finally stopped begging me to put an RBG statue in the garden."

She was here, too, waving as I walked down the aisle. I smiled back.

One row ahead of her, Giovanni winked at me, sitting between Bianca and his boyfriend, Luca, whom he met shortly after Forrest and I left Italy. He told me he knew Luca was the one because it only took two dates to make him brave enough to come out to his parents. They were more supportive than he could have imagined. He joked that his new problem was convincing Luca to stay in Rome, instead of moving in with his family at the Valeri. ("We probably will, one day, to help B," he acquiesced. "Luca loves it, and I'll be happy to move back here, too, as long as I can still do my research.")

A row ahead of him, Nonna was crying, I reached my hand out to squeeze her shoulder, and she smiled at me. There were tears among Forrest's family and friends, too. Even my mother was crying, even though she was pushing me to get Matthew back up until I told her I was dating Forrest. Now, she texted me links to t-shirts from Target's Pride Collection, mulling over what she'd wear to the parade. I couldn't tell if she was more excited to see me happy or to see herself in rainbow, but I didn't care. I was learning to draw boundaries with my parents and appreciate our relationship for what it was, flaws and all. Maybe my own desire for perfection with them sent me down this path in the first place, more than any of the pressure my mom fed me as a child.

Either way, we were both trying.

I reached the altar and gave my dad a kiss on the cheek before he took his seat.

Then came Forrest's bridal party. Her aunt, cousin, friends from college and grad school, and Monique, her maid of honor. All wore the same blue as Carter and Gemma as they took their places at the altar, to my right. As she reached the front, Monique pointed to my dress and whispered, "Wow!" I grinned back at my soon-to-be sister, who already felt like family.

Then, the tone of the music changed, and I knew.

My soulmate was here.

My heart stopped when Forrest appeared. The off-shoulder straps on her white wedding dress circled her arms and connected to a fitted, lace bodice, while the flowy tulle skirt was covered in lace flowers. Her

446

twists were tied half-up behind her head, decorated with little pearl pins that glowed in the sunlight as her long veil trailed behind her. As beautiful as she looked, it wasn't her dress or her hair or her makeup that immediately sent me into tears.

It was the pure, unfettered joy filling her face when she looked at me.

I had never seen anything so beautiful.

She clamped a hand over her mouth when she looked at me, surprise and awe flaring in her eyes as she took in the dress I designed for this moment. She almost sunk to the ground before her uncle tugged her back up, wiping tears away with his free hand. He gave her a handkerchief that she used to dab her eyes. "Sorry, but just look at her," she exclaimed, and we all laughed as she gave Uncle Artie his handkerchief back.

She didn't take her eyes off me as she walked down the aisle, her lip trembling slightly through her smile. My tears welled at the warmth in her gaze; her unabashed love was more than I'd ever dared to imagine for myself. I couldn't believe she was mine.

We were both crying when she reached me, creating a chorus of sniffed back tears as Uncle Artie grabbed my hand.

"Welcome to the family, Alana," he said, his voice filled with emotion as he placed Forrest's hand in my own.

As he returned to his seat, Forrest took a step back, clutching both my hands as she studied me from head to toe. I watched her eyes light up and her dimples twitch as she held back a radiant smile and a flurry of sobs, all at once. She was radiant.

We said at the same time, "Holy shit," then burst out laughing.

"You're so beautiful, Alana," she whispered ardently.

"Forrest, I am never taking my eyes off you for the rest of our lives," I murmured.

She smirked. "I think I can make that happen."

I squeezed her hands as Dominic stepped forward, smiling shyly at both of us before he began. "Dearly beloved, we are gathered here today..."

The ceremony progressed with a sermon from Dominic, in which he shared a quote from RBG about her own happy marriage, readings from Forrest's cousin and Bianca. I watched my fiancé as she laughed at Dominic's jokes, teared up at her cousin's reading, and watched me with tenderness through the service. Her eyes were practically on fire with emotion. I raised my eyebrows quizzically, a silent plea to know her thoughts.

"My parents would have loved this," she whispered, but not with sadness. There was joy in the way she beamed through her tears, as if she could feel them here with her.

I squeezed her hands as I whispered: "I know they would. Nothing makes me happier than knowing that."

We were interrupted by Dominic's call to our loved ones to speak now or forever hold their peace. My breath hitched on reflex, but Forrest winked as she squeezed my hands. The peace in her gaze grounded me.

This time, there was glorious, resounding silence.

Dominic continued.

Gemma handed the reverend our rings, matching platinum bands with a small sapphire in the center. Inside each, there was an engraving for only us to see. *Always in All Ways.* A vow I'd spend the rest of my life keeping.

Did I take Forrest to be my lawfully wedded wife? To have and to hold, to love and to cherish, in sickness and in health, as long as we both shall live? It was an easy question. I stared into her eyes as I said "I do," letting her know how committed I was to this. She did the same, her eyes darkening as she said "I do," affirming her intention that our souls become one, until death do us part.

This was the start the rest of our lives. Of mornings waking up to the softness in her eyes, of lazy Sunday afternoons sitting in comfortable silence, of evening questions about our days and reminder texts to buy milk at the grocery store. Maybe we'd even start a family, if we felt ready for children one day. Certainly, it wouldn't be perfect. We'd have our frustrations and disagreements. We'd suffer losses and heartbreak as life ran its course, inflicting the unpredictable. But it would be ours. Whatever the future held, I'd face it with Forrest. We'd live every day strengthened by the certainty of our devotion to each other.

Knowing that, we could to anything.

"I now pronounce you wife, and wife," said Dominic. "You may kiss the bride."

Forrest smiled as she wrapped her arms around my waist and kissed me. Her touch was gentle but firm — full of promise and our unspoken understanding that this was only the beginning.

"I love you, my beautiful wife," I whispered, only for her. "Always."

She smiled as she kissed me back, and I melted into her, elated and loved and perfectly whole.

In other words, I was right where I belonged.

Our loved ones cheered as we broke our kiss and raised laced fingers in the air. Now it was time for the party, a night of dancing, drinking Prosecco, and checking our left hands to say yes, this was real. We really were married. "I could spend a lifetime celebrating you," said Forrest.

I knew, then, that she would.

Acknowledgements

I'd first like to say that anything good I do in this world, I owe to God. Anything flawed, I owe to my own humanity. This book is a mix of both. It feels redundant to thank Him here, because He already knows the words before I write them down, and I prefer to pray in private, the way He taught us. But He also taught us to claim Him the way He claims us: loudly, lovingly, and without shame. I've recently realized I don't do that enough, so I'm doing it here. He already knows that this book, and everything good in my life, would not exist without Him, but I want you to know that, too. I don't say this with an evangelist's agenda; my goal is more self-focused. I just want God to know I love Him. So, please know that any bits of this book you enjoyed, any parts you found insightful came from Someone else. Someone greater.

Mom, Dad, Jack, Jennie, Logan, and Jane — Thank you for being my rock, always. Our family, and the peace that comes with knowing we will always have each other, is the foundation I built my entire life on. Every risk I've taken, I've taken because you believe in me. Because you make me believe I will land when I jump. Because you are my biggest cheerleaders, confidantes, and comrades, whenever I need rescuing. There would be no book, no anything without you. I love you, I love you, I love you!!

Bonnie, Carolina, Chandler, Christina, Ciana, Jamie, Ivy, Marisa, Mark, Sarah D. and Sarah L. — Thank you for the deep talks, neighborhood walks, sleepovers, vacations, visits, and late-night phone calls. Through the chaos of being in your twenties, you kept me confident and content enough to keep writing. I believe in soulmates because in this wide, wild world, we somehow found each other. I love you.

Jane, thank you for reading multiple versions of this book (even the bad ones) and believing in it, always. When I got tired and discouraged by the editing process, I'd remind myself that even if this book never went anywhere, even if it was just a story you and I could laugh about together, all the hard work would be worth it. I love you.

Sarah, thank you for designing a cover that is more stunning than I could have imagined. Your art has blown me away for as long as I've known you. You have grown into an artist worthy of the National Gallery, who our high school selves would have studied and made paintings trying to emulate. Never forget how proud you are making your childhood self, not just with your unbelievable talent, but with the phenomenal person you are, in every sense of the word. I love you so much. I cannot wait to see what you do for the next book! ;)

Ivy, thank you for being the most incredible Third Act Break-Up Coach. I genuinely don't know how I would have tied those chapters together if I didn't get to talk through it with you over drinks at As You Are. Also, one of my favorite parts of living in DC was picking apart the meaning of the universe (and walking Shelly) with you and Mark. I love you guys!

Kelly, I frequently look back on the day you met with me for smoothies in 2023, when I was just starting out as a freelancer, and patiently, generously, taught me everything I know. Working on a freelancer schedule is what gave me the time to finally finish writing this. I was able to do that because you helped me every step of the way with your advice, work referrals, and friendship. This book would not exist without you. Thank you so, so much.

Laura, and the Laura Evans Media team, thank you so much for everything you have done to empower me as a young professional. I feel so lucky to get to learn from the best, and to be part of a team of such kind, talented, and bad ass women. Your unwavering trust, mentorship, and support has made me more confident than I've ever felt in the workplace, because you help me believe that one day, if I work hard, I can be like you. That confidence has empowered me in our work together and in finishing this book. It's a gift I will carry with me forever. Thank you, thank you, thank you.

Andrew, Athans, Hans, John, Mike, Paul C., Paul O., and Tim — Thank you for teaching me the craft of telling a story. This book might seem like a hard pivot from my sports journalism career, but your writing lessons, edits, and advice mark every page. I am so grateful.

If you made it this far, thank you for reading. Seriously. I wrote this book to improve my own sense of peace, with very low expectations for the final product. There were times when I thought nobody would read it. If you're here, you proved me wrong. Thank you from the bottom of my heart.

Blake Richardson is writer who loves cozy reads with happy endings. She works as a social media consultant and learned storytelling as a sportswriter, with work published in the *Los Angeles Times*, *The DCist*, the *News & Observer*, and other publications.

She lives in Barcelona, Spain. This is her first novel.
www.blakerichardsonwrites.wordpress.com

Find her on Instagram and TikTok:
@blakerichwrites